SHADES

OF

VALHALLA

Inner Origins Book One

ELLIS LOGAN

An Earth Lodge® Publication
Roxbury, Connecticut

Published in the U.S.A. by Earth Lodge®
Cover Design by Maya Cointreau

ISBN 978-1-944396-05-3

Discover Your Inner Origins

SHADES OF VALHALLA
FATES OF MIDGARD
GIFTS OF ELYSIELLE
HEART WARD

"Myths are things
that never happened,
but always are."

Gaius Sallustius Crispus
On the Gods & the World

CHAPTER 1

There had to be a better way.

I slammed down the box in frustration. I couldn't imagine lifting one more box up into the apartment's tiny overhead attic. What would I do when it was time to move again? How would I unload everything quickly?

I definitely needed to look into the whole zen-styling thing. Seriously. How many books and knick-knacks could a girl cart around from town to town? I had way too much stuff.

The problem, I thought as I huffed a curl of hair out of my eyes, was that I was just too sentimental. I needed to cut some ties to the past. Like this box marked "Raggedy Anne and Andy." Those two sculptures had been made for me by my grandfather when I was a baby, and they were cute, but did I really need to keep them to pass on to my own babies someday? I might not even ever have children. I sighed. I didn't particularly want kids. But hey, someday I might, and then they should have heirlooms, right? Maybe, yeah. Maybe some smaller heirlooms. Maybe just mom's sterling baby spoon and sippy cup that I had used, too, as a toddler. I grinned and chucked the box of porcelain figures through the open doorway into the kitchen.

The box crashed, the unmistakable sound of tinkling broken pottery reaching my ears along with a light euphoric feeling. I could definitely get used to this whole Zen thing. There were still ten or twelve more boxes in the living room stacked up by the ladder to the attic, and I was wondering how many of them I could talk myself into throwing away when my mom burst into the room.

"Siri! Are you okay?"

"Yeah, mom, I just decided I'm going to get rid of some of these boxes instead of storing them," I said, pointing at the dented box lying on its side in the doorway.

"Thank the gods, I thought you fell down the stairs or something! How about instead of throwing them, you start another pile on the porch, alright? We just got here, don't want the neighbors to think I'm beating you already."

"Ha! Yeah right, okay, mom." I trailed after her as she walked into the kitchen to grab the abused box. "Speaking of beating, when do we start?"

For as long as I could remember, my mother and I had fought.

Almost every day, we went through the same dance – Tang Soo Do, Qigong, Aikido, Krav Maga, even a little Capoeira. Hand to hand combat, bo staffs, nun chukkas and the occasional sword. Mom said she started teaching martial arts to me as soon as I could run without holding on to something, which put my earliest days of training back to when I was just over a year old. According to her, we'd started with basic Qigong forms, building my strength and endurance. By the time I was three, she caught me on video doing flying kicks off the sofa.

Training always ended with sweaty hugs, good food, and a huge pitcher of water. There was never any shortage of treats in the house, either – mom believed in eating healthy, but also considered chocolate one of the four basic food groups. The kitchen was always the first room mom unpacked when we moved. Already the butcher block island boasted a large red ceramic bowl filled with peaches, honeycrisp apples and bananas next to several smaller turquoise plates displaying sleeves of organic dark chocolates, fresh brownies from the local market and colorful sugar cookies. The holy trinity.

I set the box down on the counter and opened a couple cabinets, trying to find where she'd put the mugs. Pulling out my favorite vibrant tangerine one with a little chip in the handle, I filled it with water and drank it half down in one go. Mom was a big believer in Fiestaware pottery, and our plates and cups came in every shade of the rainbow. No matter where we were, the bright colors always made us feel at home. They always clashed, so they always matched. Sort of like us. I'd given up a long time ago trying to match every new town we moved to. I was just me, like the mug. Not perfect, but me. If someone preferred blue and didn't want orange, chipped things in their life, that was cool. Their prerogative. Whatever.

I wondered what this town would have to offer – matched or mixed sets? Not one to ponder the unknown, I grabbed a brownie and sat down. "So what's the plan tonight?"

"Well," my mom answered as she moved the damaged box off the counter and opened the door to put it out on the front porch, "I have to check in with work and find out what time they want me to come in Monday morning. They're in a really big rush to start planning a new security protocol so they can sign a procurement deal with the NSA. Until the agency is sure their contract will be fully safeguarded, they won't finalize the contract."

"Oooh, sounds exciting." I rolled my eyes. Mom's work was mostly about numbers and angles. It was her job to determine the soft spots in a facility, where people could sneak in and out, the IT vulnerabilities, how many guards and cameras you needed to cover the weaknesses in the building, what kinds of alarms were best suited to the business, how soon local law enforcement could lend a hand if needed, and what sort of situations warranted a call to the cops. Like I said, totally riveting stuff.

Mom laughed. "Hey, it pays for those brownies you're eating. So I bet your stomach thinks it's pretty exciting. Anyhow, after I check in, I figured we could do movie night and pizza. At least it's Friday, so we'll have all weekend to buy some new school clothes, relax and finish unpacking before your big day on Monday."

"Ugh, yay, school. Can't wait." I pushed away from the counter and started to head back to my room. We were already a few weeks into the school year and I was pretty sure in a town this small I would be the only new student in my year.

"Yeah, well, before you get too excited, how about you sort your boxes while I'm getting ready. And no more tossing them around! Start a pile with the box on the porch and I'll take them to a thrift store on the way to work tomorrow."

4

"I'm on it!" The idea of ditching some more boxes was still pretty exciting. "And I'll pick out some movies for tonight, too, I still haven't unpacked my DVDs."

"Action Romance!" She yelled as I went back to the living room.

"Pride and Prejudice it is," I sang out, making her groan.

I hauled out most of the boxes, and went back to pick up the last one. Looking at it, I supposed I should go through it before tossing the whole thing. It had old photos in it, along with my martial arts ribbons from tournaments. I was pretty sure it also had some random mementos, like yearbooks and shells from beach towns we'd stayed in, that I didn't really care to keep. I carried the box into my room and stuck it in the corner. I'd deal with it later.

I tuned into some psytrance on my Digitally Imported music app, sighed and flopped down on the bed. Another town. Another school. For the most part I didn't really care about trying to fit in or joining all the little dramas each school had to offer. The last place we'd been, I had made some really great friends the first week I got there, and it had been really, I don't know, comfortable. Everything had been easy in Tucson. Nice people. Great weather. Awesome places to run and train. I wondered what this town would be like.

We'd moved into a tiny town called Falls Depot in Vermont, near Bennington and Mount Snow. Our apartment was actually part of an old farmhouse that had been split into several homes, and it had a huge empty field behind it that joined some state forest. The company my mom was working for was in Bennington – she had asked the company to put us in Falls Depot so we wouldn't be too far from the mountains. I was really looking forward to getting some snowboarding in, since I hadn't had a chance the whole last year while we were in Arizona.

I'd have to get all new gear, there was no way my old boarding clothes would fit since I had grown several inches in the last year. Now, at 17, I came in at a respectable 5'6". Not too short, not too tall. Big enough to get taken seriously, not so tall that I automatically intimidated other girls. That was good, considering how often we moved. Next year I'd be starting college, so this was the last time I would have to worry about being the new kid in town. There, everyone would be new. I was kind of looking forward to that. It'd be a whole new experience.

I realized I'd probably need a new snowboard, too, and got up to look at my old handbuilt Gnu in the closet. Checking it over, I figured I could probably trade it in for a good deal on a new one. I set to work scraping off the old Daft Punk, Mesita and Quicksilver stickers and fumbled through the box on my desk for my army knife so I could remove the bindings. Those would still work with my feet, at least. I just needed to adjust them up to fit now that I was a size seven.

Sitting on the floor, working off the bindings, I started getting warm. At first I didn't notice, but then the heat started building, more and more. I stripped off my hoodie and went to work on the last screw. Removing the old, rusted screws was pretty frustrating, but hardly enough to work up a sweat over. I almost felt feverish. I pulled the last screw out and dropped it in a bag with the other screws and binding plates, and secured the bundle to the bindings with a shoelace so I could find them all later when I got my new board.

I stood up to put the mess away and stumbled. My legs felt wobbly, my head was pounding. The room felt like it was swaying under my feet. Weird. I shook my head and reached up to place the bindings on the top shelf in the closet, and the whole room lurched beneath me, rumbling and shaking. The heat grew overwhelming, like I was going to vomit or pass out, and I reached for the wall to support myself, but all I grabbed was air.

I found myself outside in the early morning on an empty city street. Low buildings surrounded me where I stood and it was quiet, so quiet, and really beautiful. The light of the sun was just starting to shine on the horizon, and the birds were all still sleeping in the eaves.

It looked like the sort of gorgeous exotic getaway they always showed in movies – small apartments lining steep hills, cobblestone streets where no cars could pass, cream colored homes with tin and clay roof tiles, doors painted in brilliant hues of blue, green, yellow and orange. The type of place movie sets always filled with luscious accents, gorgeous men, and great food. The type of place that we all knew was probably actually filled with dirt poor families, lots of crime, and yeah, okay, probably some really hot guys and great food, too.

I wondered how I'd gotten here, I couldn't remember, had we moved to South America and I'd forgotten? I tried to think where I was, but before I could really concentrate hundreds of birds flew up from the rooftops and trees, making my breath catch.

Well, good morning to me, I thought, and I laughed.

I almost didn't hear the rumbling when it started, because of that laugh. And then, buildings were falling all around me, their colorfully painted doors disappearing under the crumbling bricks and mortar, the dust swirling all around me. Muffled screams and wails erupted in every direction. The people. The people were crying. I couldn't see, there was so much dust, but I could hear them, and they were crying.

Crying, and dying.

I coughed, and opened my eyes. The city was gone. I was on the floor, lying half in and half out of a closet. My closet. Here, in Falls Depot. Right. Not Brazil, or wherever that weird dream had taken me. I still felt hot and unsteady as I got back on my feet. Maybe I was coming down with something, or having some sort of weird allergic reaction to Vermont. My head was pounding.

I reached into my bedside table and grabbed a couple Tylenols, swallowing them down with some water. My legs started to give out again and I crawled into bed.

The rest of the boxes could wait until tomorrow.

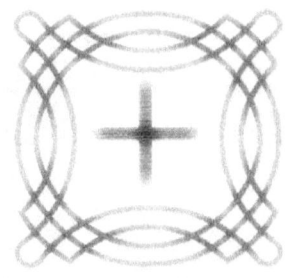

CHAPTER 2

I woke up to the muted sounds of morning coming from the kitchen. Fresh, bright sunlight slanted in through the window, pouring over the bed and hitting me straight in the eyes.

Pain rocketed through my head and I squeezed my eyes shut again. I breathed in slowly, counted to five, and exhaled. I waited, testing my senses. That was a little better. A few more moments, and the light behind my eyelids dimmed. I cautiously opened my eyes, gratefully noting the clouds moving in across the sun.

I sat up and slowly made my way out of bed. When I went to slip on an old kimono over my pajamas, I looked down and realized I was still wearing the same clothes from the day before. So much for movie night. Or wait – had we watched a movie? Some kind of 'end of days' film? I shook my head, trying to remember when I had fallen asleep, and failed. Giving up, I went over to my closet to pick out a fresh shirt, and stumbled over my snowboard on the floor. I didn't remember leaving it there, although I vaguely recalled removing the bindings. I put the board up against the wall, and pulled on my favorite grey hoodie over my shirt.

Sunlight started streaming in again through the windows, and I made a mental note to pick up some better curtains when we went out later. I swiped my sunglasses off the dresser and put them on my head. Those, I would definitely need today.

I opened my door and smelled something awesome that eased my headache down below the surface. Mmmm. What was Mom cooking today?

The kitchen was already immaculate, since Mom liked to clean up as she cooked. She claimed it was no fun to eat if she knew she'd have to clean up afterwards. I guess I saw her point, but personally I was usually too hungry to think that far ahead. Between my frequent workouts and what mom called "teen hormones", I seemed to need to eat every hour. Cleaning up was generally the furthest thing on my mind.

"Hey sunshine," Mom said as she took a bite of her breakfast. "I made some strawberry waffles. Grab a banana and come eat. I have to take a conference call in an hour, but I figured we could train a little before. You can unpack some more while I'm online, and then we can head out to shop. What do you say?"

"Sure, that sounds great." I slid down onto the stool next to her at the island. "What happened to movie night?"

"I tried to wake you, but you were out cold. I didn't try too hard, figured you must need the rest?"

"Yeah, I guess." I didn't want to tell her I didn't even remember lying down. Mom was tough, but she tended to worry sometimes. "I kind of woke up with a headache, but I'm feeling fine now. Thanks to your awesome pancakes – these are great!"

"Thanks, glad to hear it. Why don't you finish up, and I'll go set up. I have something special for you today. Oh, and here, have some of my juice, that will make sure your headache doesn't come back."

"Ew, not the dreaded juice!" I sighed as she passed me the partially full glass. Bright green, with swirls of purple and orange. "What's in this one?"

"Oh, you know, the usual. Kale. Dandelion greens. Some purple cabbage and carrots. Fresh ginger. Just drink it. You know you want to." She winked at me as she left the room

I took an experimental sip. Alright, it didn't taste quite as bad as usual. It was almost sweet, and the ginger was nice. I closed my eyes and drank most of it down in one go. Gah. Too much green. Mom wasn't just a big believer in the power of chocolate, she was a whole food fanatic. Sure, she'd eat pizza, but she also made enough fresh juice every morning to have some with each meal. And, apparently, enough for me if I needed a pick me up. Any time I was tired, she would force some green stuff at me. She claimed the fresher the food, the more pure the energy was for our body, and the better our immune system could function. I just thought it was revolting.

Although, I thought as I finished the last bit left in the glass, this time it really wasn't so bad. Either she'd finally hit on a better combination, or she was converting me after seventeen years. I had to admit, it did usually make me feel better, and I never got sick.

I put my dishes in the sink and walked into the living room, taking in what my mom had planned for us today.

Most kids had living rooms filled with Xboxes, massive TVS, chairs, side tables, huge couches. Me? We had one small flatscreen anchored securely against the wall, a DVD player connected to it, sitting on the cabinet below. A cushy old sofa was pushed against the opposite wall. And that was it. No end tables. No other furniture. Not even a decorative carpet. Sometimes, we got to live in houses with yards or basements that were perfect for sparring. Other times, we had to live in apartments. Like now. And this was where we sparred.

You would have thought that the cabinet under the TV at least held a game console or cable box. But no. Not my mom. She said that's what my computer was for – I could use that however I wanted. But TV was for movies only, we never had cable (she claimed the commercials weakened the mind) and the cabinet, that was for our gear.

Right now, it was standing open, with my mom in front of it. She had already removed a short, thick wooden staff and two small swords and laid them in the middle of the floor. She was busy putting some ten pound weights on her wrists to go with the fifteens on her ankles. She tossed two pairs of matching weights at me as I walked in the room.

I grabbed one out of the air, and ducked as the other pair just missed my head. "Hey, watch it!"

She chuckled. "Still not much better at catching, I see. No worries, we'll make a softball star out of you yet."

"Whatever." I rolled my eyes while I finished strapping on the fives and tens she'd given me.

She shut the cabinet and turned around. "Okay, today we're on defense. Grab the staff, and get ready."

I stepped into the middle of the room, removed my hoodie and threw it on the couch. I took a deep breath and bowed slightly to my mother. She bowed to me as I picked up the staff and stood up to face her with my knees slightly bent in a wide stance.

She just stood there and stared at me, not moving a muscle. I started to get impatient. She often did this, trying to force me into action, since she said my lack of patience made me impulsive, and was one of my greatest weaknesses. Suddenly, her eyes went dark, cold. Determined. It was her only tell. Fast as lightning, she dropped and rolled to the side around me, picking up both swords and leaping up on to her feet in one move, suddenly standing behind me to the right. I whirled as her swords came down on either side of me. I leapt up and just missed having a bit of my hair sliced off.

"Watch the hair, mom!"

She laughed, and came at me full force, swords flashing as they whirled and sliced. I quit worrying about my hair and stopped each move with my staff. I blocked again and again for what seemed like forever, until I was sweating furiously and out of breath. This was getting old. I decided to throw my mom's move back at her, dropped to the ground and rolled around her to the left. As I rolled, I knocked her left sword out of her hand with my staff, then reach around her and grabbed her right sword with my own hand from behind, giving her wrist a quick, painful twist to the side so that she had no choice but to release it.

"Nicely done!" Mom beamed at me, like I was a toddler coloring neatly inside the lines. She didn't look the slightest bit winded. She wasn't even sweating. At least a strand of auburn hair had fallen out from behind her ear, and her ponytail was a little messy. "Next time, you can wear the heavier weights."

I groaned. "How about next time you don't try to kill me?"

She laughed, and handed me a glass of water from on top of the cabinet. "As if that would ever happen. Now drink up, and go take a shower. I have to uplink with the IT guru from Setacom, and then we'll head out."

I trudged back to my room to grab a robe, wondering if the day would come when I won with a fight with my mom and I wouldn't feel like she had let me win. I laughed, and shook my head. It'd never happen.

CHAPTER 3

The green drink had certainly done its job. I toweled off my hair and looked in the mirror, wiping away some of the steam on the surface so I could see a little better.

My cheeks were flushed, and my silver eyes looked wide awake, reflecting the cool white light of the LED strip above the mirror. I put on a little mascara to bring out my fair, practically invisible lashes and turned my attention to my hair. Mom would probably make me try on clothes when we were out, so I should probably go with some frizz-proof style. The wheat-colored waves were already starting to curl. If I didn't blow dry it straight, which I almost never felt like doing, it would hang in waves around my head, eventually curling into ringlets down my back. That was on good days. Other days, especially when it was raining, it puffed up into an unruly wilderness. Still, it was better than when I'd had short hair in eighth grade, and just looked like an elf-boy. I hadn't cut it since then. Usually, I'd pull it back into a ponytail or plait it into a couple braids so I didn't have to deal with it. Since I was hoping to go for a run later and explore the neighborhood, I opted for braids.

I walked back to my room and picked out some jeans, hi-tops and a gray tank top. I spent some more time unpacking, putting away my book collection on the shelves by my bed and hanging up a pink speed bag in the corner of my room by the closet. Mom had given it to me when I was ten, back in my pink phase, so I could punch things in privacy. Ten had been a tough year for me, we'd been staying in Charleston and the debutante pre-teens at school had given me a rougher time than usual. I hated dresses, and I didn't fit in with the social norms there. I would come home, crying and feeling pretty frustrated. Then she gave me the speed bag and taught me how to use it, how to get into the rhythm so that the ball seemed to barely move as I hit it again and again and again. It turned out to be very therapeutic, and that year took the place of having a close friend. I'd start hitting it, angry, but as I got into that rhythm I would start to zone out and relax, and by the end I'd always feel lighter. More free. I gave it a couple swipes now, to make sure it was at a good height.

"Siri, you ready to go?" My mom knocked at the door.

"Yeah, Mom, I'm all set."

We locked up and hopped in the car. Mom had already explained that there weren't really any malls nearby. Bennington was an old Vermont town with lots of covered bridges, a few big department stores, and some cute little streets with mom and pop stores. I didn't really care, I wasn't exactly into the whole shopping thing anyways. Clothes were just something to help me get from point A to point B without being naked. I cared about my running shoes, because I hated getting shin splints and liked good traction when I ran through the woods or did obstacle training, but that was about it.

We drove into town, and Mom did a quick loop, showing me the two colleges in town and the place she'd heard had the best pizza. Supposedly, they delivered to our town, so I figured we'd be on good terms with the delivery guys soon once Mom started working late hours again, which she always did at the start of a new job.

It was the weekend, so I saw a lot of kids my age walking around on the sidewalks. Most of them were probably from the colleges or Bennington, but I figured some of them must live in Falls Depot, too. It looked like I wouldn't have to worry too much about fitting in with any debutantes here. Everyone seemed to be wearing jeans or simple miniskirts with leggings, plain shirts and sweaters. Even the adults seemed really laid back. Most people looked like they were ready to head out on a casual hike through the woods. We even saw some skaters rolling through a park. This was good, it reminded me of Colorado, and seemed even more low-key than when we were in NoCal. Vermont style seemed like it would suit me just fine.

A minute later, I groaned as I noticed my mom was pulling into JC Penneys. "Really, mom, again?"

"Hey, I can't help it if this is the only big store in town."

See, my mom had this thing for Fiestaware, right? So every new town we stayed in, she made sure to get a few pieces from the local Penneys in a new color to add to our collection. You could rely on Fiestaware for this, to roll out a new color every couple of years, so we never ran out of options. Every color we had at home reminded me of a different town. I suppose it was kind of cool. I mean, if she had to collect something, better plates than weird little baby figurines or cats.

"Don't worry," she said as she locked up the car. "We can check all the departments. Maybe get you a new backpack for school, new jeans?" She looked at my worn knees hopefully. "Maybe some shoes, too?"

I perked up at that last part. "Fine, I surrender. I'll try on whatever you want if we can get me some new running shoes."

She laughed. "Siri, you're impossible. Fine. But we're getting you some new sweaters, too, and a winter coat. There is no way your old one from two years ago will fit, and you can't just wear the one you had in Tucson. There's no way that will be warm enough in a month or two. We'll need some gloves and hats, too."

She picked up her pace and got a really determined, far-away look on her face as she started planning the massive new wardrobe she'd be picking out today. I sighed, and followed in her wake. This was going to be a long afternoon, but I could see there was no point in protesting. Besides, I'd had my eye on some really amazing (and expensive) new Asics, and this was the perfect time to get them. I'd seen a sporting goods store on the outskirts of town, so I figured I could talk her into heading there for the sneakers, and probably find some great snowboarding gear at pre-season prices, too.

She looked behind to make sure I was following, and I must have been smiling because she said something about being glad that I was getting into the spirit of things. Then, she saw a display of sage and slate platters and let out an excited little "whoop" as she rushed away from me. Yep, I was doomed.

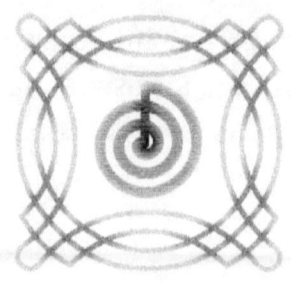

CHAPTER 4

Three hours, four jeans, six shirts, three sweaters, one jacket, two boots, 6 sage green bowls and an unholy number of accessories later, we finally emerged from my own personal shopping hell. I couldn't help but think that the sage bowls were pretty close in color to the evergreen chili crocks we had picked up when were in Charleston. I really hoped this wasn't a sign of how the year would go here in Vermont.

My mother was beaming from ear to ear. Me? I was famished, tired, and grumpy. After we'd put everything in the trunk of our ancient Subaru Forester, Mom turned to me with a suspiciously innocent smile.

"Ready for those sneakers?"

Oh, she was good. I was way too worn out now. But I wasn't letting her off the hook. "Yeah, definitely." Her smile faded. "But let's try out that pizza place first. We totally missed lunch."

"You're right," she laughed. "I was having so much fun, I totally forgot. All right, you have a deal."

Even though it was past the lunch rush, there were still a fair number of cars in the lot at Giovanni's. We headed in and found an empty booth by the door. Most of the other tables were filled with young people eating and laughing.

"Guess this is the local hangout. I suppose they never get a lull since this is a college town, and the kids all sleep in late on the weekends. I bet they are packed from noon till closing."

"Yeah, I guess." I wasn't really interested in the scene. I was just really, really hungry. I didn't see any waitstaff around, so I just folded my arms and started tapping my foot while I looked out the window. By the time the waiter came over, my stomach was actually growling at me, and I felt like I might start, too.

"Hello ladies, what can I get for you today?"

"About time," I grumbled.

"Ignore her, she has low blood sugar." The waiter chuckled along with my mother. "Siri, you want the usual?"

"Yeah." I was still tapping my foot and looking at the street view.

"Great. We'll have a medium cheese with mushrooms and pepperoni, and two waters."

"And a strawberry milkshake," I added hastily, looking up. Oh. Wow. Thank god I had placed my order already, because now I was pretty sure my mouth was just hanging open. This guy was gorgeous. Short, spiky blond hair with blue tips, an eyebrow ring, and deep dark eyes that almost looked black. Luckily he was looking down at his pad jotting down the last of the order. By the time he glanced back up again, I had at least shut my mouth.

"Okay, right. Two waters, one medium with shrooms and pepperoni and one strawberry milkshake. Coming right up." He smiled at us both and walked back to the kitchen, stopping to deliver checks at a couple other booths on the way. Once he disappeared into the back, I turned to face my mother, who had an even bigger grin on her face than during her post-spending bliss.

"Well, that was interesting. He's handsome, huh?"

"Geez, mom, come on. He's probably one of these local college kids, anyways. It's not like I plan on hanging out here in town. We're over in Falls Depot remember?"

"Oh yeah, I remember. But don't forget that all the kids around here go to the same regional high school, so everyone knows each other."

I grunted. "Whatever. I just hope our food comes soon so we can go finish our shopping."

I pulled out my phone and started looking up the sporting goods store to see what they had in. I had a pretty accurate idea of my mom's spending range, and wanted to have a good plan of attack before we got there so I could maximize my take. Some girls swooned over Abercrombie hoodies – me, I wanted to make sure I could get some good polarized goggles that wouldn't clash with the awesome grey and purple jacket I had my eye on. By the time the waiter came back with our drinks, I had picked out everything I needed.

"Here are your waters, and one strawberry milkshake." Cute boy put the drinks down in front of us and flashed a megawatt smile at my mom. "I haven't seen you two in here before, are you touring the colleges?"

"Thank you. No, we've actually just moved into town nearby, Falls Depot. My boss said this was the best pizza in town and that you even deliver to our area." My mother beamed at the waiter.

"Yeah, we deliver to the Depot all the time." He looked right at me, giving me a really clear view of his eyes. Had I thought they were black? They were the deepest indigo I had ever seen, like the blue in a starlit summer sky. Realizing I was about to get lost in that night sky, I quickly grabbed my milkshake and started poking at it with my straw.

"Welcome to town, my name's Rowan, I work here almost every day, just ask for me if you ever need anything. Your pizza will be out in a couple minutes."

"Wonderful, thank you Rowan. I'm Fredrika Alvarsson, and this is my daughter Siri," my mother volunteered.

"Nice to meet you both." I felt this strange tug, deep inside my chest, to look up at him, but I didn't dare. "Let me know if you need anything else," he said and walked away.

"Well, he certainly seems friendly," gushed my mom. "I hope the pizza is as good as Frank said!"

I rolled my eyes, and settled in to relax while my mother started to go on about her new project and what it would entail. The pizza came out a while later, and I managed to avoid embarrassing myself any further, even though every time he smiled at us it felt like the sun had come out from behind a cloud or something. When it came time to pay, my mom sent me up to the counter, where I "rang bell for service" as directed by the small sign over the register. Rowan came out of the kitchen, wiping his hands on a dishcloth.

"What, do you make the pizzas, too?" I asked in a snarky voice. As usual, my innate attitude got the better of me.

"Actually, yeah, sometimes. Gio's been teaching me the ropes. He wants to head south this winter for a few weeks, and he's hoping I can help the other guys out when he's gone." He flashed me that blindingly sincere smile again. "You guys all set? That's gonna be $16.15"

"Um, yeah. Thanks." I felt like such a jerk. Oh well, it wasn't the first time. "So, um, you go to college here?"

"Nah. I have another year left at Union High. How about you?"

"Oh, is that the regional school here?" He nodded. "Yeah, then that's where I'm starting. Can't wait," I said, rolling my eyes.

"Ha! I can see that. You'll have to check out the pep squad, then. I can tell you are totally all about the school spirit." He grinned, and I almost didn't notice how much hotter that made him. Almost. "No, but seriously, if you need help figuring stuff out, come and find me. I have lunch fifth period, if you want to meet some more people you can just look for my table by the windows."

"Cool, thanks, maybe I will. I don't have my schedule yet." I shrugged. "Here's twenty, keep the change."

"Hey, thanks. See you around, Siri." He looked right into my eyes when he said my name, and I felt a hot flush come over me, and that same weird tug in my sternum. Oh god, was I blushing? Probably. My fair skin always flushed massively at the worst moments.

"Um, yeah, sure." I stammered, and started backing away. "See you!" I turned around and just missed banging into another customer's table. If I hadn't been blushing already, I certainly was now.

My mom, of course, had seen the whole thing, and was trying really hard not to laugh when I got back to the table.

"Smooth, Siri, super smooth," she mocked.

"Thanks mom, you're the best. Ready to go?"

Apparently my angst was the last straw, because she burst out laughing as she got up, and continued on hysterically all the way to the door. Outside on the sidewalk, I chanced a glance back through the window, expecting to see a very self-satisfied and amused Rowan. But that wasn't what I saw at all. What I saw, was Rowan, looking back at me. Looking at me, with a totally serious, slightly intrigued look on his face. Like he was interested. In me.

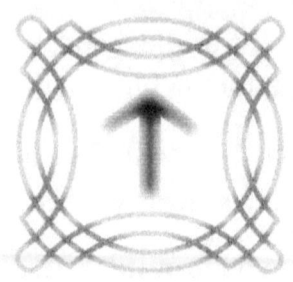

Chapter 5

By the time we got home, the daylight was already fading. I carried my bags inside, dropped them by the closet in my room, and changed into neon nighttime running clothes. I rummaged through the bags and pulled out my brand new pair of Asics Quantums and some padded socks with extra arch support. Once I'd pulled them on, I did a couple bouncy hops in place. Oh yeah, these were awesome. I went over to the closet and looked at my stinky old pair with the treads worn off, wrinkled my nose and tossed them in the trash.

Yelling over my shoulder, "I'm going running!" I headed out the front door and down the street to the west. Might as well have a pretty view of the twilight sky while I ran.

The neighborhood was quiet. Street lights were just starting to flicker on. It was awesome, living in a rural town again. Mostly we stayed in cities, since that was where the bigger companies usually were that my mom worked for. In

Tucson I'd had to run every day on sidewalks and through city parks, although we did head out into the desert mountains on the weekends sometimes. Cactuses and sand were about as interesting as it had gotten.

Here, everything was green and soft, and there wasn't any sidewalk. Even the road seemed softer. I'd seen plenty of dirt roads in the area since we'd moved in, and was really looking forward to checking them out. For now though, I figured I should explore the neighborhood. The houses were all spaced far apart with huge yards and lots of trees between them. The older houses had barns, and a lot of them had pastures behind them with horses and goats. As I walked, my body started to loosen up, and I broke into a light jog, opting to get off the street and run in the grass along the side of the road. Occasionally a dog would be out in a yard and bark quietly at me, following along the property line. At one point I had to actually jump over a chicken that was lazily pecking in the grass under one of the streetlamps.

"Better head home, chickie, it's almost night!" I called over my shoulder. "Don't want the big bad wolf to come and eat you."

I kept running, passing house after house, until I came to a cute looking housing development. This was probably a good place to turn around. I vaulted up onto the sidewalk and kept going, figuring I'd do a loop through the place. The ground level ranch houses here were newer, simpler. Attached garages, tricycles out front, little playsets in the back. Cute.

It was the type of neighborhood I'd secretly always wished I could grow up in. Not that I'd ever tell mom that.

She worried enough about all the moving we had to do, and how I had to change schools so often. Even though she wasn't in the military anymore, I lived the life of an army brat, constantly being pulled from one home and being thrown into another. Don't get me wrong. I actually kind of liked it. I enjoyed seeing so many different parts of the country, and we'd even gotten to live in Ireland and Egypt for a little while. How many kids could say that?

Still, a part of me always envied the kids who grew up in neighborhoods like this. The kids who kept their best friends all through school. The kids who got to come home, throw their bags on the floor, and dash back outside to play down the block without their parents getting worried, because of course their parents had also known everyone on the block for years. I envied the sort of comfort and stability those kids grew up with. The naïve belief that the whole world was safe, and that they had a place in it. Where was my place?

I shook my head. Focused on the running. Focused on the pounding of my feet against the pavement.

I imagined that the beat of my footsteps matched the beat of my heart, thump-thump, thump-thump. I was working up into a good sweat by this point, my body really starting to heat up, and I imagined that the air I breathed in was flowing through my heart, too, cooling it off. Every exhalation pushed the heat out with it. Thump-thump, cool air in. Thump-thump. Hot air out. Thump-thump.

The air was thick. Choked with smoke and an acrid dust. I couldn't see where I was going, and I stumbled over a body or a stone, I wasn't sure which.

I faltered in the walkway, stumbling, and stopped. I looked behind me. Nothing there. Nothing to trip over. Nothing to see.

Rumbling and tumbling noises and muffled screams everywhere.

I gasped, disoriented and put my hand out against a tree. I hung my head, trying to draw in a clear breath.

The earth continued to shake, a strange rolling and swaying, as the dust slowly begin to settle. Everywhere I looked, buildings had been reduced to rubble. The bright doorways and signs of life from before were gone, splintered into pieces and crushed. Here and there, moans emerged from the debris and rocks moved as people began to pull themselves out of the mess. But not very many rocks. Not nearly enough. I stood, alone, or at least I thought I was alone. Until I heard a voice next to me.

"It has begun."

I turned to see who was talking, but I could not make out the face of the man next to me. Darkness swirled around him, obscuring his features.

But the voice. Where once I had felt warm, I was now cold, chilled to the depths of my soul.

"We have to help them!" I cried. I ran to the nearest pile and began moving rocks. I looked behind me, and the man was gone.

There would be no help here today. I kept digging, frantically searching for the source of the nearest moans, I reached to move a large piece of wood, and felt a hand on my shoulder.

"Are you all right?" A woman was peering at me, her hand on my shoulder as I leaned against the tree. My insides heaved and I took a deep breath, trying to keep my lunch from hours ago down where it belonged. The woman had long pale hair wrapped into a bun, and blue eyes. She was dressed for running, just like I was. There was a concerned look on her face, but it didn't quite seem to reach her eyes. "You look a little sick."

"I...I'm fine. Thanks. I guess I ran a little too far."

"Are you a runner? I don't recognize you from school. I coach track there."

"Um, yeah, I usually run all the time, but it's been a week or so. We just moved here from out west." I tried desperately to block the images from a moment ago out of my brain.

"Are you transferring to Union?"

"What?" Focus, Siri. "Um, yeah, I start Monday. I'm a senior."

"Hmm. Well, you shouldn't be too far behind, we're only a few weeks into the term. Make sure you take it easy on your way home, and hydrate plenty." She looked at me closer, taking in my running clothes and expensive new shoes. "What's your name? We had tryouts last month, but you are welcome to come and show me what you can do."

"Siri Alvarsson."

"Alvarsson?" The woman looked surprised. "What an unusual name. Where are you from originally?"

"Um, my mom's family is from Norway, but she grew up in Ireland." This woman was totally weirding me out, giving me a really intense look like she could read my mind if she stared hard enough.

"Indeed? Ireland. What a magical place." She was still giving me that penetrating stare, but now there seemed to be a slight sneer to it. "Well, I'm Coach Thorn. Stop by the track any day after school."

"Okay, thanks. I'll check it out. I better get headed home, my mom's probably wondering where I am."

She nodded and grimaced in what I suppose was her attempt at a smile, and I took off, running straight back the way I came. Forget exploring. I was ready for some water, followed by a serious chocolate fest.

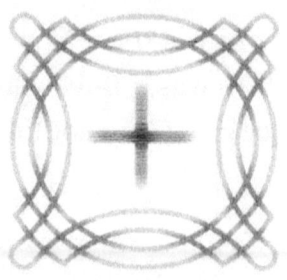

Chapter 6

I pounded up the steps of our front porch and walked into the apartment. Mom was halfway through a Wu Qin Xi set, an ancient five animal Qigong form for mastering the elements. I grabbed some water off the table by the entry, and watched her graceful movements.

"Did you have a good run?"

"Yeah, not bad." I wasn't about to tell my mom that I was seeing weird visions of people dying. I could just imagine what sort of reaction that would bring. Mom would probably assume it was some sort of emotional trauma related to the move, and bring me to the local shrink. No way was that going to happen. I wasn't exactly a "share your feelings" kind of girl.

"I'm gonna take a shower. What's for dinner?"

"I saw that Giovanni's has chicken parm dinners. I thought I'd order in. What do you think?" She stepped into the final animal stance and pushed her hand out in claw form. "Spaghetti or Ziti with yours? A side salad, too?"

"Sure, with spaghetti. And blue cheese on the salad."

"Great, I'm almost finished here, and then I'll order. We can do movie night, since you slept in last night."

"Yes! I have a chick flick all picked out."

My mom groaned, and I headed to the shower.

After washing the day off, I stepped out and threw on a black cami and sweats. My mom knocked on the door. "You done yet?"

"Yep." I stepped out of the bathroom. The two-bedroom apartment only had one. "It's all yours."

"Perfect. I left some money on the table, in case the delivery guy comes while I'm in here."

"Cool, thanks."

I sat on the floor by the sofa and worked at toweling off my hair, then put the towel around my shoulders and did a few stretches. My mom was still in the shower when the doorbell rang.

I grabbed the money off the table and opened the door. Rowan was standing there, a big brown bag with the letter 'G' on it in his hand. He looked me up and down. "Hey there," he said, a grin spreading over his face.

My stomach flip-flopped. Feeling a little nervous, I rubbed the end of the towel through my hair with one hand. "Hey."

"I've got two chicken parm dinners and salads here, and one bottle of grape soda."

"Uh, yeah." I handed him the thirty bucks my mom had left on the table. "I think this will cover it."

"Yeah, that does it. Do you need change?"

"I don't think so."

"Thanks." He pocketed the money with one hand. An awkward silence fell over us.

"So...a group of us are going swimming tomorrow afternoon at the Falls. You want to come? Meet some people before you get to school?"

"Oh! That would be great, I love swimming! Arizona was definitely lacking in the water department." I gushed without thinking. Uh-oh. I tried to tone it down a little. "I haven't had a chance to swim in anything other than a pool for the last couple years."

"Ah, an Arizona girl."

"Well, yeah, just for the last year. And before that we were in Egypt for six months. No public swimming holes there!"

"Wow, Egypt, really? That's cool." He looked at me with that intense gaze of his again, like he was trying to read my mind or something. "How about I pick you up at noon? The back roads around here can get a little confusing until you know your way around."

"Sure, that sounds good." My stomach was filled with butterflies again, but I managed to keep my tone light.

"Cool, I'll see you tomorrow." Rowan turned to walk away.

I laughed. "Hey! You still have my food."

"Oh, right!" He shrugged and gave me a sheepish smile. "Here you go."

"Thanks. See you." I backed up, shut the door and sighed.

"Looks like you've made an impression." I jumped at the sound of my mom's voice, as she came chuckling around the corner. "Aren't you proud of me? I didn't interrupt or anything."

"Oh yes, uber proud, mom. Your super spy skills are not creepy at all, either." I rolled my eyes, which really set her off laughing. I pushed by her into the kitchen, grabbing the new sage-colored bowls and a couple turquoise plates after I put the bag of food down.

"Did I hear something about you going out tomorrow?"

"Yes," I said. "Apparently there's some waterfall where you can swim."

"Ah, yes, I suppose there would be in a town called Falls Depot." She winked, and started plating our food. "That's great news, Siri. I'm glad to see you're making friends so quickly."

"Yeah well, don't throw me a parade yet. We'll see how this thing goes tomorrow. Rowan seems a little...I don't know...intense?"

"Oh, he's just friendly. Seems like you couldn't have met a nicer person your first day out and about."

"Yeah. I guess." I thought about how my stomach filled with butterflies every time I got near him. "I hope so." I carried my dinner out to the living room and flopped down on the carpet in front of the TV. "Now what will it be? *Clueless* or *Hunger Games*?"

"Like you have to ask." She laughed, and picked up the *Hunger Games* DVD. "Can't have too much romance in the house, we might combust."

I groaned, and stuffed a piece of lettuce in my mouth so I wouldn't have to respond.

After the movie, I went to my room to check Facebook. A few messages from friends in old places, lots of funny memes about kittens. Social networking at its best. My closest friend from Egypt, Claire, said her dad had transferred to the same Irish company my mom had worked at five years ago. She was totally swooning over all the accents at her new school, and had included a few snapshots of the hot local eye candy. Claire was totally boy crazy. It was good to see that some things never changed.

Next, I checked out the Mount Snow website. Season passes were still on sale at a discount for another couple weeks. I decided I'd head over in the morning and get a youth pass, apparently local students under eighteen got a great deal. It was so cheap it was practically free. I couldn't wait to put all my new gear to use in a couple months.

I turned off the computer and leaned back in my chair. What would tomorrow bring? I hoped that Rowan's friends were as nice as he was. Well, maybe not quite so friendly. His total openness and chipper attitude was a bit much for me, I didn't think I could take it from a whole group of people. But you know, it was better than unfriendly. Whatever. I guessed I would find out soon enough. I turned off my desk lamp and crawled into bed.

Moonlight seeped into the room through the curtains, casting strange shadows on the walls and ceiling. I stared up, feeling a little melancholy. Watching *Hunger Games* always did that to me. The scenes where her father disappeared down the mine, never to return. I envied Katniss. At least she'd had a father to miss. A father who had been kind and loved her.

My own father, according to mom, was a soldier she had known for less than a week. She said there'd been an instant pull and attraction between them, a knowing. She had still been with the army, stationed over in Afghanistan. He had been with a covert mercenary unit for the Brits, and both their teams had been working together to secure a biochemical facility from some terrorists. They had spent every free moment together during the mission.

Every moment, and by the time he was gone all she had was his code name. And me, of course, just starting to grow in her belly. She'd never been able to track him down. She'd tried, once she realized she was pregnant, but the Brits hadn't been too forthcoming about who she'd actually met, and where the team had moved on to. They even refused to forward him a letter from her. The army had transferred her to a desk job, since she was pregnant, and she'd pensioned out a few years later.

I'd sort of hoped that we would run into him when we lived in Ireland, because hey, it was practically right there in England. Okay, fine, it had been a longshot, but I knew my mom had been disappointed when we left without making any sort of a connection, too. It was a bit depressing. I mean, my mom wasn't loose or anything. She almost never dated. I knew my dad must have been someone really special. I could see it in her eyes whenever she talked about him. The yearning and the sadness.

I sighed, and closed my eyes. The odds were slim to none that I would meet my dad here in Falls Depot. At seventeen, I was pretty much resigned to never meeting him. Still. Sometimes it hurt to be without him, like how I imagined it felt after you lost a limb. You knew it was meant to be there. You could feel how it felt.

But it wasn't there.

CHAPTER 7

The next morning, the smell of fresh coffee woke me up. I rolled out of bed, put on some skinny jeans, my favorite pair of green Docs and an old burton sweatshirt. I was still feeling a little out of sorts from the night before, so I spent a few minutes getting out of my morning funk by working on my speed bag by the window. By the time I left my room, the apartment was quiet.

I crossed the living room into the kitchen, poured a cup of coffee, added some sugar and looked at the note on the counter.

"Running. Back in an hour."

I jotted down a note to my mom telling her I was heading out to Mount Snow, grabbed a couple bananas and the keys to the Subaru. We'd bought a new GPS at Penney's the day before, so I took that, too, and headed out the door. The GPS was pretty easy to set up; Mount Snow was even listed in the menu as a local attraction. It was just twenty minutes away, assuming I didn't hit any traffic. I couldn't imagine what sort of traffic there would ever be on these winding country roads, anyways.

My mom had been pretty upset the one time I'd gotten a warning in Tucson for speeding, so now I drove carefully, never going more than a few miles over the speed limit. Still, I got to the mountain in just over fifteen minutes. I imagined the trip would take a little longer in the winter when we got good snow, but I was pretty excited to be this close to skiing again. I hopped out of the car and wandered over to the ticket booth, where a really bored guy directed me to the lodge office to get my photo pass made.

The mountain looked huge. One of the lifts was running, the gondola pod that went all the way to the top, giving lazy off-season mountain bikers an easy ride down. Since I hated biking uphill more than just about anything, I couldn't blame them one bit. Signs were posted all over the place for an upcoming OktoberFest, and a reggae concert that had happened the week before. Gee, I was really sorry I had missed that. Not. One of the only things I disliked more than mountain biking was patchouli, which I'm sure would have been the eau du jour at that event.

I gazed back up at the mountain with mounting excitement as I pushed my way through the lodge doors. More signs for OktoberFest greeted me in the vestibule, advertising online ticket sales, beer and bratwurst. I shook my head. Again, not really my thing. Polka and tiny hats, I could do without. I looked past the advertisements and saw the lodge office nearby. The door was open, so I walked right up to the counter, where a girl my age wearing a vintage rainbow striped sweater à la Brady Bunch was leaning over her iPhone, clearly engrossed in some game.

I cleared my throat.

"Oh, hey!" She looked up and smiled. She had short, naturally red hair pulled into two tiny pigtails with bangs, clear blue eyes, and a host of freckles across a small perky nose. "You here for a pass or applying for a job?" She asked this like there couldn't possibly be any other options.

"Just a youth pass." I answered.

"You have ID?"

I handed her my Tucson driver's license. She examined it curiously.

"Well, I guess it must be real, since no one actually ever tries to pass for underage." She laughed. "Did you just move here or something?"

"Yeah, we got here last week." I shuffled my feet on the ground. This was my least favorite part of moving to new places. The constant introductions got real old, real fast.

"Okay, well you just need to fill out this form here, and then we'll go take a picture." She slid the form across the counter to me with a pen, and went back to playing her game. From where I was standing it looked like Clash of Clans, and she seemed to be in the middle of an epic siege.

When I was about halfway through the form, I heard her groan.

"Clan troubles?" I asked.

"Yeah, my friends are all offline right now, hiking the back of the mountain, so no one's got my back in this battle. Oh well, guess it's time to send in the trolls." She exhaled in frustration. "You play?"

I signed the form and slid it back to her. "Not really. Some of my friends out west did though. I kind of suck at war games. Not enough action for me, too much waiting around."

"Ah. Yes, I can get that." She looked at my form. "Oh, you moved to the Depot? Are you going to Union High?"

"Yeah, actually. I start tomorrow."

"Oh, cool! I'm one of the hall monitors, I know, totally lame but my mom really digs it," she rolled her eyes and grinned. "We usually get tapped to show new students around if they are in our grade. You a senior?" she asked eagerly.

I eyed her warily.

"Yeah."

"Sweet, me, too! So I'll probably see you in the school office tomorrow. It's the best part of being a monitor, because we get to wander around a bit while we tour the school." Her pigtails bobbed while she nodded, apparently in total agreement with herself. I liked her enthusiasm, even if I didn't have too much of it myself. She glanced at my form again.

"So, Siri, is it? I'm Rose. I know, I know, don't say it. I mean who names a redhead 'Rose'? It's just too corny. But, it's a family name, according to my mom." Rose shrugged, and I laughed.

"Now, come on and let's get your photo taken care of."

Ten minutes later I was back in the car with a new pass. Rose had made me take the photo a bunch of times until we got the best photo, claiming she didn't have any other work to do, so why not make sure I looked my best? Since I'd have to stare at the pass attached to my jacket all season, I couldn't help but agree. I wished the DMV back in Tucson had the same attitude.

I drove down the resort road, out towards Route 100 to head home. I was about to pull out, when a massive black Ford pickup came barreling down the road. I waited for it to pass, turned right and followed the truck down the road, keeping my distance.

We hadn't gone very far when I saw a squirrel sitting on the side of the road, eating a nut. The truck swerved right at it. The squirrel leaped back at the last moment, slamming into the side of the truck and falling to the ground as the truck roared away.

"Are you kidding me?!" I yelled. I couldn't believe it. I had seen some article going around on Facebook about how a guy did a study in Texas that showed five percent of all drivers would actually go out of their way to hit animals in the road, rather than go around them, but I hadn't really believed it. I mean, what a psychopath. I pulled to the side of the road, tears rolling down my face. Who would actually do something like that?

I left my blinker on and got out of the car, scrambling over to the squirrel. The closer I got, the more slowly I approached. I was scared of what I might see.

It looked like it was sleeping. The small, black squirrel had a small patch of light fur under its chin, and some blood was seeping out of its mouth. I kneeled next to it, and prodded it gently with my finger. No response. I gently picked it up and placed my fingers on its neck and chest. No heartbeat, at least, I didn't think so. I wasn't exactly squirrel certified. But, I was pretty sure it was dead. For some reason, this hit me really, really hard, and I sobbed. I clutched the squirrel tightly to my chest and tried to take a deep breath, to calm down and get some perspective. It was just a squirrel, right? I mean, they got hit all the time. But this had just seemed so – malicious.

I held the squirrel and shut my eyes, trying to center myself and get a grip. Come on, Siri, just relax, take a deep breath, and calm down. Circle of life, and all that. Calm down, lay the little guy on some grass, cover him up with some leaves, and move on. Go swim in the falls.

But I couldn't move.

I tried again to relax, concentrating on my pounding heart instead of my breath. I felt my heartbeat, strong, and willed it to slow. After a few moments, it was slower, but also stronger, louder. I breathed deeply, willing myself to get grounded and relax. I felt my pulse radiating through my body, stronger and stronger, and then it was like there was a deeper pulse surging through the ground below me, up through my legs, in time with my own. The two beats came together like a war drum pounding through my body.

Suddenly, a third beat joined in, small and quick, pulsing through my hands. I opened my eyes, totally stunned, and looked at the little being in my hand. Looking right back at me.

I was so shocked, I dropped the squirrel into my lap. Instantly, I worried that I had hurt it again, but it sat up on its hind legs, chattered at me while I stared at it, and ran off into the woods.

I shook my head. Well, that was hella weird. I got back in the car and looked at the dash clock. Somehow it seemed that I had lost a half hour there on the side of the road. I guess I had spent more time than I thought freaking out over the squirrel. Now I had less than an hour to drive all the way home, clean up my teary mess of a face, and shave my legs. Perfect.

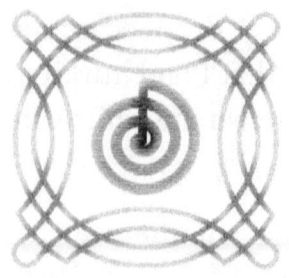

CHAPTER 8

When I pulled into the driveway there was a silver Prius sitting in one of our parking spots. I really hoped that wasn't Rowan's car, I was so not ready yet. I jogged up the steps and went inside.

"Mom? You home?" I'd taken the Subaru, but she could have gone running or hiking.

"Yeah, Siri, in here," she called from the kitchen.

I went in and saw her sitting at the counter eating pita chips and hummus. "Someone's parked in one of our spaces. I thought maybe you had someone over?"

"Ah, no. But there is something I wanted to talk to you about..." She leveled me with a serious gaze.

"There is?" I worried for a moment, wondering what I'd done. I couldn't think of anything, so I wasn't sure what this was going to be about.

She burst out laughing. "Oh, I'm sorry! I can't do this. You are just too easy. You should see the look on your face!" She got up and went over to a pile of papers, came over and waved them in my face, "I got a new car!"

"What!?"

"I know you are planning on going snowboarding every day this winter, and there's not really any good transit in the area, so I thought it was time you had your own."

"You got me a Prius!"

"Ha!" she guffawed. "As if! No, I got me a Prius, and you get to call the Forester your very own. Now, who's the best mom in the world?" She spread her arms wide and beckoned me in for a hug.

"Ha, yeah, you are, definitely. Thanks mom!" I gave her a big long hug. "You are the best, I mean it."

"Alright, gratitude session over. Don't you have a date to get ready for?"

"Oh, right, I almost forgot! And it's not a date, Mom, a bunch of people are going swimming, that's all."

"Whatever you say, Siri." She winked at me and sat down with her chips again.

I shook my head and went to take a quick shower. After I got out, I threw on my bathing suit, assuming there wouldn't be anywhere to change when we got there, some cutoff shorts and a faded Chemical Brothers concert tee. I grabbed my backpack, packing a towel and some sunglasses, along with my phone, wallet and a sweatshirt. I came out of my room just as my mom was opening the door.

"Hi Rowan, come on in."

"Hi Mrs. Alvarsson. How are you today?"

"I'm wonderful Rowan, thank you for asking. I'm actually just about to head out myself." My mom turned to me. "Siri, there are some cookies and sodas in the kitchen if you guys want to take them with you."

I rolled my eyes. "Thanks Mom, but I think we're good."

Rowan cleared his throat and I looked over at him. "Actually, Mrs. Alvarsson, I think that would be great. Thanks!"

My mom laughed, grabbed her keys off the table and headed out the open door. "Alright, well help yourself you two. Take whatever you want. I won't be back until late, Siri, Frank wants to take me out for a game of golf and then dinner with some of the team. Rowan, you make sure my daughter's home before I am!"

I groaned. "Mom, you are so embarrassing!"

"I know, isn't it great?" She tossed her hair and jogged down the steps to her car. "Back by nine -- I mean it, it's a school night!"

Rowan turned back to me. He looked sympathetic, but I could tell by the muscle jumping in his jaw that he was trying really hard not to laugh.

"Alright, come on, let's get your grub, hungry man." I led the way into the kitchen. I grabbed a couple water bottles and decided to stuff the whole bag of chocolate chip cookies in my bag, too. Served her right if there weren't any left later. I looked around the room, then back at Rowan. "Anything else you want?" I smirked at him, daring him.

He took a couple strides right toward me and looked down at me. He was standing near enough that I could actually feel his body heat. I could see tiny flecks of blue and silver in the deep dark indigo of his eyes. "How about this? He reached around me, and I froze. He was so close for a moment that my lips were practically on his collarbone. I inhaled, and smelled an intoxicating musky scent with citrus undertones. He leaned back and held an apple between us.

I felt dazed. "Um, what? Oh," I blushed, embarrassed that he'd caught me off-guard. "Yeah, sure, you can have that."

"Cool." He grinned. "Alright then, Serious, I'm all set. You?"

"Serious?"

"Yeah," he was totally laughing at me now. "Serious Siri. Come on, let's head out."

We headed out to his truck, a beat-up two-toned red and black pickup. He followed me around to the passenger side and reached around me again to open the door. "Your chariot, milady."

I laughed, glad for something to distract me and climbed in. He shut the door behind me, got in on his side and turned the key. The engine roared to life, along with some old-school rock music coming from the radio.

"You listen to Rush?"

"Yeah, you want me to turn it off?"

"Nah, I'm good. My mom and I work out to Rush all the time. I like Queen better, though."

"Really? That's cool. I don't think I know too many girls who do their yoga to Rush."

"Yoga?! Boooring. My mom and I both do martial arts, she's been training me since I was a kid."

"Wow, seriously? That's really cool. I did Karate for years with the local park and rec program, got up to a red belt before I got tired of it. How about you?"

"I'm a third degree black belt in Tang Soo Do." I waited for his face to change, like so many guys' did when they heard I could probably beat them up. Instead of looking annoyed or disappointed, though, he just looked intrigued.

"That is so totally cool! Wow. So if I ever need help, I know who to call," he laughed good-naturedly. I decided I might as well change the subject while I was ahead, before he found out about the Krav Maga and Capoeira.

"So, um, what else do you do? Do you snowboard?"

"Oh yeah, of course, you pretty much have to if you grow up around here. I also ski. My dad likes to take us in during deep-snow season and hunt for bear, so I snowshoe, too."

"You can hunt bear? Aren't they endangered or something?"

"Not around here. Hunters can get a special license to get one or two bear a year. It helps keep the population from getting out of control. One bear provides most of our meat and baking grease for the whole year."

"Oh." I felt a little ill. I wasn't vegetarian, but my mom and I stuck mostly to fish and the occasional ham sandwich, and even then only a few times a week. We got the bulk of our protein from beans and nuts the rest of the time.

"Hey, don't worry. I won't make you eat any," he teased. "Though I can't speak for my mom if you ever come over for dinner."

He glanced at me, and I heated up under his gaze again. He was talking about meeting his parents, already?

"That's fine," I rushed to reassure him, "I'll try anything once."

"Oh, really?" he drawled suggestively. I blushed, realizing what he was implying. "Hold on."

We pulled into a dirt lane and stopped. My heart started hammering. "What are you doing?" I asked him, trying to keep any nervousness out of my voice.

"We're here."

"We are?" I asked. I looked around, and noticed he had parked next to a couple of other cars. "Oh! We are!" I opened the door and scrambled out of the truck. Rowan came around and pulled our backpacks out of the truck bed. He put his on and swung mine up over one shoulder, and looked at me.

"Yeah, we are. What did you think I was doing, Siri?" He asked. Now he was the serious one.

"Um, I don't know. You kind of took me off guard, I guess. You know, city girl in the woods," I shrugged and tried to smile.

He took a step toward me and leaned in. He looked into my eyes for a minute and took a deep breath. "Okay. I get it. Look, when I want to kiss someone, I don't take them into the woods and molest them."

"You don't?" I squeaked.

"No, I don't." He looked a little angry. "I take them on a date. I take them home. And then, if they seem interested...then, I kiss them."

"Oh." I exhaled.

He stood up and took a step back. "The trail to the falls starts over here, you ready?" He pointed behind him to his left and quirked an eyebrow.

"As ever," I quipped.

"Ladies first." He swept his hand before him and I walked past, heading into the warm autumn woods.

"And Siri?"

"Yeah?"

"Just so we are clear..." He paused. "This is a date."

I almost missed a step and coughed to try and hide it. Just follow the trail, Siri, one foot in front of the other. Follow the trail. And breathe. "Good to know."

After that we walked in silence for a few minutes. The further we walked, the more beautiful the forest became. It was full of hundred year old pines supported by two foot wide trunks. The ground was piled deep with pine needles and lacked undergrowth, making it really easy to follow the springy trail as it picked its way between stones and felled trees. Amid the beauty, I started to feel melancholy the deeper in we went. A strange, underlying sadness, making me feel a little homesick. Just as I was starting to feel a little overwhelmed, we stepped around some large boulders, following the trail to come out by an old train trestle overlooking a wide river. The river was gorgeous, filled with lots of little swimming holes created by worn boulders and rock ledges.

I gasped. It was so beautiful. Right on the heels of that sentiment I was hit with a huge wave of sadness. "What is this place?" I asked, feeling short of breath. Tears pricked behind my eyes, and I had to fight not to let them out.

"These are the falls." Rowan answered, watching me closely. "Are you alright?"

"Yeah, I'm fine," I smiled at him, shaking off the weird sadness I'd felt coming from the scenic view. "But...Where are the falls? I don't see any waterfall."

Rowan's voice took on a hint of regret. "They're gone. About one hundred and forty years ago the train lines decided this was a good route to take around the mountains. The falls were over a hundred feet high, and considered a holy power place by the local indigenous tribes. The train company didn't care. They blasted the falls down so that they could save distance on their line, because distance equaled time, and time was money. What you see here is all that is left of the falls. That, and the town name."

"Falls Depot. It was a train depot?"

"Yeah. It was a busy trading station for timber, fur and wool, at least until the industrial age took over and everyone started moving to the cities." He shook his head and took my hand, smiling down at me. My heart thumped in my chest and I heard some screaming and laughter from down below. "Come on. Enough town history. Let's introduce you to the gang."

He pulled me down the trail. Below the old bridge, there was a huge, dark pool of water. Several rope swings hung down from the trestles, some in better condition than others. Rowan must have seen where I was looking, because suddenly I felt his breath on my ear as he murmured, "Stay off all the ropes except the red and white one, Serious. The rest are all rotted through. Come on." He took me a couple of steps further past some bushes, and I finally saw where the laughter had come from. Two girls and a guy were sitting on the rocks in the sun, drinking beer. The guy had light brown hair and leaned close to the water's edge. Every few seconds he'd splash a bit of water at the girls.

"Cooper, quit it!" The thin brunette in a pink bikini laughed. "Next time I am throwing you in there with the fish!"

"Hey, if that means you're touching me..." He wiggled his eyebrows and flashed his teeth, and scooped up a handful of water.

"Cooper..." she warned.

"Ooops!" He flicked his wrist and got her right in the face with a healthy dose of water.

"That's it!" the brunette shrieked and launched herself at the boy named Cooper, taking him over the ledge and into the pool. The resulting splash sloshed over the stones and soaked the blonde girl who had been watching the whole scene play out with a bored look on her face.

"Ugh." She reached for a towel and started drying herself off. "You guys! How could you! You totally got my hair wet! You are both, like, so juvenile."

Rowan burst out laughing, and the blond looked up, instantly transforming her harpy face into a sweet adoring smile. "Rowan, you're here! I was hoping you would come by."

"Yep, here we are." Rowan pulled me forward with him, setting off a fresh wave of nerves, then let go of my hand. "Emelie, this is Siri. She just moved to the Depot."

The girl looked me up and down, coldly assessing my clothes and hair. "Charmed, I'm sure," she said with about zero interest. She picked up her beer and took a swig, looking back out over the water.

"Hey Cooper, Holly. Come meet Rowan's new friend." Emelie said the last word like it was dripped in acid, and the temperature seemed to drop a couple degrees.

CHAPTER 9

The fighter in me itched to wipe the smirk off Emelie's face, but I took a deep breath and controlled myself. I'd met plenty of girls like Emelie before, and I'd stopped letting myself get sucked into their petty dramas years ago. I straightened my back while instinctively loosening my stance.

Cooper spluttered, coming up out of the water after being dunked again by Holly. She gleefully kicked more water in his face as she swam over to us. Cooper followed cautiously in her wake, eyeing her with a mischievous gleam in his eye.

"Hey there, you must be the new girl Rowan mentioned." I peeked at Rowan, surprised that he'd been talking about me. "I'm Holly, Rowan's older sister."

"Older, ha!"

"Well, I am." She gave him a cheeky grin.

"Two minutes, Holly, just two minutes. You don't need to go around flaunting it all the time." Rowan actually sounded put out. This must be one of those old sibling rivalries they always talked about in movies. Personally, I was a little intrigued by the idea that anyone could actually get under his skin that way. I found it oddly reassuring, and instantly warmed to his sister.

Rowan walked over to the cooler and popped a beer open. He swallowed about half of it and glowered at her. "I swear, Holly, only you can drive me to drink."

She laughed and winked at me. "It's what I live for. You going to offer Siri something?"

Rowan had the good grace to look embarrassed. "Sorry, Siri. In case you haven't already guessed, this is my twin, Holly. She's annoying as hell, but I love her dearly." This last bit was delivered with a healthy dose of sarcasm and had Holly laughing even harder. "Would you like something to drink? Looks like we've got beer, hard cider, and water."

I didn't usually like drinking, I wasn't a fan of anything that clouded my thinking, but I didn't want to seem weird so I asked for a hard cider. I figured it wasn't like I actually had to finish it. Rowan handed me the cider and put our bags down on the stone, opening up my bag with the cookies in it.

"We brought some goodies of our own, too. Cookies, an apple, a couple sodas if anybody wants them." Rowan announced to the group.

"Sweet, cookies!" Cooper launched himself out of the water, dripping all over Emelie. He took three and popped one in his mouth whole. "Eryumm."

"Ugh, Coop, you are such a Neanderthal. Did you have to get me all wet?"

"It's what I live for." His voiced lowered and he schooled his features into what I could only assume was his attempt at bedroom eyes.

"You are disgusting." Emelie sighed theatrically. "Well, I suppose since I'm already soaked, I might as well join you, Holly." She pointedly ignored the rest of us and dove flawlessly into the pool of water.

"You can thank me anytime," Cooper drawled to Rowan. Rowan snorted.

"What do you mean?" I asked before I could stop myself. "Shouldn't you be thanking us for the cookies?"

"Ha, good one! No, I meant for getting rid of Emelie. She's always had a thing for Rowan and doesn't take too kindly to his girlfriends."

"Girlfriends, huh?" I took a sip of my cider to mask the sudden burst of annoyance I felt. "I suppose he's got a lot of them?"

"Oh yeah, he's always got someone chasing after him, I mean just last week he–"

"Can it, Coop. You're making me look bad."

"Oh! Right. Sorry," he said to Rowan. Then he turned right back to me and continued, "It's not his fault, he's just way too nice, you know? All the chicks in my grade are totally gaga for him now that he's a big bad senior."

"Oh, so you're a junior then?"

"Yeah, Holly is our resident cradle robber," Rowan teased.

Cooper rolled his eyes. "As if. No girl can resist this..." He pointed to his well-defined chest and flexed his pecs beach lifter style, making us all crack up.

"Anyway, as I was saying, girls take advantage of Rowan all the time. He just doesn't know how to say no. That's why I'm going to ask you right now...Just what exactly are your intentions towards our Rowan?"

I sputtered, shocked, and spit out the cider I had just drank.

"Dude, you are such an ass!" Rowan laughed and punched Cooper in the arm. "Siri, I swear, I don't go out that much, and I'm not dating anyone right now."

"Whatever you say, Casanova," I replied.

Cooper nodded at me in approval. "I like this one, Rowan. You may keep her."

"Oh my God. I can't take any more of this. Siri, you want to swim?"

"Yeah, sure." I stood up and started taking off my shorts. Suddenly, I heard a whoop from above and looked out over the water. Emelie swung out on the rope swing high over the pool and let go, doing a dive into water below. "Wow, cool!" I said, and pulled my shirt up over my head. When my head emerged, I made eye contact with Rowan.

He looked at me, his eyes slowly taking in all of me, and said, "Yeah. Wow." Realizing he was referring to me, and not the dive, I sucked my bottom lip and glanced away. I felt a hot flush creep up my entire body, and was pretty sure I was blushing again.

"Okay, last one in's a rotten egg!" I shouted and cannonballed into the water. I emerged right next to Holly and Emelie.

"Hey. Awesome dive," I told Emelie.

"Yeah, thanks, no biggie. I've been coming here for years with Rowan, so I know what I'm doing." She flicked her hair over the shoulder that was closest to me, conveniently getting water all over my face. Holly disappeared from view as Cooper swam up behind her and pulled her under.

"What is it with those two?" I asked.

"Oh, them? Madly in love, together for the last two years. Totally boring, right?"

"Um, right." Having never had a serious boyfriend, I couldn't imagine being bored with being in love. Being in love for two years? A luxury I'd never dreamed of with my nomadic lifestyle. I looked around for Rowan and saw him climbing out of the water, hand over hand, up the rope swing. His wet muscles bulged and glistened in the afternoon sun. When he got up halfway he started pumping his body, getting the rope to swing back and forth. He grinned over at us and yelled "Look out below!" as he leaped into the water right next to us. He came up behind me and wrapped his arm around my waist, sending a flurry of butterflies through me.

"Your turn, Siri. Most people swim the rope over to the rocks and swing out holding onto the fourth knot." He pointed over at an outcrop of rocks under the bridge.

"Aw, come on, Rowan. Don't pressure her. She might be scared." Emelie looked at me with a false smile of concern on her face.

I laughed. "No worries. I'm not too afraid of heights." I swam over to the rope, grabbed on and scrambled up. Years of boxing and training had given me the upper body strength most girls lacked, and I was lean enough that this type of climbing was cake. When I got to the top knot, I flashed a brilliant smile down at Emelie. I started pumping to get the swing moving. The moment I had enough momentum, I let go and pushed off backward, sending my body into a tight spin. I could hear the guys cheering and yelling as I came out of a flawless double back somersault and entered the water. Swimming under the dark pool to come up between Rowan and Emelie, I shook the water gently out of my hair. A little retribution for Emelie's earlier hair flicking.

"That was awesome!"

"Where'd you learn to dive like that?"

"Falls Olympics, here we come!"

Everybody was smiling at me, except Emelie who muttered, "showoff," under her breath. I suppressed a grin and shrugged.

"We swam a lot at the Y in Tucson. Not much else to do there when it's 110F outside for half the year. Beat jogging, that's for sure."

Rowan laughed, came closer and tucked a wet curl behind my ear. "You are amazing, Serious." He gazed at me, looking pretty serious himself. Then he tapped a finger on my nose and said, "And you need some serious sunblock. You're already turning pink. Come on, let's get you protected and then you can show us some more of your awesome skills."

For once, I felt grateful for my fair skin. Because I knew I was already wearing sunscreen, and the pink in my cheeks had nothing to do with the warm September sun, and everything to do with Rowan's midnight eyes. I followed him out of the water and sat down, hiding my embarrassment behind a sip of cider. He rummaged through his backpack for a minute and then tossed me a small bottle of lotion. "Here, my mom always makes me bring this, though this is the first time I think I've used it."

I hastily smoothed some over my face, shoulders and upper chest. Then I stretched out my legs and leaned back to relax. Emelie joined us and grabbed the bottle. "Rowan, I don't think I got my back this morning. Can you put some on me?"

"Sure thing." I watched Rowan oblige her. While he was busy at task, she winked at me. When he finished, he put the bottle away, grabbed some cookies, and came to lie down next to me, resting his head against my thigh. This was all new territory for me, I wasn't used to a guy being so attentive. Or interested. Or anything. Emelie looked totally put out, so I decided to be nice and refrain from winking back at her.

"Ah," Rowan sighed, popping a cooking in his mouth, "snack time!"

I turned my attention to him, and had to fight an intense urge to run my fingers through his hair. Would that be creepy? Too forward? I totally did not get what to do in this kind of situation. Rowan was so relaxed. He acted like he'd known me forever, like we were old friends. Oh god, what if this was how he treated all the girls? I resolved not to fall straight into his arms.

I would. Not. Play with his hair. I wouldn't.

A few tiny drops of water tinged with blue from the dye in his hair shimmered on my thigh. Pretty.

I looked back at his hair, his face. Oh. He was looking right at me. With his pretty eyes. Dammit. I looked away from his eyes, down his face to his lips.

"Want one?" they moved. He had such nice teeth. Nice lips.

"Huh?" What? Was I caught? Did he know what I was thinking?

"A cookie. Do you want one?" His lips smiled upside down at me, and I dragged my eyes back up to meet his.

"Yes! Um, sure." He handed me one and I looked back out over the water while I chewed.

We sat there quietly for a few minutes, just soaking in the sun, eating and relaxing. After a while we went back in the water and swam some more. Emelie spent most of her time near Holly, ignoring me, which I was totally fine with. We all took turns showing off our best dives until the sun went behind the trees and the air took on a chill.

"Must be past seven! Mom's made lasagna tonight, I hope there are leftovers." Cooper groaned. He got out of the water and started packing up. We all did the same and hiked back to our cars as a group. Holly and Emelie got in a blue Mazda RX-7 and Cooper hopped in an old Wrangler with no doors.

"See you tomorrow!" Holly called to me out her window as Emelie peeled out into the dirt road, kicking up a ton of dust.

Rowan opened the truck door for me again and waited for me to get in, closing it gently once I did. He walked around to his side, giving me a chance to watch him move without anyone knowing this time. His tee shirt fit him just right, damp and sticking in a few key places to show off his muscles as he moved. His skin had a healthy glow to it after the day of sun and swimming, and his wet hair was a mess, sticking out in several directions. He was gorgeous. I looked out my window as he got to the door and climbed in.

He spent a minute putting in a new CD. The engine started, and we pulled out slowly into the road. Queen's "You're my best friend" played on the stereo while we drove in silence. I looked out the window the whole time, watching the sun set behind the hills. Gorgeous pinks laced through blue in the sky. Venus twinkled on the horizon, a pin of light in the deep indigo and I thought of Rowan's eyes.

I made sure to keep my gaze out the window, sure that if I looked at him now I would embarrass myself beyond redemption. Probably with some drool or something. Ugh.

The drive to my house seemed a lot shorter than I remembered, and when the truck stopped I felt a twinge of disappointment that the day was ending.

The engine turned off, and I turned to Rowan. He was opening his door, getting out of the car. He came around and opened my side, leaning in to grab my back pack. Then he turned to me, held out his hand and said "Milady?"

I laughed and put my hand in his, letting him help me out of the car. He handed me my pack. The porch light was still on, and my mom's car was gone. "I guess my mom's not home yet."

"Sweet, I've passed the first test!"

"First test?" I asked.

"Yeah, you know. On the quest to win the princess's heart, the knight must pass several tests. Impress the queen, defeat the dragon, rescue the damsel, and save the kingdom."

"Aw, you're so cute!" I laughed. "You think you could rescue me?"

"Sure, yeah, or at least fight by your side. Remember, me, the karate kid? But at least I have won favor with your queen, returning you home before the clock strikes." He grinned at me as he led me up the stairs to the porch, still holding me by the hand.

We got to the door and stopped. I dropped his hand and started going through my pack to find my keys. "So, um, thanks for the introduction to the falls today," I started awkwardly as I searched the bag. "I had a really great time."

I felt the keys and grabbed them. Shifting my bag back onto my shoulder, I looked up at him.

He was just staring at me with a bemused expression on his face.

"Um, so..."

"Remember what I said about this being a date, Siri?"

"Yeah?" I bit my lip, wondering if this was the part where he told me it wasn't.

"Yeah. Well, it was." And he lowered his head to mine, so close our foreheads almost touched. "Okay?"

His voice was so low it sent a rumbling through my solar plexus. I got the feeling he wasn't just asking if I understood him. It felt more like he was asking permission.

"Okay," I whispered.

He lowered his head the rest of the way, and gently touched his lips to mine. I'd never been kissed before, other than a few embarrassing middle school spin the bottle forays. Certainly never kissed by someone I liked. And never kissed by someone on a date. Oh, I'd been on a few dates throughout high school, but they had always ended with me rushing into house and evading the awkwardness, or with the boy and I just winding up as friends. I'd never been on a date that turned out...Well. This was turning out well. His lips seared into mine. I sighed with the pleasure of it and ran my hands up over his arms, reveling in the feel of his strength. I murmured appreciatively beneath his lips. A low growl came from his throat and he reached around my waist, pulling me closer and deepening our kiss. It was amazing. I felt like I was coming home and flying to outer space all at once. I ran one hand through the damp hair at his neck and clutched him closer. He smelled like sweet lemons and oranges and I felt like I could never get enough. He seemed to feel the same as he ran his hands through my damp hair.

God, why hadn't I kissed any of my other dates? What had I been thinking? What had I been missing? But I knew. I knew I hadn't missed anything, because I hadn't met anyone like him before. No one that lit me on fire this way. No one that made me feel home this way.

I don't know how long we kissed for. A dog started barking in the distance, and seemed to pull Rowan out of the trance we were both in. He pulled back, still gripping my waist.

"Okay." He said, his voice lower than usual. I breathed in his amazing scent and smiled up at him.

"Okay." I breathed in again.

He started to lean in for another kiss, and I eagerly went up on my toes to meet him. Halfway there, his phone rang in his pocket, The Adams Family theme song blasting out.

"Sorry, it's my parents." He took a step back and answered his phone. I heard a high voice on the other end, and it didn't sound happy. "Yeah mom, fine, sorry. I'll be home soon. Yeah, I know. Fine." He hung up.

"Sorry about that. My mom...she's a bit high strung sometimes. She's mad that I'm not home yet, she knows I have homework to do still." He leaned in and gave me a quick kiss on lips, followed by another on my forehead. "I'll see you tomorrow at school, yeah?"

"Alright." I smiled. "Tomorrow."

"Go on in," he nudged me. "I can't leave until my princess is safely ensconced within her castle, you know."

I laughed, and unlocked the door. "Great, am I safe now?" I asked from inside the threshold.

"For tonight," he leered suggestively at me and I giggled.

"All right, get out of here, you."

He laughed and hopped down the stairs to his truck.

I shut the door and leaned against it, listening to his truck roar to life and drive away. My heart was hammering in my chest. Oh, I was so not safe. Not from him. And it was so good.

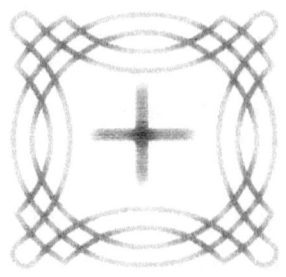

CHAPTER 10

Twelve hours later I was sitting in the parking lot of my new high school, staring in dismay at the hundreds of kids parking their cars and getting off buses. Everybody looked happy and relaxed. Everybody already had a group of friends to catch up to, to walk with, to high five.

I looked at the school entrance, watching until most of the kids had walked inside. It was now or never. I leaned down to grab my backpack off the floor of the car and banged my head on the dashboard when I heard a loud rapping above me on the window. I glanced up, rubbing the sore spot on the back of head. Rowan and Holly were staring down at me. Holly covered her mouth, obviously trying to stifle a giggle, while Rowan mouthed "Sorry" and shrugged through the window. I smiled and shrugged back at him and got out of the car.

"Hey guys, what's up?"

"Guess you're not as graceful as you are agile, huh Siri?" Rowan teased.

"Hey," Holly punched him in the arm. "Give a girl a break! If it was me I would have probably shrieked in surprise, too." She smiled at me as we started toward the school. "You should hear my bug scream."

"Ha, yeah. Let's go find a spider. Holly has an awesome spider shriek." Rowan snickered as Holly actually paled and started shaking her head.

"Whatever. I think I see Emelie. See you!" And she jogged off into the school.

"Guess she's not a fan of spiders?" I asked.

"Nope. Not at all. I have a great collection of rubber ones in my room that I save for extra special occasions."

"Such as?"

"Oh, you know, breakfast, showers, prom. Whatever."

"Nice. Remind me not to tell you about the things I'm afraid of," I laughed.

Rowan examined me as we walked into the building. "Somehow, I imagine you're not afraid of much, Siri Alvarsson." He stopped and reached for me. Was he actually going to kiss me right here? My heart sped up with excitement and just a little bit of nerves. Instead, he straightened my backpack on my shoulders and tucked one of my curls behind my ear, just like a mom. "The school office is over there," he said, angling his head to point to the right. "Go get your locker number and schedule, and hopefully I'll see you soon in one of my classes. And don't forget to come find me at lunch by the windows in the caf." And then he did kiss me, well, more of peck really, on the nose, but it still caught the attention of a couple younger girls walking by, who started whispering furiously and giggling.

I smiled up at him shyly. "Alright, I'll see you later."

"Get on with you then," He smiled and started walking backwards. "See you later, Serious!" He yelled the last part loudly, and everyone still in the halls looked around at him curiously. I rolled my eyes and ducked into the school office as quickly as possible.

The woman behind the counter glanced up and smiled kindly at me. "What can I do for you, my dear?"

"Um, yeah, hi. Today's my first day, I'm Siri Alvarsson," I said, approaching the counter.

"Oh yes, Miss Alvarsson! I'm Mrs. Kite. Your mother had all your transcripts faxed over to us last week. So many places you've lived in. Wonderful to have seen so much of the world, isn't it?" She beamed at me.

"I guess it is." She was so open and warm, I felt compelled to smile back at her, even though I usually tried to stay off the radar at school.

"Well, based on your past performance, we've placed you in all honors history and science classes, and senior lit. You have room for some extracurriculars, and I saw you seem to like the arts so I would suggest trying Mr. Brown's film class. It's pretty popular with seniors, and you get to watch so many great classics. Also, we have a really great horticulture class that people love. Not too many high schools offer a class like that, but with all the agriculture in the area, we take plants pretty seriously."

"Um, sure, yeah, those both sound good."

"Alrighty then." She gave me my new class schedule. "Hold on just a minute." She picked up the phone, pressed a couple buttons and spoke into it "Mr. Fein, could you please send Miss David down to the office? Thank you." She hung up and looked back up at me. "Now, all I need is your driver's license and license plate number for campus parking, since your mother indicated you wouldn't be taking the bus?"

"Yes, right, here they are."

"Perfect. I'll just get these copied down and you can follow Miss David to class when she gets here. She'll show you around this morning until you get your bearings. Can't have our new student getting lost on her first day!" She cackled to herself, as she walked over to her desk, apparently thinking the very idea of it was pretty funny.

I stood there, looking at the framed inspirational posters scattered throughout the office walls. It was your typical mix of "Determination," "Achievement," "Dream Big," "Teamwork". I did a double take when I saw one of a kitten standing with its paws up that said "Busted: You know what you did." I laughed in surprise. Just then Rose came running in.

"Hey! Siri, right? Guess who gets to be your tour guide of the day!"

Mrs. Kite looked up and greeted Rose happily. "Rose, darling, so nice to see you this morning! Ms. Alvarsson here is just starting in your class." She handed Rose a copy of my schedule. "Can you please show her around for the day?"

"Oh, yes, of course, Mrs. Kite, I'd love to!" Rose grinned at me. "Siri and I are old friends. Come on, off we go. Wouldn't want to miss your first class!" She grabbed me by one arm and steered me out of the office. "Have a great day Mrs. Kite!" she called over her shoulder. The door closed behind us, cutting off whatever the woman said in reply.

"Okay, so, let's see." Rose looked over my schedule as we walked, her arm linked through mine. "Ooh, you're a smart one!"

"We have lit and weeds together. The rest I can show you where they are. I'll walk you to your first class, that's math – ugh, what sadist thought anyone should start the day with numbers anyway? – and I'll be waiting outside when it's over to walk you to the next one."

She talked a mile a minute while I just let her drag me along.

"Oh, I love this job. Because of you, I get to miss half of every class today! You are the best!" she gushed and squeezed my arm. "SO. What is this I hear about you kissing Rowan Carey?"

I stopped walking. "What?!"

"I saw you guys this morning, all cute and up close and personal, and he kissed you right there in the hallway. Everyone's talking about you, the mystery girl Rowan's sweet on. So spill."

73

I blushed. "I don't know. We met a few days ago, and we went to the falls. He wants me to have lunch with him today."

"He's a smooth one, our Rowan. He hasn't dated anyone in a while, as far as I know." She bumped shoulders with me. "Must have been waiting for someone special, eh?"

"Ha, right. I don't know, we'll see." I tried to blow the whole thing off. But on the inside I felt bubbly. So he'd been telling the truth about not dating that much.

"Yes, we will. As your self-appointed Union mentor, I'll come with you at lunch and help you assess the situation," she teased me. And with that, she opened the door to my first class and propelled me forward. "Enjoy!"

I turned around, ready to glare at her, but the door had already closed behind me and she was gone. I turned back around and realized the whole class was staring at me, including the teacher who looked none too pleased to have been interrupted. Ah, perfect.

"Can I help you, young lady?"

"Yes, hi, I think I'm in this class?" A couple of kids in the back started sniggering, only to be cut off by the teacher's glare in their direction.

He looked back at me, "You think?"

"Um, yes, here, see?" I handed him my schedule. He quickly scanned it, snorted, and handed it back to me.

"Well, you're going to have some catching up to do. Find a free seat and like it. You'll be in the same seat all year."

I nodded and scrambled into a chair by the window.

"Everybody, meet Siri Alvarsson. Siri, meet everybody," the teacher said, and started back in on the lesson. I spent the rest of the class vacillating between paying attention, and drawing a picture of the large eastern pine that towered outside the window.

When the bell rang, I joined the rush for the door. I felt a tug on my backpack and turned around, annoyed. "Hey watch–"

"Hey yourself," Cooper grinned at me. "If you need help catching up, let me know. Math is kind of my thing."

"Oh, hey! Thanks, Cooper, that's really nice of you. I think I'll be alright, but I'll keep it in mind. Thanks."

"No problem," he smiled. "See you later, Serious."

"Aw, come on, not you, too!"

He winked at me. "Later!"

He walked off, just as Rose came up. "Hey, looks like you made another friend already!"

"Yeah, I met Cooper and Holly yesterday at the falls with Rowan. Emelie, too."

"Oh, that's cool." Rose's tone cooled down for the first time since I'd met her.

"Let me guess. Not an Emelie fan?" I drawled.

"Oh thank God. I was worried she had tried to claim you into her group of minions. She is such a hag. She has this whole clone group of girls that follow her around and do whatever she says." She eyed me up and down from my green Docs to my Social Distortion tank top. "But I guess you didn't win her favor, huh?"

"Not quite," I chuckled. "She was really pissed when I showed up with Rowan. I ignored her for the most part, though."

"Oh, I bet that really pissed her off. Especially since you showed up with Rowan."

"Yeah, what's up with those two?"

"Oh, they dated for about a week in ninth grade, broke up because she decided she had crush on some senior, then she changed her mind and she's been trying to win him back ever since. He never got back with her, but he hasn't really dated anyone else much, either. At least, not anything serious. Their parents are best friends, so she and Holly are besties, even though Holly isn't a mindless minion."

"Ah, so all is revealed." I wiggled my eyebrows.

"I know, right?! Anyhow, I'll introduce you to some of my friends when we get to class. We're all in weeds together."

"Weeds?"

"Horticulture 101. Anyone who likes plants or farming is in it, plus all the hippies and stoners. Or any seniors who want an easy grade." She must have seen the doubt on my face because she rushed on. "It's a really fun class, actually, I promise. A couple of the guys I board with take it, because they want to do forestry when they graduate. Plus, the teacher is way cool. You'll see."

We wove through the halls, finally coming to an outside door that led to a covered greenhouse inside a large courtyard area. I was a little nervous about taking a class all about plants, we'd never really bothered with having any gardens anywhere we lived, since we wouldn't be able to keep them. My mom did buy a few houseplants for every new place, but we always had to leave them behind when we moved. I had no idea how to do anything with a plant, other than to give it some water when it started wilting.

The hot, humid air of the greenhouse poured over us as we entered. I was glad I had worn a tank top today, and made a mental note to always wear layers to this class. A short, plump woman was standing in the far corner, and a bunch of students were already standing around her attentively. We hurried over and stood on the edge of the group.

"Well hello there, Rose, nice of you to join us today. And who's our guest?"

"Sorry Ms. Anjali, this is Siri Alvarsson, a new senior. I'm showing her around today." Everyone turned to look at us.

"Hi," I said, smiling and doing a little half-wave. A few people smiled back, while most looked bored and turned back to the teacher.

"Wonderful, wonderful! Welcome, Siri!" She gushed in a sweet voice. "I was just telling the students about today's project. We are going to be rooting Begonia, Forsythia and Echinacea cuttings with vermiculite to plant around the school in the spring. So step up and listen in. You can work with Rose today."

Thank goodness we were working in pairs, because I had no idea what she was talking about. Cuttings? Vermiculite? It was like she was speaking a whole different language. This was going to be interesting. I looked around the room while she started talking about buds and hormones. Everything was so green and vibrant. I could practically feel the energy humming around me. I breathed the sweet air deep into my lungs and felt a calmness that I hadn't ever really felt before. The plants all looked so happy and full of life. Without realizing it, I zoned out for the rest of her talk, just staring at the lush blooms behind her merging together in a sea of corals and pinks.

It wasn't until Rose nudged me forward to gather our own collection of plants to work with that I noticed how much time had passed. Luckily, Rose had been paying attention and was able to guide me through the simple process of cutting small, healthy stems off the living plant, dipping them in a fine powder and then gently planting them in a light soil mix that Rose called "rooting medium." Soon enough, we heard the faint echo of the bell ringing indoors, washed up and headed out to the next class.

The day continued on easily. Most people seemed nice enough, and my classes weren't bad. By the time lunch rolled around I was starving and looking forward to just sitting quietly for a while. Of course, with Rose meeting me right after History, that last part was pretty much not going to happen. That girl could talk!

But she was really nice, and seemed to have decided that we were going to be good friends, so I'd resigned myself to the happy chatter. It was great, actually, to have been able to fit in so quickly in a new town. As we walked to lunch, linked arm and arm again with Rose pulling me speedily along, I thought about the fact that I was about to see Rowan again. Suddenly, Rose didn't have to pull me so much as she needed to keep up.

"Whoah, slow down there, speedy!"

"Sorry, I thought I smelled tacos," I lied. "I'm starving!"

"Sorry, no, Taco Tuesday's tomorrow, today I think it's burgers. Or pasta salad if you're a veg."

We stepped into line, grabbed our food and I followed Rose out into the cafeteria. "So, I usually sit over there," Rose pointed at a table nearby filled with a few guys and girls I recognized from our hort class. "We all work at the mountain together. But you said you're meeting Rowan? You want me to come with?"

I looked over at the table where Rowan was sitting, and saw Holly, Emelie and Cooper, along with a couple strangers. I smiled at Rose, glad to have her with me. "Definitely."

She beamed back at me before leading the way to their table. "Hey guys!" She said as she sat down next to Holly. On the other side of the table, Rowan slid away from Emelie and motioned for me to sit down between them.

We all introduced ourselves and then everyone got back to their previous conversations. Rowan smiled at me and picked a fry off my tray. "So, how's Union treating you so far?"

"Not bad. I have this crazy guide taking me around, but other than that it's not so bad." I grinned over at Rose, who threw one of her own fries at me. I grabbed it out of the air and popped it in my mouth. "See? I even get free food."

Rowan laughed. I started in on my burger, which was pretty overdone but not terrible with the "special sauce" the kitchen had come up with. I practically jumped out of my seat when Rowan put a hand on my knee and squeezed. He leaned in and whispered, "I was thinking about this all morning."

I looked back at him dumbly. "About burgers?"

He let out a huge bark of laughter. "No Siri, not burgers." He winked at me, took his hand off my knee, and went back to eating. Everybody else looked at us, wondering what he was talking about. Emelie glared and turned her back to me, talking to the girl on her other side in hushed tones before they got up and left. Definitely no love lost there.

I stared down at my plate, suddenly all thoughts of hunger had left my body, and all I could think about was the hum in my leg where his hand had been. What was happening to me? I had never felt like this before. I couldn't even tell if I was nervous or excited, hungry or nauseous. I took a cautious sip of my juice, decided that it was acceptable, and went back to picking at my fries.

"So, what class do you have next?" Rowan asked me.

"She's got AP Physics." Rose answered before I could check my sheet.

"Sweet, so do I. So we do have a class together after all." Rowan bumped shoulders with me. "You gonna let me walk you to class, or do I have to fight Rose for the job?"

Rose giggled and gave me a knowing look. "Oh, I think you can handle it. I'll even let you walk her to her class after, too. Just make sure you get her there on time."

"What am I, a dog?" I grumbled at the same time he answered with a chivalrous bow. "I swear it will be done."

"Ooh!" Rose clapped. "Princess Bride! I always knew you were a keeper, Mr. Carey."

"Yeah, well, this one over here," he said, inclining his head at Holly, "gets to choose half the flicks we watch on movie nights, so I've watched it a few billion times."

"Perfect," I chimed in. "Now I know what to make you watch when you come over."

He looked back at me. "Oh, really? Am I coming over?"

"Um, well, you know, maybe some time." I stammered. Ugh. If the floor could just open up now that would be good.

He leaned into me. "Maybe definitely."

"Oh. Good. Great." Great. More stammering. I was so not good at this flirting stuff.

Rose laughed and got up. "Okay, well I don't think I can stand any more of this young love. I'm out." Everybody at the table laughed, too, and started getting ready to go. I ate a few more fries while the table emptied out.

Finally, Rowan stood up and took my tray on top of his, "Ready?" He looked down at me kindly, with a little smile teasing the corner of his eyes. It was so not fair. He was obviously way more socially adept then I was. A little flare of jealousy for the stability he had enjoyed all his life flashed through me for a second, and I shook it off. I stood up and followed him.

"So what's this class like? Am I super far behind?"

"It's not too bad. Mr. Adiletti is pretty awesome. He has this hair that sticks up everywhere and makes him look like a young Einstein. And he's pretty cool, gives hard tests but not too much homework other than reading. I have next Friday off, so you should come over to my house that afternoon. I can help you catch up before our first test. Plus, then you can enjoy the fabulous Carey Friday Family Movie Night tradition afterwards. And, lucky for you, it's my turn to pick the movie, ha ha!"

"So is it studying or is a date?" I asked before I could think better of it.

We walked around the corner into an empty stretch of hall, where Rowan stopped and turned, pinning me up against the wall. "Oh, it's a date." He leaned in and I tilted my head up, closing my eyes, ready for a kiss like Sunday's. Instead, I heard someone clear their throat and felt Rowan let go of my shoulders. Disappointed, I opened my eyes to see Union's track coach glaring at me.

"Mr. Carey, Ms...Well, I don't remember your name, but this is not the time or the place for that sort of thing. Get to class now before I think better of it and send you both to the school office." Ms. Thorn crossed her arms and started tapping her foot. All the blood drained from my face. I never got in trouble at school, ever. She threw a pointed look at Rowan. "Mr. Carey, you, especially, know better than this. I would hate to have to call your father. Go on now, you two. Get!"

"Sorry Ms. Thorn, it won't happen again." Rowan looked almost as pale as I felt. He placed his hand on the small of my back and steered me around her.

"See that it doesn't," she called after us.

"Whoa." I exhaled. "That was intense. What's her problem?"

Rowan ran a hand through his hair, ruffling the little blue and blonde spikes, and looked down at me, clearly distracted. "Um, what? Her? Yeah, she's always like that. And she's old friends with my dad."

"Oh. I hope your dad isn't as scary as she is." I joked.

Rowan looked at me with a weird expression on his face. "My dad is...well, he's my dad, you know, so I wouldn't say he's scary, but he can be kind of tough. He takes school pretty seriously, always talking about my duty to excel and all that."

"Wow, that sounds kind of rough, no offense."

Rowan nodded. "It's not so bad. He just wants me to do well so I can join him running the family business someday."

"Oh, well that's cool I guess." I shrugged. "What's he do?"

"Just business stuff. Nothing too exciting." Rowan didn't quite meet my eyes, and I got the feeling that he didn't really want to talk about it any further. "That's why he has me working at Giovanni's, so I can learn all about how regular businesses are run."

We stopped in front of a door.

"Here we are," he opened the door for me and in we went, finding a couple seats next to each other.

I spent the next forty minutes trying to keep up with Mr. Adiletti as he talked about quasars and black holes, and how some people theorized they led to other dimensions or hid worm holes inside them. Once, I flashed back to Ms. Thorn's cold, dark, almost black eyes, and shivered.

Thank God Rowan was going to help me catch up on Friday. I could tell this teacher didn't just mindlessly follow the text in the book. I would definitely be needing some help.

The rest of my classes flew by without incident, and when the day was over I was relieved to be able to climb in my Forester – I still couldn't get over the fact that it was now mine and mine alone. I turned up the music and headed home.

CHAPTER 11

I poured myself a big glass of milk when I got home and looked over my assignments. Most of it was pretty easy, what my mom called "busywork," so I got it out of the way right then. I also had some chapters to read for physics and lit, but I figured I'd do that later in bed. After being pent up inside all day and having to meet so many new people, I was feeling twitchy. I really needed to get outside, go for a long run.

I changed clothes and headed out, deciding to go in the opposite direction I'd gone last time. I definitely wasn't in the mood to run into Coach Thorn twice in one day. She'd said I should consider trying out for track, but I wasn't sure I wanted to have to spend that much time around her. As it was, I was sure I'd have to see her enough. Besides, if I did track, I'd be stuck running in circles all the time.

I pushed the issue out of mind, and concentrated on my pace, just running and breathing, step after step. I'd noticed a small nature trail a mile down the road a few days before that I wanted to check out. Within a few minutes I arrived at the small dirt pull-off where there was just enough room for three or four cars to park. The trail was blocked by a single wooden lockgate so that vehicles couldn't go off-roading down the trail, complete with a large red and white "no vehicles" sign, though I could see some tire marks from dirt bikes that had snuck around the gate recently. There was a small trail map posted by the entrance, too, designating this area as "Mine Creek Preserve."

I walked over to it and did a few lunges and stretches while I studied the trail system. According to the map there was a small creek that led to a beaver pond, and the main green trail looped around both for about four miles. There were also a couple of little trails that led off the main one, one of them leading to an old garnet mine and another one marked in yellow that seemed to follow the edge of the preserve along some of its boundaries. If I wasn't mistaken, that path actually would run through the woods right behind our home. I decided to run to the pond, then double back and take the yellow trail to the end to see if it went all the way to our house.

I took off down the trail at a fast pace. After about half a mile the woods became denser, the path more rocky and rough. I started looking at the trail less like a road and more like a cross-country obstacle course, jumping from rock to rock as I went, bouncing through the woods on the hard packed dirt. I was so happy I had bought the new Asics, they were awesome. Every rock I bounced off of felt like a cloud, seriously.

A huge old tree had fallen across the trail, but that didn't faze me. I cat vaulted over it parkour style to gain maximum distance over the obstacle without slowing down. Whenever the path went to curve around a boulder, I would tic tac off the side of the stone, leaping and pushing off with one foot to change direction and follow the trail. At one point the trail split and I saw the yellow trail go off to the right. I made a mental note of where I was so I wouldn't miss it on the way back, and continued to the left. After another mile I came to the pond, a beautiful clearing in the woods complete with a cute little bench facing west so you could watch the sunset over the water if you were here at the right time.

I stood for a moment, catching my breath and marveling at the vivid reflection of the trees on the surface of the pond. The fiery reds and sunny yellows were so bright, the water looked practically black by comparison. The pond must have been really deep. The water looked super clear right by the shore, but after just a few feet I couldn't see the bottom. Far across the way I could see a huge pile of sticks that I could only assume was the beaver lodge, but I couldn't see any inhabitants at the moment. Some geese swam by and honked a few times at me, apparently outraged that I was invading their afternoon swim, and floated closer to the lodge. I took a deep breath, inhaling the clean, fresh air. It tasted like pure sunshine and fallen leaves. Perfect.

I turned around and went back the way I came, ready to tackle the yellow trail. The map indicated it was less than a mile long, and that it ran behind some houses by the main road, so I was hoping I could link up to my back yard from it. How cool would it be to have access to my own private running trail?

I hadn't lived in such a rural place for years. While I ran at a more sedate pace, keeping an eye out for the trail split, my mind wandered. What was Rowan doing right now? Rose had mentioned at one point during the day how having a boyfriend that practically ran Giovanni's would be soooo awesome ("imagine all the free pizza!") so I guessed he worked most days after school. He hadn't mentioned getting together for another date before the following Friday, so he was probably pretty busy. That or he was taking it slow. Or he just wasn't as into me as I thought.

I didn't really know for sure how to tell with these sorts of things. We'd just met, really, so I figured it was actually a good thing to have some time to myself. I mean, he seemed awesome, but I didn't really know him at all. Not to mention the fact that he was friends with Emelie. That wasn't exactly a great recommendation. Not that it was his fault, I mean, she was his sister's friend, really. And Holly seemed nice enough.

If I didn't get to go out with Rowan again right away, it was probably a good thing, I decided. I could take it slow, get to know the school better, take some time to settle in. I mean, hey, it's not like he was even my boyfriend. Maybe I'd date someone else, too. Have a whole posse of boys. I laughed at myself. As if that would ever happen. This was my senior year, and I was only just now getting my first real kiss. I started thinking about that kiss, the way my stomach had somersaulted again and again, the firm press of his lips against mine. Totally not paying attention where I was going, I stumbled over a root in the ground. I caught myself before I actually hit the ground, and it was just in time, too, since I looked around and there was the trail split.

I veered off to the left, following the yellow patches of paint on the tree trunks that appeared every twenty feet or so. The trail grew narrower – obviously this path wasn't used nearly as often as the main routes. Leaves and small branches were everywhere, hiding smaller rocks and divots. I increased my focus and got back into parkour mode, becoming more springy and ready on my feet as I took in every detail along the way. After a while I started seeing the occasional house or barn on the right through the trees. The trail seemed to follow the boundary of the preserve, with small buffer zones of twenty to fifty feet of woods before reaching people's lawns. This looked promising. I jogged past several more places, and then saw our multifamily converted farmhouse through the trees. Curious to see how much further the trail continued, I kept going, only to stop in front of a sheer rock face another quarter mile down the way. There was an old fire ring a few feet in front of the cliff, with some logs nearby and crushed, faded cans on the ground. It didn't look like anyone had used the spot for at least a year. It seemed like a really good, quiet place to hang out, minus the old beer cans. I picked them up and put them over by the cliff face, resolving to bring a small bag next time I came so I could clean the place up. I saw some small dead branches nearby that has fallen, so I broke them up and put them by the fire ring. Sitting on the logs by the ring, I gazed around.

It was so peaceful here. Huge white quartz boulders surrounded the area. The birds seemed quieter here, and the rocks had an ancient, knowing feel to them. Like if I sat long enough, they would tell me something special, impart some indigenous wisdom or something. Whatever, I shook my head. Where did that come from? What a weird idea.

Still, I could see that this would be a great place to come to think and read as the days started turning colder. Maybe I'd even bring Rowan here. Just the thought of it made me feel as if I had already lit the sticks in the firepit.

The light was starting to fade, so I got up to make my way home. It seemed even closer on the way back than it had the first time down the path. The undergrowth wasn't too thick by our yard, so I was able to easily pick my way between the trees to reach the lawn, exiting the forest next to a huge old sycamore tree. Awesome. I would be able to find my way back to the trail anytime with no problem, and the trail complex would insure that I could do any length run I wanted, or just sit and hang out by the rocks again. No way was I going to join track now, not when I had my own wonderland to explore until the snows came.

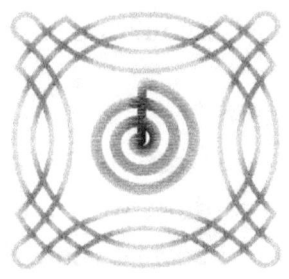

CHAPTER 12

The next day passed quietly until lunch, when Rose and I sat with Rowan and his friends again. A fight had broken out between a few kids on the other side of the caf, so most of the short period was wasted with everyone watching the drama unfold. I'd barely eaten or spoken to Rowan at all, in fact, although I noticed that he and Cooper both managed to eat their whole meals without distraction. Watching them, we might as well have been at the movies considering how little it affected their appetite. Boys. Clearly, the old sayings about men and their stomachs were all true.

After lunch Rowan and I walked to our AP class. I was still sort of out of it, thinking about the excitement at lunch, and he steered me through the halls with his hand on my back. The warmth of his hand burned through my shirt, sending strange pulses up my spine.

"Everything good with you?" he asked.

"Huh, what?"

"You seem a little distracted." I looked up at him, and saw that his eyes were dark with concern. My head was starting to pound, and I sort of wished that he would stop looking at me. I was feeling a bit warm, too hot, actually, and the heat from his hand was just too much. It seemed to be going straight to my head, lighting a fire under the pain that was just too much to bear. I tried to shrug his hand off, but it didn't budge.

"Yeah, sure. I'm just starting to get a headache. Guess the excitement at lunch was too much for me." I picked up the pace, grateful when his hand slipped off my back.

"Those guys were pretty loud. Stuff like that doesn't happen too often here, hope it didn't freak you out."

I laughed, despite the building pressure in my head. "Yeah, right. As if. Back in Tucson we had fights like that almost every day. Same at my school before that. Both of them were majorly jock infested, way too much testosterone going on there. I was just surprised, that's all. I didn't think Vermont had so much potential for excitement."

"Oh, don't worry," he said suggestively. "I can think of plenty of exciting things we could do."

If I hadn't been feeling so crappy, I'm sure I would have been filled with butterflies at that comment. As it was, I just felt a little nauseous. "Mmm, I'll keep that in mind." I gave him a queasy smile and walked in through the open door to Adiletti's class.

There was a desk right by the door and I took it, while Rowan slid into the seat behind me, giving me another concerned look. I turned to the front and tried to keep my eyes open as more waves of nausea poured over me. It felt like the floor under my feet was rumbling, like the whole classroom was at sea and I thought I might suddenly get sick, right here in class.

Oh no, I thought. Not again. Not here.

Again, I was back on the scene of a lovely city built on a hill. Bright stucco houses with rainbow colors for doors, simple tile roofs, narrow cobblestone streets built into steep hillsides. Vespas outside doorways, chickens and dogs roamed the streets quietly, the sun just starting to rise over the sea. Or was it an ocean? I couldn't tell. It was quiet, early morning, and everyone was abed. I knew this place. I'd been here before. But when?

And then before I could think of what was happening, flocks of birds took to the skies in a raucous migration, all at once, and I remembered where I was. The rumbling. The swaying.

And then it began. The street lurched beneath my feet, sending me to my knees, and I closed my eyes. It's just a dream, I thought. Just a dream. The whole world groaned as buildings broke under the strain of exertion and tumbled to the ground on every side. Everyone had been sleeping, but now they were awake. Babies were crying. Mothers and fathers moaned. Voices raised up and then went silent, while others sobbed and whispered. Dust choked the air, so I couldn't breath and my head ached, and all around me the people were crying.

I crawled to the nearest pile of rubble and began clawing at the rocks, trying to reach some of the moans.

Before they stopped. Before it all stopped. Before I stopped. I didn't know if I could do this, if I could go on. How did people go on in disasters? How did they survive?

I'd always thought I was strong. But what good were my fighting skills against something like this? What good was anything? What could I, one girl, possibly do?

"So it begins."

A man spoke behind me. His voice was cold, uncaring. Not upset at all. Not like me.

"Do something! Help me. Help them!" I yelled at him. I couldn't see his face clearly, but I hated him. I hated him being here with me, for being another person standing, for being another person who couldn't really do anything. And I hated his voice, his detached voice. I turned away from him and kept digging.

"There is nothing to do here. It has begun."

I screamed in rage as the stones I had dug out collapsed in upon themselves, and turned to yell at him again, but he was gone. Everything was gone. He was right. There was nothing I could do. I shut my eyes in horror and frustration, trying to gather my strength, trying to figure out a way to deal with this,

and when I opened them again I was lying on the floor, staring up at the flickering glare of Union's brilliant fluorescent tube lighting. Rowan was kneeling next to me and Mr. Adiletti was staring in confusion over his shoulder, while a couple of girls snickered together nearby at their desks.

"Siri, are you okay?"

"Ms. Alvarsson, can you tell me how many fingers I am holding up?"

I blinked at them. "Um, yes, I think so. I don't know, maybe. Two?" I answered them both. "What happened? Why am I on the floor?" My head was pounding in full force now, and I was pretty sure that if I sat up I might hurl. And I really, really, so did not want to do that.

"You fell. Are you sure you're alright? Mr. Adiletti, I think I better take her to the nurse."

"Certainly, Rowan, I think that would be best. Ms. Alvarsson, do you think you can walk?" The girls snickered some more behind him, and I resolved to get up. Screw them. I didn't know what was happening to me, but I wasn't some weak invalid. I was woman. I could roar. And I could certainly damn well walk.

"Yes, I can walk." I tried to get up and was overcome with nausea. I'm pretty sure I actually turned green. Rowan quickly scooped me up in his arms, grabbed my backpack and carried me out to the hallway. I looked over his shoulder and could see that the girls were no longer laughing, but instead were sighing with stars in their eyes. Yeah. Rowan was pretty swoon worthy. Too bad I was too out of it to really appreciate it. I mean, he was actually carrying me. Carrying me. Like some kickass hero out of the Princess Bride. Talk about swoon. I leaned my head on his shoulder and closed my eyes.

"So, you going to tell me what happened back there?" Rowan asked. He sounded mad at me, which I couldn't figure out.

"I don't know. I had a headache, then I sort of started daydreaming and felt like the whole room was shaking, and then I just passed out."

"The room was shaking?"

"Yeah, I told you. Maybe I'm anemic or something?"

"Maybe. Did you feel anything else? What were you daydreaming about?" The anger in his voice gave way to concern, just like my mom when I hurt myself doing something stupid and she couldn't stay mad at me.

"I don't know. It's all kind of foggy. I just got nauseous and dizzy and wobbly. It happened over the weekend, too, I forgot. I must be getting sick."

"You know, you said something while you were out. You fainted and fell on the floor, and before you came to you said 'It has begun.' Was that part of your dream?"

"What? I don't know. I don't remember. Can we stop with all the questions, my head is pounding." I closed my eyes and breathed in his warm, citrusy musk. "God, you smell amazing."

He chuckled. "I do, huh? Way to change the subject. But I'll let it slide. This time." His breath washed over my hair and I thought I felt the brush of his lips on my head before we entered the nurse's office.

The school nurse was young and capable, and had me lying down in no time. After she sternly ordered Rowan back to class, he squeezed my hand and told me he would check in on me later, all the time apologizing with his eyes for having to leave. I probably should have felt upset, but honestly I was just so tired and aching all over, I didn't really care if I was alone or not. After he left, she assured me that a stomach bug was going around town and that once I was feeling more the thing I could go home and sleep it off. I thought that was a great idea. Maybe if I rested, the rest of my daydream would come back to me. Somehow, it seemed important, but whenever I tried to reach for the memory it felt like dust slipping through my fingers.

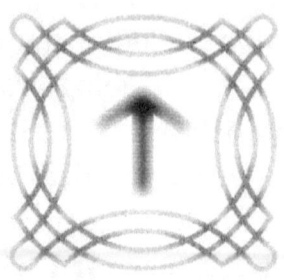

CHAPTER 13

I wound up staying at school until the end of the day, sleeping through a couple of periods in the nurse's office. When the last bell of the day rang she gently prodded me awake and helped me up.

"Time to go home, sweetie. You think you can get there alright or do you want me to call your mom?"

I insisted I was good and made my way home, driving slowly through the quiet afternoon streets. When I got home I sat on the floor in the living room doing homework while I watched a couple shows on a local TV station through my laptop. Hey, what my mom didn't know wouldn't kill her. At least I usually skipped through the commercials. She'd left a note on the counter saying she'd be working late again tonight, so after a couple hours I decided to order a pizza from Giovanni's. Rowan took the order and said he had a break coming up, so he'd bring it over when it was ready. Mmm. Pizza and Rowan. Delish.

My appetite grew even stronger, though whether for the pizza or for Rowan, I couldn't say with any certainty.

I spent a few minutes picking up and making sure there weren't bras hanging around on my floor or in the bathroom, and put on a fresh coat of lip gloss. I didn't want to be one of those girls, primping just for a guy, but I also figured it didn't hurt to make sure I was at least presentable. And sporting kissable grape-flavored lips. Why not?

The doorbell rang just as I was walking out into the living room. I could see that the TV show had segued into the early evening news, and they were leading with some news about Rio in Brazil. I walked past the sofa and opened the door.

"Hey Rowan," I smiled.

"Hey yourself," he smiled back and leaned against the doorframe. "One medium mushroom pizza, and an order of jalapeño poppers."

"What? I didn't order any poppers."

"I know, but I look out for my own, you know?" He winked at me, and then got more serious. "Are you feeling better now? You kind of scared me back there in school today."

"Yeah, I'm fine. The nurse said there's a bug going around."

"Well, you don't look ill. At least not anymore."

"Hey, thanks! Please, tell me more about how craptastic I looked earlier today." I laughed as I took the bag of poppers from him. "Do you have time to hang out a bit? Come on, I can't eat all this myself." I turned and nodded for him to follow me into the living room.

He started saying something behind me about how he'd have to get back to work in a few minutes, but I wasn't paying attention. Because there, on my laptop screen, I could see pictures of dusty rubble.

"What—" I started to say as I slid down onto the couch. The screen was showing images of the hillsides of Rio de Janeiro, which had been devastated that morning in a 6.3 earthquake, flashing back and forth between images of the poorer favela communities before and after the earthquakes. Everything I had seen earlier, all the visions I'd had, cascaded through my head.

"I was there." I whispered.

Rowan sat down beside me. "Siri, you're pale as a ghost. Are you alright? I mean, what is it?" He looked at the screen. "Rio? You've been there?"

"No," I said, and then realized how that must sound. "I mean. Yes. I was there. I've seen these places. I've been there." A very familiar image of the street I had seen at dawn in my visions flashed on screen and I pointed at it, "There. I've been on that street, right there. Oh. My. God. All those people!"

Tears were running down my face, and I knew I must look like a total freak to Rowan, but I just didn't care. The news was flashing numbers across the bottom of the screen, tallies of the dead and the missing. The numbers were sure to go up because it was still early. Because I knew. I knew how many had died. On that street alone, it had been almost everyone. Those poor, weak buildings hadn't been built to withstand earthquakes. And now the people inside were all dead. So many. Just gone. I stifled a sob and shut my computer. "I think I've lost my appetite. Rowan, would you mind very much if we didn't..."

He hopped up instantly. "Yeah, sure, no problem." He ran a hand through his hair nervously. "Look, I'm sure they'll find most of the people. I have to get back to work anyways, but listen," he knelt down and gave me a quick hug, "text me later, okay? Just to let me know you're alright? I worry about you, Serious."

I gave him a wan smile. "Okay, I will. Thanks Rowan."

"Anytime, gorgeous." He smiled at me and walked out the door.

As soon as he left, I opened up my laptop again and ran a Google search for news articles about the earthquake. The articles already listed several thousand people dead, and the numbers were expected to keep climbing over the coming days. Or weeks. Some articles said it might take weeks for the rescue parties to make it to certain parts of the city. It had happened early that morning, as far as I could tell. So what now, I was some sort of seer? I could tell when big disasters were going to happen? And then, if this was something real, something that had really happened, then who was that man in my vision, the one I couldn't get a good look at? And what did he mean, "It has begun?" What had begun? The earthquake? Or something else, something worse?

God, this was all so creepy. I shut the laptop again and stood up, suddenly feeling very twitchy again. I needed to be outside. Immediately. I put my shoes on and ran outside, down the porch steps. Without even thinking where I was going, I turned around the side of the house and was in the woods before I even realized what I was doing. Coming out on the tiny path, I made my way back to the rock ledge and the fire pit. Everything looked the same, no one had been here in the past day. I stood still, staring up at the rock face, taking deep breaths. Within moments, I felt better, but I still needed to move. I dropped into a solid horse stance and began flowing through some Qigong forms, weaving my way around the circle several times.

Better.

But I could still hear the startled screams of the sleeping Brazilians as their homes swayed and collapsed without warning around them. I expanded my circle, and started incorporating the quartz boulders into my routine, pretending they were part of my internal kung fu movie set, leaping over them, onto them, around them. The moans of the fallen surrounded me. I fought my way clear of the pain and the confusion. The noise of the dying began to subside as I worked my way through the pain, striking and lunging to defeat an unknown army so I could see another day. Finally, I collapsed into a full lotus position on top of a large granite outcrop, and leaned back into the face of the cliffs behind me.

I closed my eyes and breathed deeply.

The voices were gone. The ground was still. Everything was as it should be. I was in the right place, at the right time, doing the right thing. Everything was going to be okay.

I repeated the last like a mantra in my head, over and over again. I almost believed it. The stone all around me felt comforting, like home. I thought that maybe if I just knew how to ask the right way, the rock would be able to tell me what was going on. And it, most definitely, would say to me that everything was going to be okay. Could I truly believe that? Or was it just wishful thinking? I heard movement in the forest nearby and tensed, hoping someone else wasn't making their way to my new spot. I opened my eyes and looked around. No one was there. The birds were quiet, and the leaves rustled on the trees, even though I didn't feel any wind where I was sitting in the lee of the stone. Each tree had its own vibrant, unique shade of green, red or yellow. The foliage here was amazing this time of year. The stone beneath me felt warm and cozy, not hard and cold like I would have thought a rock should feel. It felt alive. I felt alive.

I heard some more noise in the woods, coming closer, fast. My heart sped up for a moment, and then stopped when a little dark blur of fur passed behind a stone nearby. A moment later a black squirrel clambered up onto the rock across the circle from me and stood on its hind legs, scenting me with its small twitching nose. It had a small patch of white just like the one I had held a few days before by the side of the road. But that couldn't be. Could it?

"Hey little guy," I cooed in what I hoped was a reassuring tone of voice. "Have you come to say hello?" The squirrel cocked its small ears forward in interest.

"Is this your special spot, too? We can share." The squirrel chittered back at me and ran back down behind the rock. Seconds later, it came back up, an acorn its mouth. It settled down, and started snacking away.

"Lunchtime, huh? I like nuts, too. I guess we can hang out," I chuckled.

The squirrel looked up and clicked at me, and went back to eating its nut. For some reason, I felt reassured, like the squirrel was keeping me company on purpose, like a sentinel. Not as useful as a guard dog, but for some reason I felt as safe as if it had been. Everything was so peaceful. I closed my eyes again, and continued sitting for I don't know how long. Eventually I heard the squirrel chattering away again, and when I opened my eyes I could see it had started getting dark.

I was reluctant to move and scare away my companion, but couldn't stifle a yawn as I stretched my arms over my head. "Guess it's time to head home, little one." The squirrel flicked its tail twice and scampered off into the woods, leaping up into an oak tree with another acorn in its mouth. I got up and started heading home, and as I walked I could see that the animal almost seemed to be following me, leaping from tree to tree in the canopy above until finally it ran up high into an old pine tree. "Good night, little one, sleep tight!" I called.

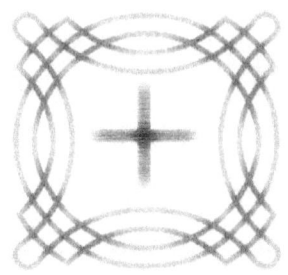

Chapter 14

Back in the house, I grabbed the box of pizza and settled in at the kitchen counter with some water. The food was cold by now, but it was still awesome. I heard the front door open and close.

"Hi Siri, I'm home!" my mom called.

"In the kitchen," I yelled back.

She came in carrying the bag of forgotten poppers, holding it up. "What are we having?"

"Pizza, Jalapeño poppers. We should probably nuke the poppers for a minute. Rowan delivered them a couple of hours ago."

She took them out of the bag and popped the container in the microwave. "Everything alright? The school nurse called and said you had to lie down for a while."

"Yeah, I guess. I don't know. I sort of passed out in class."

"What?!" She sat down next to me and brushed the hair out of my eyes, peering into my face intently. "Are you sure you're not sick? I can't believe the school didn't tell me!"

"Yeah, yeah, I'm fine. At first I thought it was just a cold or something. I've actually been feeling a little off all week. But then today when I came home I heard about the earthquake in Rio..." I trailed off, not quite knowing what to say.

"Oh." My mom took a deep breath, like she was preparing herself for something.

"Yeah, so the thing is," I stared down at my plate and steadied myself. I had always told my mom everything. She was my best friend in the world. And I had to tell someone what was happening to me. I just hoped this wouldn't buy me a ticket to the therapist's office. "When I saw the images on the news, I...well, I sort of remembered them. Like I had seen it all before. When I passed out in class, I saw the earthquake, Mom. I saw it happen. I've been seeing it for days, actually. Except I didn't really remember until it happened."

"Oh, Siri." My mom looked at me with tears in her eyes, reached out, and gathered me in her arms.

As soon as she held me, I broke down. "I saw it, mom. I was there. I felt the earth shaking, and then I heard...I heard all those people dying. I saw them all die. And I couldn't do anything about it." She rubbed my back and soothed me.

"Oh, Siri, I am so, so sorry. I had no idea."

"Well, how would you?" I wiped my eyes, giving her a weak smile. "It's not like I have a big sign over my head saying 'Crazy girl, step right up to see the freak show,' right?"

"Don't say that. Ever. You are not crazy."

"Well, then what else am I?"

She sighed. "I should have told you before. It's just, I thought we had more time. This shouldn't have started for months."

That got my attention. I stopped feeling sorry for myself and stared at her. "What are you talking about?"

"Do you remember when you had that family tree project in fourth grade and your teacher asked you to map out your genealogy going back several generations, and to check out the meanings of your names?"

"Yeah?" I looked at her, not getting at all where she could possibly be going with this.

"Do you remember how excited you were to find out what your name meant? You were still young enough to not have completely grown out of your Tinkerbell addiction, and when you found out that Alvarsson means "Child of the Elven Warrior" you ran around for weeks in your old fairy wings, chasing me with a sword. You thought that was just about the coolest thing you'd ever heard."

"So? What does this trip down memory lane have to do with anything?"

"It's not just a name, Siri. It's who you are." I just stared at her, not comprehending. She sighed again. "Look, Siri, the people we are descended from, our family, we are fae. We don't have wings or pointy ears, and we don't really fly, but we are fae."

I gaped at her. This had to be some kind of joke.

"Our people are what all the old legends are about," she continued. "Our family, in particular, has a strong tradition of defending the Earth. It's part of why you are so good at fighting, and why I started training you at such an early age. All the companies I work for, they all have connections to our people. At least the owners do. And I help protect them. I make sure that our race stays safe among the humans."

"I'm sorry, what? You mean we're not even human? Are you kidding me?" I looked at my hands. They looked normal to me. Why was she saying these things? None of it made any sense, and I said as much.

"We can't be fairies. They're just stories. I don't know why you would even say something like this to me," I frowned at her. "Here I am, thinking I am all kinds of crazy, and now you're messing with me? Why would you do that?"

"I promise you, Siri, I am not messing with you. You're human, but you are also fae. We both are."

I snorted, not ready to believe any of it.

"Look," she sighed, "it's a long story, one that I think calls for some hot chocolate." She got up and set the tea kettle on the stove to boil after filling it at the sink. She continued talking while she opened a container of high-end dark cocoa mix, pouring equal amounts into two mugs, bright poppy pink for me and clear cerulean blue for her.

"The ancient fae were like all those magical people you loved in the old Celtic stories I used to read you. They lived hundreds of years, sometimes even thousands. They were incredibly strong. But then there was a fight for power among the ruling families, a disagreement about how to live. Some of the fae decided they wanted more power, and the easiest way to do that would be to use humans to their advantage – they turned Dark, and lost their respect for the natural order of life. The Light fae, they decided to close off part of their domain in order to protect themselves from the dark. That meant that they also had to close themselves off from the rest of the world. But we didn't want to just leave the humans at the mercy of the Dark, either, to be manipulated and enslaved."

She reached out and held my hand. "A large contingent of fae guardians stayed behind – our family was just one among them. There are many stories about this time throughout the world, especially in Celtic, Tibetan and Norse mythology, since there are several main gateways to the fae domain in those areas. Over the generations, humans joined our family, so most of us are really only part fae now."

She paused, and I looked at her, stunned. As strange as everything sounded, I could hear the ring of truth in what she was telling me, almost as if the universe had just shifted slightly to the left, and suddenly everything was clicking into place.

"What does that mean for me?"

"Well, normally our fae side starts to develop after we finish maturing, after the age of eighteen." The water started boiling for our cocoa, and she poured it into our mugs, gave it a stir and topped it off with a couple handmade vanilla marshmallows shaped like cats.

"But how could you not have told me before?" I shook my head, wondering what else she'd hidden from me. "Don't you think I deserved to know?"

"I guess I waited too long," she gave me a sorry look as she handed me my mug. "I swear I was planning on talking to you about all this soon, but I wanted to give you a chance to settle in first. Like I said, I figured I still had plenty of time, at least a few months." She sighed.

"I guess that makes sense," I granted.

"Anyhow, part of what it means for you is that you'll always be healthier than a regular human. Fae have much stronger immune systems so we almost never get sick. Viruses that take down regular people for a week or more will manifest in young fae as a mild twenty-four-hour bug, or in mature fae not at all. And because our body is stronger and continually repairing itself, we don't age as quickly as humans or get more serious diseases like cancer, either."

"Like, how quickly?"

"The Ancients lived nine hundred years or more. Some still do, if their blood is very pure. Most fae on earth live around two hundred years. As I said, your fae DNA kicks into gear when your hormones stabilize and you stop maturing, so by the time you reach twenty five your aging process will have slowed to be no more than one-third the rate of a normal person."

"Wait so that means you're actually...?"

"Fifty eight. I joined the army when I was thirty seven, although my license said I was twenty two. I couldn't have a full military career because they would have noticed that I wasn't aging."

"Oh my God, you could be my grandma!" I stared at her in horror, the full implications of what she was telling me hitting me like a ton of bricks. She laughed nervously but quickly sobered up.

"Actually..."

"Oh please, now what?"

"You've met your grandmother. Aunt Jade's not really my older sister."

"Oh, wow. You weren't kidding all those times you said we had good genes."

She laughed. "No, definitely not."

I took a cautious sip of my cocoa. "So, then, what does this have to do with my visions?"

"The fae are ancient, as I said. We were here before the humans. Our stories tell that we came from the stars to create the earth itself, and we became its keepers. As humans evolved, we took care of them, too. Part of our innate ability as fae is to be in tune with the earth. It's a part of us, and we love all of it as we would a child. At least, the Light do. The Dark have turned away from their duty, and over the years have lost much of their ability to connect with Nature the way we can."

I raised my eyebrow at her in question.

"Our heartbeat is the beat of the earth – we are her pulse, and she is ours." My mother looked sad for a moment.

"The darkness some fae have nurtured, it is the source of so much of the strife and degradation of the planet right now. Their inner distortion creates the darkness you see in the world. They are angry, power hungry, greedy, and the disease of their thoughts infects everything around them and spreads through the world like a virus. The Alvarsson line is descended from Tyr, the son of Odin. Just as Odin had visions, many of us know when the earth is rising up in cataclysms to cleanse away the darkness. We can feel all the pain of the earth, all the joy of the earth, and of all beings on the earth. It is why we have always defended against the darkness. Our empathy made us the finest warriors, and legend has it that the strongest among us can decide entire battles. We can feel the beauty and the love we protect. We will do anything to keep it alive," she finished fiercely.

"My visions..." I murmured while she gingerly took a bite of one of the marshmallow cat's ears. "There was a man there, more of a dark blurry shadow, but I couldn't really see him. He said, 'It has begun.'"

My mother looked at me, stunned.

"It can't have... You..."

"What, Mom? What is it?"

"Well, are you saying that there was another person sharing your vision?"

"Yes, that's what it seemed like. I didn't like the way he felt, either. He made me feel, I don't know, icky. Dirty, somehow, just hearing him."

"There are old stories about Ragnarok. The end of the world. It is something the Dark have tried time and time again to bring about, but they always fail." She shook her head and sat up straighter. "Listen, he was probably just talking about the earthquake itself. We can't know what he really meant. I'll call my mother and see if she has heard anything, but I am sure it's not a big deal." She pasted an overly bright smile over her face.

"Awesome. I feel totally better now." I retorted and looked at her skeptically. "So what about you, did you have the same visions? I mean, if this is a fae thing and all?"

"No, I don't get too many visions anymore. And I never had visions so far ahead of the actual occurrence of an earth event. There may be more going on with your visions than we can understand yet. But I can teach you to control them better – I've learned to only tap into the earth when I need to, if I'm in battle or I need to send a message to someone. Or if I need to check up on someone I love," she winked at me.

"You can spy on me through the earth?!" I flashed back to the hard cider at the falls and wondered if she'd been there then. She seemed to know just what I was thinking, because she smirked at me and nodded her head.

"Yep, if I feel the need. Thank god you are such an angel." She drawled out the last word sarcastically.

"Yes, you are very lucky I am so perfect." I grinned at her. "So, what about healing? Or animals? There was this squirrel that I thought was dead last weekend at Mt. Snow, but after I picked it up and held it for a while, it got up and ran away. And I swear I saw it behind the house today, too."

My mom looked at me speculatively. "I don't have any special healing abilities, but there have been those who do, mostly pure fae who still live in Valhalla. Perhaps your father…"

"Wait, Valhalla? You mean as in Valkyries? We're descended from Valkyries?" My voice rose in excitement. The old Norse tales about the Valkyries had always been my favorite, and I had dressed as a Valkyrie warrior at least three times for Halloween over the years. My mom laughed, again knowing just what I was thinking.

"There are many names from the domain of the fae that are recorded in human history as legend. As I said, we created the earth. The heart of the planet was our most protected, purest land. Although we have always shared the outer realms of the Earth with them, humans have almost never been allowed to enter within our domain. There are many stories about man crawling out of the earth or being created from earth, and about the "little people" living underground."

I nodded, remembering all the stories she'd read me over the years.

"Every story contains echoes of the truth. This planet is actually quite hollow inside, with a vast land that is inhabited by the Fae and an inner energy source that warms and lights the lands beneath."

"Shut. Up." I deadpanned. I couldn't really think of anything else to say. I mean, come on. Hollow Earth? Could this get any weirder?

She gave me her best sit-down-and-be-quiet look. "We call it Aeden, which is of course where the original story of

Eden comes from, as well as tales of Asgard, and the Elysian Fields. The ruling city of the realm is called Valhalla, and it is where their most able warriors have always been trained."

"So? What does that have to do with my dad?"

"It is, most likely, where your father is from. We recognized each other as fae when we met, our hearts let us know right away," my mom said in a soft voice, getting all starry eyed. "But we were on a black op and we had very little time to talk about who we really were and where we were from. We never even learned each other's real names, because the army insisted we use code names. I always figured he would turn up eventually, but I haven't been able to find him. Either he is very good at hiding, or he is living within Aeden. You'd be surprised at how large the fae world really is, both above and below."

"Wow." I looked in my mug and realized that all the chocolatey goodness was gone.

My mom peered over my shoulder and sighed. "All done, huh?"

I nodded, suddenly feeling oddly bereft, as empty as my cup.

"Look, Siri, I know this is a lot to take in. It's getting late. How about we turn in, and you can google your heart out for the next few days, like I know you're going to, and anything you want to know more about, no matter how silly it seems, you come and ask me. How's that sound?" She opened her arms for a hug, and I fell right into them.

"It sounds great, mom," I mumbled thankfully into her shoulder.

Pushing away, I laughed. "You know, if I didn't know you better, I would be sure this was all some elaborate joke. But you're just not that funny!" I cracked.

"Ha. Watch out, Siri, because guess where you got your sense of humor from?" She winked at me and put the mugs in the sink. I groaned and went to my room. My brain really couldn't process everything I'd just heard. I lay in bed for a few hours in the dark, trying to make sense of it all until I just gave up and fell asleep. Google would have to wait.

CHAPTER 15

The next day I woke up early and went for a run, followed by a round of punching on my speed ball. After I showered, I stood looking in my closet. I really wasn't in the mood to wear anything other than my pajamas and was tempted to stay home from school. Too bad I was already several weeks behind in school. I supposed I should catch up before I started ditching.

Resigned, I pulled on some jeggings with a long grey and black camo cami and my silver sk8-hi Vans. I looked in the mirror, brushing out my damp hair. It was already starting to curl up around my shoulders, and I really wasn't in the mood to do anything so labor intensive as blowing it dry.

I huffed a strand out of my eyes, annoyed at its unruly ways. Braids or a ponytail? I remembered what my mom had said about the Valkyries and grinned. Oh yeah, definitely braids.

I finished up quickly and headed into the kitchen, where I guzzled down the fresh pink juice my mom had left out on the counter for me with a note to have a nice day. It tasted like papaya, lemongrass and strawberry. Not bad. Then I grabbed a couple bananas from the kitchen to eat on the way to school in the car.

On the way to school, I went over what had happened the day before again in my head. Could we really be fae?

It seemed like some sort of dream.

Thinking about the visions I'd had, I guessed it was as good an explanation as any. My mom wasn't exactly the fantasy type. That was so more my thing. Mom liked to watch action movies and go over the tactical errors the characters inevitably made. Even in training, she never pulled any punches, and she had never been anything less than straight with me.

Well, unless you thought about the fact that she'd managed to hide our family origins from me for seventeen years. Aunt Jade, indeed.

Going on autopilot, I barely registered the fact that I had driven all the way to school and parked. I blinked a few times, clearing my head, and looked around the student lot.

So many normal kids. Just doing their thing.

I'd always envied them the life they had. Growing up in one place. Knowing where they belonged.

I'd had no idea how different I really was.

I hopped out of the Subaru and made my way inside with everyone else. Suddenly, someone bumped into me hard from behind, making me drop my bag.

"Nice braids, Heidi," Emelie sneered at me, passing by as I bent down to retrieve it.

Seriously, what had I ever done to her? What a jerk. A rush of irrational hatred flooded through me.

"Thanks, Emelie, nice heels." I flashed her a sweet, innocent smile. "Want one through your eye?"

"What?" She stumbled a little and her eyes widened in surprise. "What-ever, freak. Go back to where you came from, flatlander." She flipped her hair and walked away quickly.

When I got to my locker Rowan was leaning there waiting for me again. God, he was gorgeous. And he clearly wasn't even trying. Today he was wearing dark jeans and a faded black tee from some Indie rocker band. His short, blue-tipped hair was sticking up in several directions and it took all my self-control not to reach up and run my fingers through it and fix it. Or just grab it and bring his well-formed lips down to mine. Either way would be a win-win, as far I could imagine. My stomach flopped in that weird way it did whenever he was nearby. I made a concerted effort to look away from his mouth and up into his eyes.

Those deep blue, starlit eyes.

I really had to get a grip.

He smiled down at me quizzically.

"Dude, what did you say to Em? She sounded wicked pissed."

Ah, apparently he hadn't noticed me staring. Thank. God.

"Oh nothing," I answered breezily. "I just complimented her shoes."

"If you say so." He eyed me with just a hint of disbelief. He drew himself up to his full height, away from the lockers, and looked down at me with concern.

"So, what about you? Are you sure you are well enough to be at school today?"

I don't think anyone other than my mother or aunt had ever looked at me with that much concern before now. Well, aunt, grandma...Whatever. Still, I didn't usually have any friends that were close enough to really care about my actual well-being. Then again, I couldn't recall ever being sick, beyond the occasional sniffle, so I suppose no one had ever had the opportunity to show me if they cared. I enjoyed his concern.

"Siri?" He looked down at me, waiting for an answer.

"Hey, what are you trying to say?" I smiled up at him coyly. "Do I look sick?"

His eyes gazed into mine, then traveled down the length of my body. Slowly, they made their way back up and I felt my face glowing with what I was sure deep, dark red. So much for coy. I cursed my fair Viking heritage. Wait, were we even Norwegian at all? I would have to ask mom about that.

Rowan locked his eyes back on mine and he leaned in slowly, touching his forehead to mine.

"No," he whispered. "You look fine. Really, really, fine."

I giggled and he drew back, kissing me lightly on the nose. "Still, I'm keeping my eye on you. Can't have my best girl getting sick on me."

"No?"

"No. Who will give me such great pizza tips if you're not eating?"

Pretending mock outrage, I elbowed him in the abs. He doubled over, cracking up and protecting his stomach at the same time.

"Come on, joker, we're gonna be late." I turned and sauntered away. Rowan followed, still laughing. I did my best not to reach up and rub my elbow where I'd ribbed him. It was actually smarting from the contact with his rock hard abs. I'd never felt a set like that, not even in tourneys with other champion mixed martial artists. That boy was in shape, almost freakishly so.

Not to mention freakishly nice, awesomely funny and hella hot. Or wicked hot, as the local kids said.

I could get used to living here. I really could.

Oh, who was I kidding.

I was already head over heels in like with a guy, and had a pretty awesome gal-pal in the making with Rose. Everyone here was uber-nice. Well, with the exception of Emelie, but honestly, I was so used to girls like her it didn't really phase me.

"And what the hell does flatlander even mean, anyway? Is that, like, some Game of Thrones thing or something?" I remembered to ask him as we arrived at my class.

"Nah, it just means you're not from Vermont. And honey, I wouldn't have it any other way." He swatted me playfully on the butt and strolled off to his first class. Still laughing. Jerk.

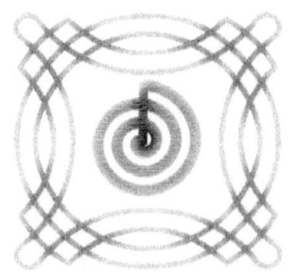

CHAPTER 16

It had been two weeks since we arrived in Falls Depot. It was hard to believe that we'd only been here fourteen short days.

Fourteen rather blissful days. Fourteen totally normal days.

I'd fallen into an easy routine, running each morning, heading to school, hanging out with my friends, training with mom each night, stealing kisses with Rowan between classes and whenever I ordered in from Giovanni's.

Obviously, pizza became my new favorite food, if it hadn't been already.

It felt as if I had lived here for years. Rose and I had become best friends already, texting each other every night about the guys we loved and the teachers we hated.

Everything I'd always wanted. The normal life I'd always envied in other kids. I had it. And the best part? I could keep it. It was my last year of high school, so I could enjoy a totally regular senior year, planning for college like every other kid. And when everything changed next year, I would, again, be just like every kid at school. Well, except for the fact that I was destined to age a little (yeah fine, a lot) more slowly, and I could feel the heartbeat of the Earth. No big deal.

Still, totally normal.

Totally fae, and finally, totally normal.

Mom had added some new meditation techniques to our after-school training sessions, with instructions to continue practicing even on the days when she worked late. Yeah, like that was going to happen. Meditation was so not my thing. I know it was supposed to help me control the visions, but I hadn't had anymore since the disaster in Brazil, so I figured I would deal with it when I needed to. Right now, I really just wanted to spend every free moment basking in the sheer sensation of feeling...home. I finally felt home.

I'd been so many places. Lived in so many houses and apartments. We'd even lived on a houseboat once. They had all been great. Lots of fun times with mom. Lots of interesting new things to do and see. I'd always felt loved. But this was the first place I'd ever felt I actually belonged, like I wasn't the new strange girl who had to carve out a space to fit between all the people who had history together. It had been so comfortable, I'd just eased right in like a deadbolt sliding home.

That was how easily I'd fallen for the Depot.

And that's what was going through my mind when my mom dropped me.

I slammed to the ground and lay there staring up at my glorious mother, her wooden bokken sword pointed at my throat. Outside, I could distantly hear birds chirping and a squirrel chittering. From my position, it almost sounded like it was laughing at me.

"You're not paying attention, Siri. Where's your mind at?" She reached down and helped me up.

"I don't know. Just out of it, I guess."

She poured us each some water and handed me one.

"Come on, sweetheart, let's take a break. Want to go out on the porch?"

The light was just starting to fade, and the sky was turning a luxurious shade of gold over the trees. The porch was pure country chic, complete with a double swing hanging to one side. It was pretty much ours, since the other tenants both used entrances around on the other side of the building.

We settled in on the swing and we both tipped back our glasses to drink. More often than not, this is what it was like with my mom. We were always in sync. Sometimes, people even thought we were sisters, we tended to move so similarly. Of course, now that I knew our family secret, I could understand why she still looked so youthful, too. She didn't really look more than thirty. Good genes, she'd always joked. No kidding.

Out of the corner of my eye I thought I saw movement in the shadows across the porch. I turned my head to see a black squirrel run across the deck and stop at my feet. It cocked its head and made series of strange clicks and purrs, and then hopped up into my lap. Stunned, I kept my arms still at my sides and watched as it turned in several circles and then settled down into a little ball, curling its tail neatly around it.

"Uh, Mom?" I squeaked.

I turned my head to look at my mother, and saw that she looked just as surprised as I felt.

"Looks like you've made a new friend."

The squirrel turned its head up sideways, coquettishly exposing its little chin like a cat waiting to be petted. A small patch of white gleamed under its mouth.

"I think this is the same one I told you about, the one that got hit a couple weeks ago."

"How can you tell?"

"That squirrel was all black, too, except for that white part." I pointed to the squirrel's chin and it stretched out further, encouraging me to pet it. Still nervous, I gently stroked the soft fur with one finger.

"Aren't rabid animals supposed to get really friendly before they go psycho? I mean, are you sure this is okay?" My voice shook a tiny bit, pitched high from a combination of nerves and wonder.

She smiled gently at me. "I'm pretty sure that's a different type of friendliness. This little guy, he looks totally relaxed. Go with it, Siri."

"Is this part of the whole fae thing, too?" I imagined myself traipsing through the forest like Snow White, animals trailing behind me, birds flitting around bringing me gifts. It was too weird for words.

"Well, like I told you before, our family is more in tune with the Earth. The ancient fae did have the ability to speak with animals, even plants. They were truly one with the Earth. I know a few fae who still have that ability, but no one in our family. Probably, he just decided he likes you and has followed you home. Guess he needed a friend, and now you're it." The squirrel started purring on my lap. Without even realizing it, I had been petting his whole body and he was stretched out, totally basking in the attention.

"This is so wild."

"You know, some Earth fae, like your grandmother, have the ability to awaken plants in their time of need, and many Ancients had animal familiars. There are those who can call up the elements to do their bidding. Some more powerful fae have created tidal waves or made the earth tremble beneath your feet, or so the stories go."

She looked like she was going to say more, but a car pulled up in front of the house just at that moment. Moments later, Rose got out and slammed the door. In a flash, the squirrel was off my lap and scampering across the yard up into a tree.

"Hey, Siri!" she called.

"Hey, Rose!" I had totally forgotten she was coming over to study for our first horticulture test.

"Mom," I stood up as Rose made her way up the stairs to the porch, "this is Rose. We're going to study for our test tomorrow."

"Hello Rose, nice to meet you. I've heard a lot about you." She smiled up at Rose. "I'm so glad Siri has made such a nice friend already."

Rose blushed, the hue clashing furiously with her red hair. "Thanks Ms. Alvarsson. It's nice to have a girl to hang out with who likes to talk boarding. Usually it's just me and the guys from the mountain, and that gets a little old sometimes."

"Alright, well you girls have fun." Mom stood and finished her glass of water, setting it on the porch rail. "I'm going to head out for a run. Please help yourself to whatever food's in the kitchen." She gave me a quick hug and jogged off down the stairs.

"Kicking butt?" Rose looked at my sweaty clothes and the wooden sword by my feet. She knew all about my martial arts training and had made me promise to teach her some self-defense moves before she headed off to college next year.

"More like getting my butt kicked," I laughed.

Rose looked down the street admiringly towards where my mom had run into the night.

"Your mom is so cool. My mom's biggest skills are gardening and cooking. I mean, don't get me wrong, I love her apple pie and her roast lamb is to die for, but having a hot mom who can do hand-to-hand combat is just off the hook cool."

I shrugged and opened the door to inside, leading the way to the kitchen.

"Not everyone see it that way. Most of the girls I've met over the years think I'm kind of a freak. Of course, since I could kick their butt they wouldn't usually say it to my face."

She let out a snort. "I bet."

She started spreading out her books on the counter while I took out all the fixings for sandwiches.

"Roast beef or ham?"

"Mmm, roast beef, yeah, thanks."

She piled up the beef on a mini baguette with some cheddar, horseradish and sun-dried tomatoes, while I heaped Swiss cheese and ham on some dark rye bread with mustard. I opened a bag of kettle chips and sat down at the counter with her.

"Yum, I am so hungry," she moaned as she dug into her sandwich, and I nodded in agreement, my mouth too full to answer her properly.

We scarfed down our food in relative silence, and got down to studying. We went over plant propagation methods for a while and quizzed each other on the Latin and common names of perennial herbs, along with how to properly cultivate each one.

"Echinacea purpurea."

"Purple Coneflower. Indigenous to North America. Grown by seed, root cuttings or division. Hardy and drought resistant, attracts butterflies and honeybees." I ticked off the attributes of the last plant on our list one by one. Echinacea was easy, I'd always loved its rosy purple petals and bright orange center, and it seemed to grow almost everywhere we'd ever lived.

"Perfect!" She leaned back on the stool and stretched. "So, what are you up to tomorrow night? The guys and I are going to see a preview of the new Star Wars movie in Burlington. Chuck got extra tickets from his dad's job. Want to come with?"

"Oh, that sounds awesome! I would totally love to, but Rowan invited me over to his house for dinner. We're going to go over the stuff I missed so I'm definitely caught up for our physics test on Monday."

"Oh yeah. Studying, eh?" she waggled her eyebrows at me.

"Shut up," I swatted at her with my notes. "Yeah, studying, and movie night with the fam he said."

"Ooooh, meeting the fam. Big night then! Rowan and Siri, sitting in a tree –"

"Ah, stop it! We're just...We're not even..."

"Yeah, what, you're not even what?"

"Well, we haven't had that talk. You know, we've only been on one date."

She snorted. "And he kisses you every chance he gets. Honestly, you guys are sick, I think I've seen you smooch in every hallway in school this week."

"Oh come on, as if! We're not that bad." I groaned. "Are we?"

"Oh yeah, totally. You guys are wicked in love." She laughed. "And now you're meeting the parentals. Good luck with that one."

"Yeah, I'm a little nervous actually. Rowan hasn't talked about them much, but his dad sounds kind of intimidating."

"Bah. I'm sure he'll love you. What's not to love? After all, I befriended you," she winked at me. "And I have killer awesome taste."

She got up and grabbed my hand, dragging me out of the kitchen.

"Now come on and let's figure out what you are going to wear."

"Seriously?" I protested as she pulled me to a stop in front of my closet. "I didn't think you really cared about those kinds of things."

"Siri, you wound me! A lot of thought and effort goes into finding the perfect mix of vintage boho tomboy chic. Anyhoo, even if I don't care, and you don't care, this date requires some seriously difficult planning."

"It's not a date," I protested as she started tossing random items of clothing out of my closet onto my bed. "It's just studying and a movie."

"Exactly! And you're meeting his parents. We need to find the perfect blend of not-trying-too-hard, girl-next-door-every-parent-loves, and hot librarian. This is so not easy!"

"Can't I just wear a sweater and some jeans?"

Rose snorted and dug deeper in my closet, now on her hands and knees searching for what I could only assume would be the "perfect" pair of shoes.

I sat at my desk and leaned back to watch the show. She crawled out the closet triumphantly, holding two pairs of ballet flats in her hand, one black and one navy. She put them on the floor by the bed and started picking up tops, matching them against various pants that she had selected.

"Alright, stand up, let's see these against your skin tone. Don't make that face, my aunt's an aesthetician in Bennington at the Oasis. I know these things."

She clucked and made faces as she held up shirt after shirt. Finally, she lit up with approval.

"Lavender is really your color! I mean, the gray you wear all the time is good, too, it brings out your eyes, but the purple really warms up your skin tone and highlights the gold in your hair."

I just stared at her, bemused.

"You'll wear these jeggings with this lavender tunic with the three-quarter length sleeves, it makes you look sweet and relaxed and pretty all at the same time. The navy flats are classic, but say you're a good girl, too. Wear some small simple stud earrings, and your hair down. Definitely down. No braids tomorrow, Siri! I mean it."

I rolled my eyes, "Whatever you say, Madame Chanel."

She giggled, turning back into the Rose I knew and loved. Or at least so I thought. "So, fashion torture is over and studying is done. How about we do our nails and eat some of those brownies I saw in the kitchen earlier?"

"Nails, too, really? Who are you?!"

"Something purple or blue. Or silver. Take out what you have and I'll go get the brownies." She bossed me, bouncing off to the kitchen.

I shook my head in disbelief. Who was this girl and what had she done with Rose? I giggled as I went through my nail polish collection. I actually had quite a few. I couldn't ever keep it from chipping off my fingers, but I loved having bright toes. Every time I went to a pharmacy I seemed to walk out with a few new colors.

I supposed there wasn't any harm in having some deep, "Vixen Violet" toenails. Rose would be so proud. I took out a few hot pinks and oranges from the collection, figuring they'd complement her usual Rainbow Brite thrift-store look perfectly.

She walked back into the room with a plate, and peered at my selection.

"Mmm, that is a gorgeous purple! Perfect. But what are those colors you picked out for me? Hot pink?? Do you know what that does to my hair?" She pretend squealed, putting her hands to her head dramatically, and we both broke down laughing at the ridiculousness of what she had put us through for the last twenty minutes.

When we finally stopped, she reached over me and grabbed some gold polish. "This is much better. Don't you know, it brings out my freckles?" And with that she tore up laughing again.

I watched, smiling warmly at my new friend.

Laughter, brownies and Violet Vixen. I don't think life had ever been better than this.

CHAPTER 17

So I was wrong. Life could get better. Infinitely better. Our test in weeds had gone great, I was sure I'd gotten every answer right. The rest of the day had been easy, and I'd rushed home after school so I could get in a quick run and change into Rose's date-ware before I headed over to Rowan's.

The address he gave me led to the historic district in the center of town where the houses were both huge and ancient. They all dated from before the revolutionary war, when Vermont had apparently been a country, and not a state. Just like Old Main Street with its war-era cannons on both ends, these houses looked like they contained their fair share of antiques. Even the streetlights in this part of town used special lightbulbs so that they looked like they still burned gas.

I pulled into his driveway on South Street and marveled at his home. It was gorgeous. A huge old colonial painted in rich cream with white trim and a pumpkin-colored front door. A couple of real carved pumpkins sat on the huge stone steps, each step made from a single granite slab. I wondered if his mom painted the door a different color every season. His old beat-up truck looked incongruous sitting in the cobblestone driveway, but at least I knew I had the right house.

I parked behind his truck and climbed up the steps to the huge orange entrance. Before I had a chance to knock, the door opened inwards.

"Hey, come on in. I heard your car come in."

"Thanks," I said, shouldering my book bag. "I love your house. What a great neighborhood."

"Yeah, it's not bad. My mom complains because she has to get permission for every little thing she wants to do on the property, since it's historic and all. But she can paint it whatever she wants so she picks a new obnoxious color for the door every month, just to annoy the stodgy old neighbors."

"I wondered if the orange door was seasonal."

"Actually," he chuckled, "she's going for a spooky black this weekend. The orange is left over from September."

"That'll freak the kids out something fierce." I laughed.

"Oh, you have no idea. My mom gets so into Halloween. She makes my dad dress up as Dracula and she has him lie down in this antique coffin she got on sale at an auction. She dresses like Bride of Frankenstein, and then she has the kids come in two at a time to get candy, at which point my dad sits up and scares the daylights out of them. It totally terrorizes all the kids. Cooper says he still has nightmares about it."

"He's such a sweetie," I murmured. Cooper was like Scooby Doo and Shaggy, all wrapped up together in a tall, cute package. I had a soft spot in my heart for his goofy ways.

Rowan gave me a look that sent shivers down my spine, and not in the best of ways. He looked...cold.

"Really?" he said.

"Well, yeah," I said. "He's so goofy and funny. Like a big kid. And he's so nice to everyone. It's sweet."

Rowan narrowed his eyes and grunted. "Come on, we'll study in the library." He spun on his heel and stalked off, leaving me wondering what his problem was.

After a moment, I rushed after him, catching up at the end of the hall. "In here," he nodded. Books upon books lined the walls. A large marble fireplace lay dormant on one wall, flanked by two large windows. Two comfy leather couches faced each other with a large wooden table between them, already covered with textbooks and an open binder. I flopped down on the one where Rowan's sweater lay draped over the edge, figuring we would sit next to each other.

Apparently, he had different thoughts.

He sat down on the other side, perching close to the table and leaning over his notebook.

"So, I figured we could begin with the basics of what you missed, starting with Newtonian theory and working our way up to quasars." He ran a hand through his hair while he flipped through his notes. A muscle in his cheek twitched on and off, on and off. My stomach muscles clenched in response to the tension.

"Sure, whatever," I sulked. Not that he noticed, since he seemed to be sulking mightily himself. Why the hell had he invited me over if he was going to act like this the whole time? Grabbing my textbook, I kicked off my shoes and tucked my feet up under me.

He started shooting questions at me from his notes, rapid fire. Surprising myself, I actually knew most of the answers. We fell into a rhythm, despite ourselves. At one point I looked up and noticed that he was staring at my toes. What, did he think I was I getting his couch dirty or something? I decided not to play along with his drama.

Wiggling my toes, I saucily asked, "You like?"

"They match your shirt," he huffed and hastily looked away, focusing once more on his damn binder. I had so had enough of this crap. The fighter in me rose up and decided to call him out on whatever his damage was.

"Dude, what's your problem?"

"What do you mean?"

"You invited me here, remember? And now you are acting like a complete douche. I mean, I walk in, we laugh, you smile, and then you start acting all weird like you're pissed at me or something. If you don't want me here, just say so."

He ran a hand through his hair. The muscle in his jaw flexed a couple more times, and he sighed.

"No, I...of course I want you here. But you...You..."

"Oh. My. God. Spit it out Rowan. What?"

"I know you spend a lot of time with Cooper in school, and you're right, he is a really great guy, and you only just met all of us, so I mean, if you like him better than me, you know, you can just let me know." He shrugged and looked back at his book, like he hadn't just dropped some sort of ridiculous bomb of full-on craziness on me.

"Are you serious? What are you smoking? I'm at your house, Rowan. Not Cooper's. And Cooper is in love with your sister, hello?" Mystified, I continued, "Why would I be interested in him, anyway, I mean, you are just perfect, I have no idea why you even like me so much and I—"

I didn't get to finish because suddenly Rowan was on the couch next to me, kissing me like his very soul depended on it, crushing me into the sofa. His rich scent mixed with the library aroma of books and leather and I drank it in. He abandoned my lips to nuzzle my ear, trailing kisses along my ear. Heat rose through my body and my stomach flip-flopped.

"Lunatic," I moaned. I grabbed him by his hair and dragged his lips away from my clavicle so I could look him clearly in the eyes. "Moron."

His eyes darkened with passion, his pupils almost fully dilated and gleaming as they searched my own.

"Absolutely. I'm an idiot," he emphatically agreed and claimed my lips again. More gently this time, like I was something precious he wanted to cherish forever. "I'm sorry," he murmured against my lips.

I threw my arms around him again and pulled him down on top of me so we were lying down on the couch. I surrendered to the heady scent of him, surrendered to him, wrapping my legs tightly around him, trying to get closer to him. I couldn't get enough of his mouth, his hands, his—

"Just what the hell is going on here?" a voice boomed from the doorway. My stomach dropped out to the bottom of my feet as Rowan scrambled off of me and I struggled to tame my hair.

A tall, extremely fair man with broad shoulders stared down at me. Rowan's dad, I could only guess. He was pale enough to almost be considered albino, except for his eyes which were practically black right now with anger. I shrank behind Rowan's shoulder. Not having a father myself, I wasn't too familiar with this side of angry authority, but I knew I didn't like it.

"Dad!" Rowan struggled for composure. "I didn't expect you home yet."

"Obviously." His dad answered drolly.

"No, I mean, we were just studying, and then...Anyways, I thought Mom was coming home soon. Where is she?"

Ah, nice one, I thought. Turn the question around on the parental. Always worth a shot. Too bad it didn't work.

"She left stew in the crockpot before she left; she texted to let me know she should be back in an hour or so. Then we can eat." He eyed me like I was yesterday's fish left out on the counter and I went cold all over. "Introduce me to your friend, Rowan."

"Oh, right. Yes, sorry. Dad, this is Siri Alvarsson. Siri, this is my dad, Sullivan Carey. Siri just moved here from Tucson."

"Alvarsson, did you say?" His face changed, and he looked at me with interest. "I had a friend from Norway with that name. Such a wonderful country." He smiled wolfishly at me as I stood to shake his hand. He took mine in both of his and grasped tightly. Even though he only held my hand, I felt like he was squeezing the air out of me. Out of the room, even. A sick feeling came over me, and I was pretty sure I was flushed from head to toe. Still, this was Rowan's dad, and I had vowed to Rose that I would try to make a good impression.

"Yes, sir. It's nice to meet you, sir." My mother had taught me the importance of sirring and maaming, which I assumed had been hammered into her in the army.

"Wonderful, wonderful. Well, why don't you children finish up with your studies and your mother will call you when dinner's ready," he directed this last bit at Rowan. "And keep your feet on the floor at all times, hmm? Or else your mother will have all our heads." He gave me another once over, barked with laughter and left the room. Ew. Well, now I felt just completely dirty and gross. How embarrassing.

"Well, that was embarrassing," Rowan echoed my thoughts.

We looked back at each other and burst out laughing.

"Is he always like that?" I wondered.

"He's not easy, that's for sure. But since he's never found me in his library necking with a girl before, I can't be sure."

"Just boys, huh?" I cracked up at my own joke.

"What do you think?" he questioned me.

"I don't know, you could be bi," I could barely breathe now, I was laughing so hard. "I'm sorry, that was just so...Intense. That was so freaking intense!"

He reached out and pulled me to him again. "I'll show you intense." And then he started tickling me mercilessly.

We fell back on the couch. Me, breathless from laughing. Him, still torturing my ribs.

"Hey," I reminded him, "feet on the floor, remember?"

"Right, feet." He grinned devilishly, stood up and grabbed my left foot. And started tickling that one.

"Argh! Get. Off!" I kicked him back with my other foot, careful not to knock him down, and flipped off the couch.

"You!" I panted, and pointed at the opposite couch. "There. Now."

I scrunched up my nose and glared at him with mock anger.

"Hey, whatever you say, Serious. Don't go all ninja on me, please."

After that, we got back to studying. Rowan's mom breezed in at one point, saying a quick hello and looking me up and down with undisguised curiosity. Rowan was still sitting on his couch, and me on mine, so at least we weren't treated to any lectures about propriety. She didn't linger, practically flitting back out the door, calling over her shoulder that dinner would be ready soon.

Just as she left we heard the front door bang open and shut again, and some giggling in the hall.

A moment later Holly and Cooper appeared in the doorway, flushed and smiling.

"Hey guys!" Holly flounced in and crashed on the couch next to Rowan. Cooper followed, and sprawled out on the other end of my couch. I caught Rowan glaring at Cooper's leg, which was just a couple of inches from mine. I guess he wasn't over the whole jealousy thing yet. I scooted over a little and put the book I was holding down between us. Rowan looked at me and I smirked pointedly at him, quirking an eyebrow. I mean really. He so had to get over that.

"Wow, so, you're really studying?" Holly eyed all the papers out on the table. "When Rowan said you were coming over, I figured that was just an excuse."

"Subtle Holly, really." Rowan rolled his eyes. "Besides, Dad's home, didn't you see his car?"

At that, everyone in the room adjusted their posture a bit. Holly even leaned forward and started nervously straightening up the mess.

"Ah, so you met the Grand Poobah himself," Cooper drawled. "Lucky you. How long did the interrogation last?"

"Grand Poobah?"

"Oh, you know, the big cheese, head honcho, der fürher, whatever. Sullivan takes his job as protectorate of this family very seriously, I should know." I watched Rowan to see what he thought of his friend talking about his dad this way, but he avoided my glance. Holly was giving Coop a wide-eyed 'shut up' sort of stare, but he was oblivious, as always.

"I could tell. But no, no interrogation really."

"Right. Well, no worries, we still have dinner to get through." He winked at me and patted me on the shoulder. Butterflies flitted through my stomach again, none too pleasantly. I swear, if this kept up, I was either going to have to get checked for parasites or sign up for a Xanax prescription.

I spaced out for a few minutes while everyone else chatted and I tried to settle my nerves. I had just started to get a grip on myself when a bell jangled in the hall.

"Ah, we've been summoned." Holly rolled her eyes.

"That's the dinner bell." Rowan explained to me. He stood and walked over to me, holding out his hand to help me up.

"You have a dinner bell?" I whispered as we followed Holly and Cooper down the long hallway, our steps muted by the plush oriental runner lining the floor. The rich red walls were hung with antique oil paintings of foxhunts and snowy mountain landscapes.

"Came with the house. I think it dates back to the 1800's. Mom gets a kick out of using it." He rolled his eyes, showing me into the dining room.

The huge table was blanketed in crisp cream linen, complete with candles and a massive cornucopia in the middle filled with all manner of tiny gourds, Indian corn, and cranberries. I scanned the room, wondering where Martha Stewart was hiding. Each plate had a decorative bronze charger underneath it and the glasses all had wreathes of red and yellow bittersweet vines around the stems. A huge copper tureen sat on the table, steaming. Popovers sat in baskets at both ends of the table.

"Wow," I breathed. "This is amazing, Mrs. Carey."

"Thank you, Siri." She smiled at me graciously, although it didn't quite reach her eyes. Dark blue like Rowan's, they studied me as I sat in the empty seat next to Rowan's father at the head of the table. Holly smiled at me across the table. I felt Rowan's hand clasp mine, and watched as everyone held hands to say grace. Reluctantly, I placed my left hand in Sullivan's. Coldness seeped into my hand as he took it in an iron grip. Everyone bowed their heads. I peered at Rowan out of the corner of my eye and he gave my hand a reassuring squeeze.

Sullivan's gravelly voiced rasped through the room, and everyone else murmured along with him.

"We accept this feast today with thanks to our Lord who has given us dominion over the Earth. May it give us strength to find the light, so we may live blessed in His abundance and power and glory forever and forever, amen."

Okay. So Rowan's family was Episcopal or something. Or was it the Lutheran's who liked to talk about dominion and toil? I couldn't remember. A little intense for me, having been raised up with no particular spiritual beliefs other than some decidedly pagan folktales, but I could deal. I'd had enough sleepovers that ended with Sunday morning mass that I could follow along with the motions. So long as they didn't try and convert me or anything, we were good.

Rowan gave my hand another squeeze before he let go. I started to pull my hand back from Sullivan, but realized he was still holding it captive. I glanced at him, and he locked in my gaze with his dark, cobra-like eyes.

"I'm glad you have joined us tonight, Siri."

"Thank you, Sir. I'm glad to be here?" My voice rose at the end unintentionally, making my words come out like a question.

He gripped my hand more tightly, crushing my fingers momentarily. I winced as he released me, the blood rushing back to my fingers bringing more pain.

"Indeed," he smiled. My eyes widened, and I turned away to regain composure. The rest of the family was serving themselves stew from the copper bowl and passing around the popovers, chatting easily amongst themselves. No one had noticed a thing. But I had.

Rowan's father was one stone-cold freaky bastard. My heart ached for the sweet boy I knew, and wondered how two such easy-going kids could have come from a guy like this. Rowan's mom must work overtime to make up for his deficiency. No wonder everything looked so *Home & Garden* perfect.

I took a couple popovers and cracked them open on my plate, slathering their moist cavities with butter. Rowan handed me the soup spoon and I ladled some stew over the rich pastries. I really hoped it didn't contain any bear or other woodland creatures, but I didn't have the courage to ask. Either way, I'd have to be a good guest and eat up, so I figured ignorance could definitely be a blessing.

"This smells fantastic. I don't think I've had popovers since we lived in Ireland," I gushed. I wasn't lying about the smell. And I did love popovers.

"Oh, did you grow up there?" Mrs. Carey asked. "I can't quite place your accent."

"Just nine months. We move around a lot for my mom's work. I've lived all over the U.S."

"Oh, how fascinating. What about your father? Does he work from home?"

"Um, no, he doesn't live with us. The last I heard he was working with the British forces." Generally, I tried not to share too many details about my lack of patriarchal influence. I figured these parental units would be especially lacking in understanding so I tried to steer the conversation back to my mother. "Ireland was a great place to be, especially because I got to see more of our family there."

"So is your mother Irish, then?" Mr. Carey interjected.

"Yes, she's mostly Norwegian and Irish." At least, that had always been the story. Now, I wasn't actually sure.

"Hey, we might be related then!" Holly exclaimed. "We are mostly Irish, too."

"Hopefully not too closely," Cooper smirked at Rowan. I blushed at the implication.

"No, hopefully not," Rowan's father frowned at him, obviously thinking the same thing. Thankfully, his wife didn't seem to pick up on Coop's reference to kissing cousins.

"It must have been wonderful for you to meet relatives away from home." Mrs. Carey said sweetly. "I always so enjoy traveling to the U.K. for that very reason. Sullivan often travels there for business, and I love reconnecting with family when we are there. I hope when Sully retires and Rowan takes the reins he will take his tired old mother along with him sometimes."

Rowan coughed. "Yes, well. That's a long way off still. Plenty of time to figure that out, isn't there?"

"Not too far off." She winked at him. "We're hoping Rowan will go to university at Trinity. Our families have legacies there going back several hundred years. My brothers all went, and Sully, too."

Rowan looked down at his plate, pretending disinterest. Only I could see the edge of the tablecloth fisted in his hand near his lap, the pale fabric matching the whiteness of his knuckles.

Holly spoke up. "Lucky for me, Mom paved the way for me to go to Smith College here in Massachusetts. I don't know if I'd like being so far away from home. I'm still pushing for Rowan to apply to some of the colleges in that area, like Amherst or UMass, then we could even take some classes together still. They have a five college system that shares courses."

"Rowan knows where his best interests lie," his father growled. "There's no need for him to apply anywhere other than Trinity."

"I'll apply where I want." Rowan put his glass down forcefully, sloshing a bit of water onto the tablecloth.

"Where are you applying, dear?" his mother asked me quickly, a forced bright look on her face.

"I don't know yet. I really like it here so far, so I was planning on looking at Bennington and some of the other local schools. I hadn't really thought about it too much, actually, but I did love Ireland. Maybe I'll look at some schools there, too. I have dual citizenship, actually, so I could probably get in pretty easily."

Under the table, Rowan reached over to lace his fingers through mine. Warmth spread through me at his touch and my pulse sped up.

"Bennington is a great school. I'm sure you would fit in there well." Rowan's father emphasized the last part, making it clear he did not think I would fit in well in Ireland. Or maybe he just didn't think I'd fit into the life they seemed to have planned for Rowan? "I'm surprised your mother hasn't encouraged you to think more about your education. Or maybe you don't take your future that seriously?"

"Dad!" Rowan blurted.

"What now?" Sullivan sounded bored. "I'm just saying that maybe she should think about her future more. Do you get good grades, Siri?"

"Yes, sir." Geez, I felt like I was on a college interview already. Applying to work at the mountain had been way less stressful than this.

"Siri's in my AP Physics class, Dad, that's what we were studying for earlier."

"Ah, yes, studying." His dad sneered, looking at me now like I was some sort of back-alley prostitute. An awkward silence fell over the table.

I stared down at my plate and picked at my food. So much for my appetite.

"Um, what does your mom do, anyways, Siri?" Holly asked cheerfully.

I sent her a grateful smile. "She's a security expert, actually. She helps firms implement better systems to protect their data and facilities."

"Wow, that's so cool!" Cooper exclaimed. "So she's a computer expert, too?"

"Not really. But she understands the security end of it really well. She did a lot of classified work for the army before I was born. After she left the military this was a pretty natural way for her to apply her skills."

"Nice!" Cooper practically bounced up and down in his chair. "Sounds like Mission Impossible!"

I laughed. "Some of her stories do read a little like Bond."

Rowan squeezed my hand and gazed proudly at me. "Yeah, she's taught Siri all sorts of martial arts techniques."

I blushed. So much for girl next-door. Maybe I should have just worn a slutty Bond girl outfit and had done with it.

Holly's eyes widened.

"No. Way! That is so cool." She mock glared at her mom. "All I ever learned was piano and jazz dancing."

She threw up her arms and demonstrated some dance-squad worthy jazz hands.

"So, what do you know? Can you throw down some Krav Maga?" Cooper demanded.

"Actually, yeah."

"What?! No way, you didn't tell me that!" Rowan exclaimed. "What else? Come on, spill."

I chuckled, and started ticking off my specialties on my fingers. "Well, I started with Qigong and Tai Chi as a kid, then Aikido, Tang Soo Do, boxing and Krav Maga. Lately I've been experimenting with Capoeira...Oh, and parkour is kind of a new hobby. I'm going to miss it when everything gets iced up for winter. Although of course, I already have a pass to Mount Snow, so I guess I'll be too busy snowboarding to miss it, actually."

I finished ticking off my hobbies and saw that everyone was just kind of staring at me, even Rowan. I laughed nervously. "Well, you asked."

"And you, Jason Bourne, have answered," said Cooper. Everybody cracked up at that, even the Careys. I almost missed it when Mrs. Carey just looked at her husband and gave the smallest of nods.

"You've been trained well, Siri." Sullivan studied me.

"Yes, sir, I have." I answered him, unable to hide the pride in my voice. "My mother and I work out almost every day. It's a great outlet for nerves whenever I find myself in a new place."

"How wonderful," Mrs. Carey murmured, sounding like it was anything but, "to have such exceptional skills and be able to defend oneself."

Holly giggled. "Sounds like Siri could defend a whole village."

"Doesn't it, though? I wonder what else Siri can do?" Rowan's dad peered at me like I was some sort of science experiment. "Any other fantastic abilities you'd like to share with us?"

I froze, caught in his cobra gaze again. Oh, yeah. Totally, I thought. Let me tell you all about my freaky ability to predict earthquakes and bond with squirrels. Oh, and who knows what else, since I'm a frickin' fairy and my powers are still developing. How about you?

"I make killer brownies." I innocently replied.

There, perfect girl next door. Kapow. Take that.

Everybody laughed and went back to eating. Mrs. Carey asked Holly about the play she was trying out for, and Holly launched into a long description of the part she wanted.

I pushed my food around on the plate, trying to eat and be a good guest, but still suffering from a nervous stomach. The conversation around me faded against the sound of rain pattering on the windows.

I looked up, but the moon was shining brightly through the curtains. A passing storm, I thought, and shook my head as I put my spoon down.

"Something wrong with your food, dear?" Mrs. Carey interrupted Holly to ask me with concern.

"Claudia, I'm sure she's fine. Leave the poor girl alone," Sullivan brusquely admonished her. His wife blushed, and I felt a rush of pity for her, having to listen to his pompous posturing day after day.

"I'm fine, ma'am." Unable to help myself I glared at him and turned to her with empathy, "I just thought I heard some rain outside and remembered I left my car windows down."

"But it's not raining," Rowan said, looking at me oddly.

"No, it's not. Hearing things, I guess." I shrugged.

"So, anyways," Holly continued, "I'll have more lines than in last year's play and I'll get to dress up as a guy and a girl. It's awesome! There isn't anyone else who could do—"

Her voice cut off and suddenly all I could hear was roaring wind. Driving rain flew all around me in an almost horizontal pattern, pounding the ground with force. Opulent houses lined the hill above me and rivers of water and mud sluiced their way down the barren landscape. Through the wind, I could hear ragged laughter.

Wait, I knew that voice. I spun around, but I couldn't see the man clearly through the rain.

"Who are you?" I accused. "I remember you from Rio! What's happening? What's begun? Tell me!"

The laughter increased. "You ask the wrong question, young one. You should be asking, how does it end?"

I couldn't see his face, but I could hear the sneer in his voice.

"Join us Siri, you can't stop us. Join us, and live. Join us, and win. Fight us...and we will bury you."

As he spoke, the ground screamed in fury, and the rivers of mud grew in size, huge pieces of land and rock joining them, avalanching down the side of the hill, carving out the ground below the houses. Suddenly, a massive cracking sound split the air and one of homes splintered apart. Terrorized, I watched as it slid down the hillside in slow motion towards me.

"Join us, Siri," the voice cackled maniacally. "Join us, or we will bury you."

The house loomed over me.

I cringed and shut my eyes, preparing for the worst. And—

—nothing happened.

Just, silence.

Like, you could hear a pin drop, silence. I opened my eyes, still cringing.

Everyone at the table was staring at me. Rowan's dad was giving me his x-ray investigator look again.

"Will you be joining us?" His question echoed my vision, and I could only stare back at him open mouthed.

"Huh?" I asked.

Super casual. Super smooth. Yep, that was me. My head pounded and it was all I could do to get the word out.

"For the movie? We're watching Revenge of the Sith, and we have caramel corn for dessert."

"Oh, um, you know, I would really love to, I would," I apologized and the words just ran out of me, "but I'm not feeling too well, actually. My stomach's been bothering me all day. I mean, I'm sure it's fine and dinner's been great, but I think I better head home and get an early night."

"More popcorn for me," Cooper whooped and leapt up from the table, grabbing plates to clear as he went.

"Classy, Coop, as always," Holly laughed and got up to help him clear the table.

Rowan's dad smiled at me, creepy as ever. He took my hand and my stomach lurched. Pain raged through every synapse in my brain, radiating down through my neck and shoulders.

"I'm sorry you can't join us, Siri."

Funny, he didn't look sorry. But whatever.

"Me, too," I lied through clenched teeth.

Rowan laid a hand on my shoulder and the pain eased somewhat.

"I'll walk you out."

I nodded, and he moved his hand down to the small of my back, gently steering me through the house, down the stairs and out to my car. He opened the door for me, but before I could climb in he turned me so we were facing. He leaned down and buried his head in my hair.

For a moment we just stood like that, breathing in the scent of each other. My bed at home called for me. I felt wrecked. But his deep, citrusy scent soothed me as always, like a balm for my soul.

"I am so sorry," I exhaled, anguished to have caused a scene.

"No. Don't say that. It's all my fault. I should have known..." His hands fisted at my sides, clenching the fabric of my shirt, drawing me closer. "My dad. He's just a jerk. He puts up with Cooper and Emilie, because they're practically family, but he's got a lot of rules that he expects the rest of us to live by."

"Still." I ran my fingers through his hair. "I'm sorry I ruined movie night. I want to stay, I really do, but I'm honestly feeling sort of run down still. I don't know what's wrong with me."

Except I did, of course. I was a wingless fairy. But I couldn't exactly tell Rowan that.

"Okay, well, as long as you leave here knowing two things."

"What's that?"

"One: you are adorable even when you are green." He said kissing me on the nose. "And two: I swear I will never be like my dad. Please, don't judge me by my parents."

"Oh god, I would never. I mean, that's just wrong and evil and all sorts of unfair. I mean, they're like ancient!" I kidded him.

He regarded me uneasily.

"I mean it, Siri. Please. No matter what ever happens. Remember I am nothing like my father." He stared into my eyes intensely.

"Pinky Promise." I held up my pinky. We linked pinkies and shook on it. Satisfied, Rowan took a step back, and I climbed up into the Wrangler.

"Take it slow on the way home. I don't want anything to happen to my best girl. I think I might be falling for her and I haven't told her yet."

Pausing mid-buckle, I tossed him a glance over my shoulder. "I'll make sure she knows you said that."

He crossed his arms over his chest, his shadowed biceps standing out in the moonlight, and nodded at me. I finished buckling and turned the key, T. Swift reminding me to 'shake it off' on the radio. Rowan stayed like that, watching me like a night sentinel, and I drove away.

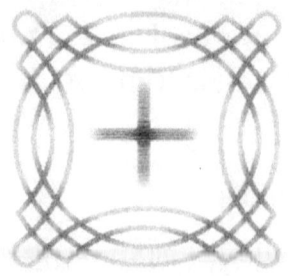

CHAPTER 18

Another day. Another butt-kicking.

I'd woken up to my mother singing in the kitchen, prepping plates of Nutella on toast and tall glasses of fresh pineapple juice with hints of kale, ginger and cilantro. I'd asked her if the juice was a fae thing, and she nodded her head, saying our constitutions healed better that way. The more fruits and vegetables we ate, the more optimally our fae cells could repair themselves. The better we would feel, and the better our fae abilities could operate.

Still. Bacon. Am I right?

Now, here I was, getting my butt kicked. Again.

Mom lunged out at me with a cross body punch, coming at me as she advanced a front kick.

"Honestly, Mom?" I spun out of reach with some defensive Capoeira, cartwheeling gracefully into a macaco, which is basically a back flip performed low to the ground. "Krav Maga should be illegal this early in the morning."

"What's the matter? You went to bed early enough. Up all night dreaming about your beau?" She teased, feinting left and then catching me lightly in the shoulder with a right hook as I came out of my flip.

I dove behind her and kicked her gently on the butt.

"No. Dinner last night was lousy. I had another crappy vision, and Rowan's dad was a total creep."

Mom whirled around and put her hands up in a gesture of surrender.

"Alright, time out!" She tossed me a towel and I tossed myself gratefully down on the couch while she stood there stretching. "So, what happened? Start at the beginning."

I thought back over the evening and blushed, realizing I couldn't actually tell her all about the beginning without mentioning how Mr. Carey walked in on Rowan and I making out. I decided I would just gloss over that part.

"Well, Rowan and I were studying, and then we had dinner with his family. His dad kind of grilled me about school, which was weird, but then I think it was going pretty well. Until, of course, I started having another vision. They all noticed me spacing out, and I felt pretty out of it afterwards, but at least I didn't pass out." I rolled my eyes to emphasize how ridiculous I thought the whole situation was.

"What did you see?" My mom switched legs, lunging to the left now.

"Rain, lots of rain, and a mudslide. But the worst part was that awful man was back, and he was just laughing and laughing at me, or at the disaster. I don't know. It was horrible, mom." I grimaced. "Then he started saying I needed to join him, or he'd bury me, that I'd die. Then I came to."

"I'm so sorry, Siri, we will work more on the meditation techniques today, okay? You don't need to be seeing these sorts of things. I'll let Jade know about what the man said, too. Do you think you could write out everything that happened for me, so I can send her a detailed report? It sounds like maybe the Dark are reaching out to all the faelings."

"Faelings?

"Young fae."

"Oh." I raised my arms up over my head and cracked my neck a few times. "Oh! And you want to know the best part? The part that just cinched my date as a disaster last night? Afterwards, when I came to, Mr. Carey was asking me to 'join them' for movie night, but I was still half in my vision and could only stare at him like a total freakazoid. And then I practically ran out of there before I could embarrass myself any further by puking or passing out or something." I buried my face in my hands and groaned.

My mom didn't say anything. I peeked up at her through my fingers and saw that she had gone pale, and looked totally wigged out.

"What now?"

"Did you say Carey? As in Rowan's last name is Carey?"

"Well, yeah. So what?"

I wouldn't have thought it was possible, but my mom went even paler. "Oh no. Oh god. Siri, I think I've made a huge mistake coming here. I had no idea they were here." She straightened and started muttering to herself. "How could Frank not know? Siri put on your shoes, we have to go out, right away."

She threw my sneakers at me and I managed to catch them just before they hit my face. Mystified, I leaned down to lace them as she raced to the kitchen and came back with her purse and keys. She tried to dial a number on her phone, cursing to herself when the call didn't go through. "Come on, we'll just go over there and wait for him if he's not home."

"Wait for who?" I demanded.

"For Frank. I'll explain more on the—"

All of a sudden, our apartment door splintered inwards and crashed into the wall, hanging off its hinges. A burly man barged through the opening, heading straight for my mom, followed by two more men and a familiar looking woman. The three men rushed my mother and subdued her quickly, fighting as one team. Shocked, I could only stand there, gaping at the female intruder.

"Coach Thorn?" I stammered. My mother struggled against the two men holding her as the third moved quickly to pull my arms behind me.

"Hello again, Siri. What a lovely daughter you have, Fredrika. Sullivan was so happy to hear that you had moved to our little outpost here in Vermont."

She sneered at my mother and my mom went wild, fighting against the two men holding her with everything she had. It made no difference, though. Clearly they were just as well trained as she was. Which of course meant I was screwed, too. I tested the waters with my own captor, confirming that he had me properly secured. Unfortunately, he did.

"I will never help you," my mother insisted.

"Oh. But we don't really need you anymore, Freddie. Not now that we have your sweet, sweet Siri." She trailed a fingernail down my cheek and I kicked out at her, just brushing her leg with my toe before Goon Number Three pulled me back out of reach.

"Screw you," I growled.

At that moment I saw a streak of dark fur blaze across the floor through the open door, and a burst of angry chattering erupted behind me. The squirrel ran up my captor's leg and back, and proceeded to furiously claw and bite at the man's neck. Surprised, he released his hold on me and the squirrel jumped into my arms.

"Siri, run!" my mother ordered me.

I hesitated, not wanting to leave her.

"GO!" she screamed, "now!"

She was my mom. She'd raised me well. So I listened and I ran, throwing all my weight into my right shoulder as rammed into the coach and flew out the door. Hopefully that would give my mom a chance to break away.

I reached the street, pausing for a moment behind their SUV, hoping she was free, too.

"Go, Siri, don't stop, run!" she yelled as Goon Three and Thorn stumbled out onto the porch.

And I ran.

CHAPTER 19

I suppose I should have tried out for track after all.

At first I ran without direction, just going as fast as my feet would carry me down the road. After a minute it became clear that Thorn, despite her advisory position to runners, was not much of a runner herself. At least, she couldn't keep up with me. I heard her yell to the man puffing behind her to go back and bring their car around. She continued after me, but the moment the road turned and I was out of sight I veered off into the woods, clutching the small squirrel in one arm like a football.

My mind raced.

What. The. Hell?! I leaped over a series of downed trees and felt myself getting really, really pissed.

Why would a high school coach bust in my door and attack my mother and I? Nerves started to take over. What should I do? Where should I go? I thought of Rose, but I hadn't been to her house yet and without my phone I wasn't sure how to find it. I knew I couldn't go to Rowan's house, either. Not after Coach Thorn rambling about Sullivan.

I felt frustrated, bewildered and betrayed. I took out some of my angst on a boulder, leaping up and pushing off of it with a flying kick as I continued running. Who were those guys? Our skills had been practically useless against them.

My mind returned to Rowan. I trusted him. He'd been nothing but a friend to me since I got here. Hoping I was making the right decision, I ran through the woods for over an hour, crossing several roads when no cars were near and sneaking through backyards until I came to the outskirts of Bennington. I grabbed a huge worn navy blue hoodie off of someone's clothesline and threw it on, stuffing the squirrel inside. I pulled the hood down over my eyes and hunched my shoulders, trying to shrink into myself as I tried to keep to the midday shadows of buildings. Every time I saw an SUV I'd duck into a store and wait for it to pass. Finally, after what felt like another hour, I made it to the back entrance of Gio's.

The kitchen was hopping with Saturday lunch orders, the fragrant sweetness of fresh marinara sauce wafting out the screen door. I hadn't realized how hungry I was, but running eight miles through the woods could do that to a girl.

I took a deep breath. Now or never, I thought. I opened the door to the kitchen.

"Hey, you can't be in here!" The cook yelled at me and gestured at the front window with his knife. "Use the front door like everybody else."

"Sorry, I'm here to see Rowan. Can you tell him, please? I'll wait out back. Thanks."

I ducked out back and stood behind the dumpster so no one walking by the alley would be able to see me. Inside, I heard the guy with the knife yell "Rowan, get your teen-aged Romeo butt back here."

"Romeo butt, really, Franco? Come on. What's up?"

"There's a girl out back says she needs to speak to you. Go on, Sal will cover for you, but this counts as your break."

"A girl? Who?"

"Didn't say."

The screen door opened and Rowan peered out.

"Rowan!" I emerged from my hiding spot and propelled myself into his arms. The full horror of what had just happened crashed down on me, and I sobbed as his arms came around me. The squirrel squeaked in protest between us and I leaned back.

"Siri! What's wrong?" His eyes roamed over me, looking to see if I was hurt. They widened when he saw the squirrel peeking its head out of the sweatshirt. "What happened?"

Swiping a hand across my eyes to clear away the stray tears, I wasn't sure where to start.

"Coach Thorn. She came to my house with these three guys. They broke down the door and attacked us. I got away, but they have my mom and I don't know why."

Rowan chewed on his lip. "How did you get here?"

"I ran. My mom told me to run and I did and I left her. I just left her there, Rowan."

"Hey, I know you're a ninja and everything, but if your mom couldn't take them, what chance would you have? I mean, three guys? Come on, you had to run."

"Well, what now? I don't know what to do."

A black car rolled by slowly, and Rowan pushed me into the shadows behind the dumpster again.

"Listen to me. I have an idea of where we can go for help. But you can't stay here. It's not safe. And we can't go there until tomorrow. I'll have to take you to my house to get some things, and put you somewhere safe for the night. Do you trust me?"

"I wouldn't be here if I didn't. But Rowan, Coach Thorn said something about your dad. Do you know what is going on?"

"Maybe. I'm not sure. We shouldn't talk here." He looked around the alley like people were about to materialize out of the walls. "I'm going to get my truck and pull up to the alley. When you see me, come out and get in as fast as you can, and stay out of sight. Okay?"

He leaned down and brushed his lips against mine softly. Filled with nerves, I nodded back at him.

"Okay."

He went back into the kitchen and I could hear him arguing with Franco about how something had come up and he'd work a double shift next week to make up for it. I assumed he'd left when I heard some pots clattering in the sink and a string of Italian curses lit the air.

I shrank down further next to the wall. The squirrel scolded me, pawing at my chin to get my attention. I looked down and he launched into a whole tirade of squirrel speak.

"I know. It's a risk. But I'm all out of ideas, little guy. Now pipe down." I gently pushed him back down inside the hoodie. A moment later I heard the familiar rumble of Rowan's truck and sprinted down the pavement to hop in.

I ducked down right away, laying my head on Rowan's leg. The smell of pizza filled the air, and I could see a couple small takeout boxes on the ground. Thank god, I was starving. Rowan reached over me and put a protective hand on my side. I sighed and closed my eyes. Even if it was just for a moment, I felt safe.

Ten minutes later, he switched the engine off.

"We're here."

I started to get up but he pushed me back down.

"No one else seems to be here, but let me just check first."

He grabbed the pizza, got out and slammed the truck door. I winced as the sound rattled my ears. A moment later I felt a breeze on my bare legs as he opened my door.

"All clear, come on." He held out a hand and helped me out of the truck.

The house was cold and dark inside.

"Go upstairs to the first door on the right. That's my room. Close the door and wait for me, have some of these if you want." He handed me the pizza boxes. "I'm just going to grab some things from the kitchen. You want a soda?"

I nodded. He waited until I started heading up the stairs before he jogged off down the hall. At the top of the stairs I pushed open the door to his room and looked around. I could feel Rowan's energy in here, but nothing really screamed 'this is Rowan's room.' There were his favorite sneakers next to the closet, and his book bag on the floor next to a small dark walnut desk with a gleaming black laptop taking up most of the surface. The walls were a dark, cool navy blue with white trim, and all the furniture was dark, heavy wood. The comforter set on the bed was blue and white pinstripes with dark, solid pillows with thick white edging. It looked more like a guest room than the room of a fun-loving teenage boy.

I quietly closed the door behind me and moved to sit on the bed. The fabric was as cool as it looked, chilling my legs below my shorts. I put the boxes down on the bed and dove in, eating like I hadn't seen food for days. Mmm. Pizza was so good for the soul. The little squirrel crawled out from my shirt and scampered down my sleeve to curl up next to me.

"Hey there, little fellow." I smiled down at him.

Rowan silently stole back into the room and handed me a can of soda. Next he went to his closet, pulling out a large pack. He threw in some food and cans of soda. He went back in his closet and grabbed a fleece blanket, stuffing that in there, too.

A door creaked downstairs and we heard footsteps echo through the quiet house.

"I don't know how it happened. Yes, yes, I told them they were trained. Thorn was supposed to bring our best men." Rowan's father snorted. A pause.

"Yes, I know...Look, don't worry about it. I'm sure we'll find her, we've got everyone out looking for her."

I locked eyes with Rowan, cocking my head in silent question. Did you know about this? I tried to put the question in my eyes.

He shook his head frantically and shrugged. Okay, so he was clueless, too. I couldn't decide if that would end up being a good or a bad thing. Obviously, it was good because it meant he wasn't an evil bastard. Bad, because it meant we knew less about what was going on.

"No, I already sent her mother to Mikael, they should begin processing tomorrow...Yes, alright. I'll check in when I have more news... Yes, sir, I promise, sir. We won't lose her again."

Footsteps started up the hall steps, and Rowan gestured for me to hide in the closet. I quickly scooped up the squirrel and slid into the closet. He shut the door most of the way behind me, along with the backpack. Through the crack he'd left open, I saw him sit on the bed and start eating the slice of pizza I'd left behind.

There were two quick raps on the door. Sullivan didn't wait for Rowan to answer, he just barged right in.

"Have you seen that girl today?"

"What girl?" Rowan asked cluelessly and stuffed more pizza in his mouth.

"That girl from last night, Siri, I think her name was? Your mother says she left her scarf in the library. Why don't you call her and see if she can come get it?"

"I can give it to her Monday, I'll see her at school."

I couldn't see Sullivan, but I could just imagine how he tensed up at Rowan's lackadaisical attitude. "Your mother," he ground out, "would like you to call her now. She is worried about Siri catching a cold."

"Okay, sure. Um, right now?" A short pause. Sullivan was probably burning laser holes in him now with his eyes. "Okay, okay. Geez."

He picked up the phone and dialed. Another pause. "No answer. Just a busy signal, weird. I'll send her a text, okay?"

"Fine. Thank you, Rowan. Let me know when you hear from her." Footsteps retreated to the hall and down the stairs. "Oh, and Rowan, next time eat that pizza in the kitchen. You know the rules," he called back up the stairs.

The front door slammed. Minutes later a car revved and peeled out the driveway.

I peeked out of the closet. Rowan was sitting on the bed with his head in his hands. I exhaled. Safe, again. Padding over to him, I laid a hand on his shoulder.

"Thank you, Rowan."

"Oh, Siri, I wouldn't thank me yet." He laughed and raised his head out of his hands. My stomach knotted up, fearful of what that could mean. Was he going to turn me in after all?

"What do you mean?"

"This is all my fault!" He stood up and kicked his book bag. "I told my mom who you are."

"But...what does that even mean?" My mind raced. He didn't know I was fae. So what could he be talking about?

"Come on, Siri, I know you are fae." He turned to face me. "Did you really think I wouldn't know? I told my mom the day we went to the falls, I told her how every time I touched you I felt a tug. All fae feel it when they are around another fae that could be a possible mate. The stronger the pull, the more compatible you are. I was so excited to meet another faeling. I mean, I've met other fae girls, but none that affected me like you. Didn't you feel it?"

I just stared at him, dumbfounded. Another fae? Rowan was fae and I hadn't known. Had my mom known?

"Look, my mother must have told my dad, even though I asked her not to. Coach Thorn, she works for the same group as my dad. You heard him, they're in on this together. This is all my fault. My dad is a jerk, I always knew it, but I never thought he would involve a girl in his work."

"Rowan, what are you talking about? What work?"

"Look, we've wasted too much time already. I have to get you out of here before he comes back. Get the backpack, and let's go. I have somewhere safer for us to talk."

He closed up the pizza boxes, scooped them up and made his way down a narrow staircase that led out to the back of the house.

I followed him, fuming. I wanted to know what was going on. Now. I was seriously starting to doubt the wisdom of trusting Rowan with anything, especially my safety. I resolved to hear him out and give him a fighting chance before I kicked the life out of him.

The backyard was perfectly manicured with beautiful gardens and rock walls. Clearly his mother had a green thumb. Which, I supposed, was no surprise if she was fae. I followed him into the woods, treading a small deer path through between the bushes and trees.

They're dark fae, a small voice whispered in my head. I stumbled at the thought.

No. They couldn't be. That would mean...no. There was no way Rowan could be dark fae. He was good. He was sweet. He just couldn't be.

Rowan stopped and I crashed into the solid wall of his back. Even in my annoyed state, I noticed he smelled divine.

I peered around him to see why we'd stopped. A huge tree stood before us, wide 2 x 4s nailed into its trunk to create a ladder. About twenty feet above us the treads disappeared into the canopy of leaves, obscuring whatever was up there.

"What is this place?"

"This," Rowan beamed, "is my top secret hide out. Well, mine and Coop's. Normally it's no girls allowed, but I think tonight we can make an exception."

He took the backpack from me and started climbing up the tree. I grinned and followed.

"Did you guys build this yourselves?"

"Yeah, about five years ago. Our mom's helped us get all the wood and supplies, and we put it together."

"Are you sure it's safe?"

"My parents never come out here, I'm not sure they even remember it's here."

"That's not quite what I meant," I laughed. I thought of a twelve year old Cooper handling a hammer, and was not reassured.

"Don't worry." He sounded offended. "It's sound. I still come up here all the time, and I shore it up every spring. It's one of my favorite places to come and think. Cooper doesn't come here anymore, either."

Rowan disappeared through the leaves. Following him, it felt like I was creeping into a huge green cocoon of happiness. The light filtered softly through the canopy, tinting everything jade. Pollen sparkled in little streams of sunshine cutting between the leaves.

I heard a hollow thud above, and saw Rowan crawling through a large hole in the floor of the hideout. I peered closely at the weathered planks, noting that there didn't appear to be any water damage. Well, that was a plus.

Not expecting much, I pulled myself up into the space and gazed around in wonder. This was everything that Rowan's room at home was not. Four stacked milk crates in the corner were stuffed haphazardly with old paperbacks and comic books. An antique glass kerosene lamp and several candles in jars sat on a small table by the window. The space was bigger than I would have expected, the size of a small bedroom with a low peaked ceiling. The wooden walls were decorated with faded drawings signed in young boy's hands, and more recent pen and ink sketches of superheroes and monsters. A camping bedroll was laid out along one side, with colorful pillows lined up along the wall.

Glass windows covered with blue, green, yellow and red cellophane cast a mellow rainbow aura of light over the room, the dimmed light making it seem later than it really was. Rowan's back was to me as he lit a couple of candles and the lamp.

"This is amazing." He turned around and smiled shyly at me when I spoke. "I always wanted a tree house." I trailed my fingers over a crude drawing of a gnome eating a flower, signed Rowan, age 12.

"Yeah, this is kind of my home away from home. Sometimes I tell my parents I'm working, but really I'm up here."

I sat on the bedroll and he moved to settle next to me, threading his fingers through mine. I leaned back against the wall and rested my head on his shoulder.

"So," I dragged out the word. "Now what. Are you going to keep me here forever, your princess in a castle?"

I felt him shake his head in denial. "It's tempting. Honestly, I'm not sure what is going on, but I know someone we can go see who we can trust. She'll know what we need to do."

"Another fae?"

"No, she's human. Vala's house is on neutral ground, it's located on old holy ground, no one can fight there. She's a Druid priestess and seer. I think she'll be able to help you."

"Rowan, who does your dad work for? What do they want with me and my mom?"

Rowan leaned forward, drawing his legs up and clasping his arms around his knees. He swallowed.

"You know, you're the first fae I've ever met who wasn't introduced to me through family."

He paused and I waited, sensing he was having a hard time knowing where to start.

"My father works directly with the council of Shades. To the rest of the world, he's just a businessman, but for the Shades, he's one of the main forces behind financing all their operations. He has businesses all over the world. We live out here in the sticks so that we can be near Vala, she helps my dad sometimes, giving him insight for investments."

"Wow, talk about insider trading. Look, I just learned about all this fae stuff recently. You probably knew I was fae before I did. You're going to have to explain everything to me from the beginning. What's a Shade Council?"

He just stared at me.

"What?"

"Siri, it's not A Shade Council. It's THE Shade Council. My mom and dad are shades."

"So?"

"Shades, Siri. It's what the Dark fae call themselves. Because there is no true dark, only shades of gray. Didn't your mom tell you any of this?"

My stomach plummeted. I swear, it dropped clear through the treehouse to the forest floor below. I realized he was still looking at me, waiting for an answer.

"A little. She told me the Dark use humans to gain more power and fight the Light in Valhalla. But, then...does that mean you are Dark?"

"No." He gripped my upper arms, his fingers digging in a little too hard. "Not officially. I haven't chosen yet. My father, of course, he wants me to work with him. But I have until I am eighteen to decide. Just like you, just like all faelings."

"Rowan," I peeled his hands off my arms gently and took his hands in mine. "You know I am a Light fae, right?"

"No, you're not. Not yet. Not until you are eighteen, remember. All fae choose when they turn eighteen, in the binding ceremony. There is good on both sides, I swear. I mean, look at me. Look at Holly. We're not bad people, Siri. But yeah. I sort of figured your mom must be Light after the whole 'let's attack Siri's family' thing going on. Honestly, I thought it was weird when my dad wasn't friendlier to you last night, but I figured it was just because he has his mind

177

set on me marrying Emelie eventually. He's convinced it would get him a position with the Council."

"Wait, Emelie is fae, too?" Blech. There wasn't a doubt in my mind that she was Dark, too.

"Yeah, her mother attends the Morrigan, the leader of the council, and Coop's dad works with mine, too. We are all Shades. Still, it shouldn't have mattered if your parents are Light or Dark, faelings are supposed to be granted safe passage at all times by both sides, since we are considered neutral until our binding ceremony."

I couldn't wrap my head around it all. My boyfriend was on the wrong side. But I knew him. I think I maybe loved him. He didn't have an evil bone in his body.

I stared at him, trying to see into him, through him, to see if I could really trust him.

"Look, we'll go to Vala's tomorrow," Rowan continued. "I'll text her tonight and let her know we are coming. She is bound by oath not to take sides, and she will keep everything confidential when we are there. We'll be safe, and I am sure she'll be able to help us. Okay? I swear, I will protect you from whatever is going on. I am not like my father. You're the first light fae I have ever met. I never really thought Shades were bad, most of them are pretty nice, actually, just regular people from what I can tell, but now that I know you...Siri, you make me feel so different, so free. Your mother, too. I was taught that the Light are all zealots who want to hide away underground and leave the Earth to rot in the hands of the humans, but I can see that's not true. If all the Light are like you and your mother, then I'm going to choose Light."

He beamed down at me like a small boy, filled with hope. I hated to burst his bubble.

"What if they aren't?" I demanded. "Or what if your father won't let you?"

Rowan's smile faltered. "I don't know." Then he straightened with determination. "I graduate this year. I'll go to Trinity in Ireland and while I'm there I can travel to see the other fae communities. Come with me. We can find out the truth. We can make our own decisions."

"Ireland?"

"Ireland." He grinned at me.

"Ok, assuming we can find my mom, and I survive the next few days, Ireland. It's a plan. If Vala person can't help me, I'll have to find my Grandmother who lives over there, anyway."

"Yes!" He fist pumped the air, and we both cracked up. Then he swept me over onto his lap and we sealed the deal with a kiss. Or a few hundred of them. Give or take.

Eventually, he had to go. The plan was he'd check in at my apartment, pretending he was sent by his dad, and grab some more clothes for me, plus my wallet and passport. The last was just a precaution in case I actually had to go see my grandmother, which I was really hoping it wouldn't come to.

He left me with a promise to return in the morning after his parents had left for church. Did they go to a fae church? I wondered. Maybe 'church' was code for some nefarious Dark community hall? I shuddered and huddled up with the ancient worn comforter on the bedroll. The squirrel was sleeping by the window, having eased out of my sweatshirt when Rowan was kissing me. Feeling totally wrecked, I decided to do the same.

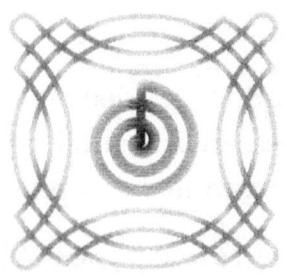

Chapter 20

I lay down and curled around the comforter. It smelled like Rowan, like allspice and cloves and the fresh lemons. I held it up to my nose, inhaling deeply.

I closed my eyes and started drifting away, only to be jarred wide awake again as the familiar, rough voice echoed through my refuge.

We will find you, Siri. Make it easy on yourself. Join us, or your mother will suffer.

Oh god. Mom.

Join us, and live like a queen.

"No," I whispered.

Rasping, deviant laughter filled the air, or my head. I couldn't really tell. I'd felt the voice thrumming throughout every cell of my body, practically blasting apart my head. I almost wondered if it had shaken the leaves off the tree.

So much for sleeping.

Totally awake now, I decided to go through Rowan's pack and see what he had brought. I grabbed a slice of pizza and started munching while I unzipped the bag.

Sharp cheddar cheese and a pack of Saltines. A couple of apples. No chocolate. I sighed, thinking about my mom. She would never have packed an escape bag without chocolate.

"I miss you, mom," I whispered. "What are we going to do? I don't think you trained me enough for this."

"She did, you know." My head spun around at this new voice. It sounded suspiciously like the one I'd heard earlier, the one that had whispered that Rowan was Dark.

Small. Wise. A little snarky.

There was, of course, no one there.

No one except me, and the little squirrel who was now sitting in front of me on his haunches, sniffing at one of the apples.

"No one here." The squirrel huffed and took a nibble of the apple. "Honestly, you're going to give me a complex."

"I'm sorry," I stuttered. "Did you just...are you talking to me?"

"Who else would I be talking to?" He looked up at me with big, glistening eyes.

"But...but...you're a squirrel."

"Way to state the obvious, kiddo. Look, it took you long enough to hear me, I gotta say. I thought your fae powers were further along than this, but I've been talking to you for days and you never acknowledged me. Thanks for healing me, by the way."

"Healing you?"

"Yeah kid, I was on my way out after that truck hit me. Saw the big white light, gramma and gramps, the whole deal. Then you picked me up, and they started to fade away. You healed me. Didn't you know?"

"I figured you were just stunned or something. No, I had no idea." Just like I didn't know I could talk to animals.

"Yeah, well you can. Hey now, don't look so shocked. I can hear your thoughts, too. Animal speak, you know? All us animals can hear thoughts. I gotta say, you humans talk non-stop in your heads. It's kind of exhausting to listen to. I don't know how the cats and dogs do it all day, hanging out in your houses. Stupid animals."

"Um, okay. Well, so, then, why are you here? You know, if I'm so noisy?"

"You saved my life, kid. Squirrel code of honor dictates a year of service now. I'll be dogging your steps for the next eleven and a half months. Good thing, too, or you'd be stuck with your mom right now with those shades."

"You know about that? I mean, I know you heard us talking, but do you know anything else?"

"I don't know where they are keeping her, but I do know that guy you're hanging out with doesn't know the whole story. Those Shades, they are bad news. They aren't trying to guide humanity. They want to control humans. Animals, too. Every time they get near a forest they tear it down or strip mine it. They think the whole planet is theirs for the taking. You think humans are bad? Shades are ten times worse. Most every horrible crime against nature or humanity you can think of, a Shade is behind it."

"But, Rowan said that Shades preserve the Earth."

I was so confused.

Who should I believe? Once again, I wished my mom was here.

"Shade faelings are brought into the fold slowly. They're raised with lies, and then they're sent away for training and education after they join the Shades when they turn eighteen. That's where they get mind-warped, and brought over to the Dark side. But believe it Siri, the Shades are bad news."

He sniffed at the cheese, and I broke him off a small piece.

"Do you want to know why they are really called Shades?" He asked me with a cheek puffed full of cheddar.

I nodded.

"We forest dwellers gave them that name." He puffed up proudly. "When they broke off from the rest of Aeden, they would meet in the darkest parts of the woods, always hiding their gatherings and plots from the Light warriors. They stuck to the shadows like ghosts, and if they saw any animals spying on them, they would cut them down like angels of death so we couldn't report back to the Light. That's why they are Shades. Everything they touch turns dark or dies. And now they've cast their net of darkness over the whole world."

"Cheery," I said uneasily.

"Look, even if you don't want to believe me, part of you knows it's true. Your body knows. I've heard your thoughts, how your stomach rolls over every time Rowan or one of his family touch you. That's not a mating thing. I mean, part of the rush you feel with Rowan is, but the stomach clenching, that nausea – that's a natural Light reaction to the Dark, even to faelings. It's your fae senses giving you a warning, Siri."

"What about Rowan, does he feel it, too?"

"Nah," the squirrel muttered as he stole a cracker off my lap. "He just feels lighter when he's around you, more energized. Happier, you know. It's a natural reaction to the Light. Once Dark go through training, they find the feeling distracting, and are taught to associate joy with weakness."

I felt deflated. My body had been warning me all along.

"Don't worry kid, you've got me now. I'll help you learn the ropes. And you can practice your animal speak with me. Not all fae can hear us, you know. We can hear you, and you can usually pick up things empathically from us, but actually hearing us talk? And healing us? You got some special skills, kid."

"What about this woman Rowan's taking us to tomorrow? Is she Dark, too?"

"No, he's right about Vala. Her house is on a special energy spot that's been sacred to the fae since the beginning of time. She is descended from a long line of Druids that has always maintained neutrality so that they can maintain the energy centers of the earth for the benefit of both humans and fae, and she really is a seer. She should be able to help us."

I chewed on some more cheese, trying to take it all in. Trying to remain calm, and have some faith in what the talking (talking!) squirrel was telling me.

"Hey, by the way, I do have a name you know. As much as I enjoy being called Talking Squirrel and all."

I came out of my daze and looked at him, really looked at him.

"Okay, what is it?"

"Mikowa. My friends just call me Miko."

"Oh yeah, what do your enemies call you?"

"Lunch!" He made a long string of clicks and chitters that I could only assume were the squirrel equivalent of laughter. I chuckled.

"Okay, Miko it is. Anything else I should know before I go see this Vala woman?"

"Your mother is a really strong Light warrior, but that doesn't explain why the Dark would have openly attacked you both like that. I think something else is going on...I think you're going to need to be both Tyr-wise and Tyr-brave to figure this out, Siri."

"Tyr, isn't he the Viking god of war? Mom mentioned we were descended from him." There was so much to figure out, I was so new to all this. I wondered if I'd ever get a handle on it all.

"A lot of people remember him now as a god of war. But really, he was one of the greatest leaders of the fae before Odin. He was concerned with justice and honor, setting most of the laws of the land, and anything he said could always be trusted. He was very wise, but he was an incredible warrior, too. When he said he would do something, he did it. He'd never give up. He was dauntless. One time, trying to prove that his council was honorable and meant no harm, he put his hand in a shifter's mouth, the fae-wolf Fenrir."

"I remember that story. My mom used to read it to me at bedtime."

"Yeah, well, the wolf smelled the deceit behind the council's promises, so despite Tyr's sincerity he bit off the hand in anger. Many people thought Tyr had been foolhardy to brandish his own honor so carelessly, so there is a saying: are you Tyr-wise or Tyr-brave?" Miko snorted. "As if you can't be both. Tomorrow, Siri, and in the days that come, you will need to be both."

Wow. Heavy, I thought.

"Ain't it though, kid?" Miko quipped. "But you are a fighter. You're just in a bit of shock now. But look how well you've done already. There aren't many faelings who could escape a trained Dark squad, help or no help."

"Hmm. Thanks by the way. I couldn't have gotten away without you."

"Yeah, I have a feeling my year of service to you is going to be a lot more demanding than I bargained for. But, a debt of life is no small thing. I will stay with you through this, Siri, I swear."

He solemnly squatted on his haunches before me, and held out his little paw. I put mine out, and we shook on it.

Not so tired anymore, I reached over to the book bins and pulled out a stack of comic books. Wolverine, X-Men, Avengers. A couple manga issues. I lost myself in the colorful graphics and stories for a while, losing track of the time. Eventually, I fell asleep, huddled up with Miko under Rowan's blankets, comforted by the gentle snoring of the squirrel and the feel of his soft fur in my arms.

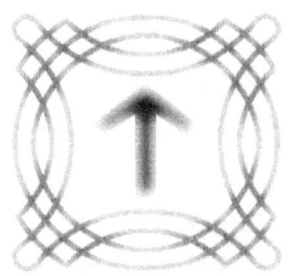

CHAPTER 21

I awoke just before dawn to the incessant chirping of birds. I tried to go back to sleep, but my bladder had other ideas. I nudged Miko awake and told him we needed to venture outside. Did he think he could check it out first to see if it was safe?

"No need," he yawned, showing perfect and tiny rows of teeth. "The birds are singing the all clear. If anyone was in the forest, it would be mentioned in their morning report."

"What, like, their morning songs carry the daily news on them?"

"Sort of. News. Stories. And just some song. Eventually you'll probably be able to understand them, too."

"Alright, well, here I go. Let me know if they sing out any warnings."

"Will do," he said as he settled back into the blanket.

I scurried down the ladder and took care of business quickly. I stretched, relishing the feel of the morning air and lack of confinement. I yearned to go for a jog or even just stay outside and do some basic forms, but I figured I better not risk it. Spying some wild concord grapes nearby I picked a couple bunches and returned back to the treehouse.

Miko smelled the grapes right away and claimed one of the clusters for himself. We ate in silence, him watching out the window and listening to the morning "news" and me, reading another comic. By the time we finished the sun was cresting the horizon, its orange rays filtering through the trees, and I could hear someone crashing through the forest below.

Panicked, I looked up at Miko. "Is it...?"

"Calm down," he admonished. "It's just Rowan. The birds call him *the lone one*. He must come out here by himself a lot."

How sad, I thought. I thought about what a refuge this place must be for him, how different it was from his room at home. I couldn't imagine living in a home where I had to hide the real me, even from my parents.

"Oh, now they are singing about how his nest finally has a mate and they are wondering when you will have chicks."

"What?!" I spluttered. "No way. Chicks?"

"Songbirds. They aren't all there, if you know what I mean. Light brains for flying, if you get my drift."

"Siri?" Rowan opened the hatch. "You okay? I thought I heard you yell."

"Oh, um, yeah, I'm okay. Just reading this comic to myself." I put the books aside and sat up on my knees. "Is it time to go?"

"Soon. We need to wait for my parents to leave first. It'll be a couple hours. But I brought breakfast, and some more of your stuff."

I went through the bag, noting he'd brought some of my favorite jeans and shirts, and my silver vans. I blushed to see some underwear in there, imagining him going through that drawer. When I saw my shampoo and basic toiletries I let out a whoop. Who would have thought I'd ever be so happy to see a toothbrush. I sent Rowan outside and freshened up, whistling softly to call him back up when I was finished.

We dug into the muffins he'd brought (yay, chocolate, finally!) and I asked him how everything had gone at my house. He told me they'd fixed the damage to the door by the time he got there, so no one would even suspect what had happened.

"They're taking shifts watching the house, it's a good thing you didn't come with me. Last night, my dad said they were trying to find you because they were worried some Light zealots were after you, so he asked me help find you. As soon as I got to your door a huge guy materialized asking me what I was doing there." He gulped down some water. "I told him my dad had asked me to try and find you, and that I'd had the idea to get some of your personal items to bring to the Seer to try and get a read on where you were. It's the perfect cover. And this way we don't have to worry about them showing up at Vala's while we're there, since they think I'm on their side, doing it for them."

"How very Mission Impossible of you." I grinned. I brushed off any unease I felt at how easily the lies had come to him.

"I know, right? I've got all the moves." He gave me his best Bond pose. "As soon as I was in your room I texted my dad to let him know my brilliant plan, in case they decided to check in with him, and he said he was impressed since he hadn't thought of it himself. Anyhow, it was easy then grabbing what you needed. All your things were right where you'd said they would be. I took some clothes from a basket of clean laundry by your door, figured they would be the things you wear most often."

"Yeah, well, lucky for you I entered a new Zen phase last month and got rid of half of my stuff. Otherwise you'd probably never have been able to find anything."

When he finally noticed Miko, I told him about how he'd helped save me from Thorn's goon and how I'd taken him with me when I ran. I didn't bother going into the whole talking to animals thing. I really wasn't in the mood to talk any more about my fae abilities. And I most definitely did not want to talk about Miko's version of what Shades were like and what the squirrel said being Dark truly meant.

Rowan seemed to understand my mood, and just held me for a while as we watched the sun send cathedral colors playing across the walls inside treehouse. Now when he held me, I knew what the butterflies in my stomach were really about. It was depressing. My first real boyfriend, a guy I really connected with and my own body was trying to warn me away from him. Just the thought of it made me feel even more sick to my stomach, so I just focused on the warmth and comfort of his arms, rather than dwell on something I couldn't change. Just because he was born to the Dark didn't mean he would choose to be a Shade.

His arms tightened around me almost as if he could hear my thoughts. I hoped he never let go. Surely he must know now that he'd never be able to be himself or be truly happy if he had to work with the Shades. He had to be just as shocked about everything that had happened as I was.

Finally, it was time to go. I repacked everything snugly into the larger of the two packs Rowan had brought. Miko nimbly balanced on my shoulder, his tiny little claws gently keeping him in place on my tee shirt like he was velcroed to it, and we headed out.

The ride to Vala's took over an hour, climbing over mountains and winding dirt roads. When we turned onto a narrow off-road trail in the woods, I imagined our destination would be some tiny rustic cabin in the woods. Maybe look like something out of Hansel and Gretel. Instead, after a few minutes of slow travel the truck emerged onto a well-maintained gravel driveway and we pulled up to the back of a gorgeous antique colonial house overlooking a small lake. A huge marble fountain depicting children playing under a gnarled old oak tree created a circular rotary in the large driveway.

We parked to one side and got out, Rowan taking my pack again, and me, just staring in awe at the view.

The land around the house had been cleared enough to let in plenty of sunlight. The house seemed to be the only one on the lake. Paths wound through the grounds between well-tended gardens, many of them still in bloom despite the lateness of the season. Trellised roses trailed romantically over half-hidden benches and multiple bird baths and ethereal sculptures made of wood and stone adorned the property.

"This is amazing."

It wasn't just the grounds. There was an energy to the place that literally hummed. My entire body was practically vibrating with the joy of it. I don't think I'd ever felt so alive.

"Yes, the lake and the land surrounding it has been hidden from humans for centuries. It doesn't even show up on maps or satellite images. The magic of Vala's family has always been adept at cloaking places like this from humans."

"But why does it need to be cloaked?" I asked. "Shouldn't everyone have access to places like this? I mean, the way it makes me feel..."

"I know. That's just it. Or part of it. Vala's family has safeguarded this land for generations, mostly to make sure the land is maintained and kept safe. Too many other sites, left unattended, have been destroyed or used in the wrong ways."

By shades, Miko snorted. Rowan continued unaware of Miko's contribution to the conversation.

"The water here holds special healing energies for humans and amplifies seer's visions. Drinking it daily allows Druids to increase their lifespan so that they age more slowly. Not as long as fae, but long enough to allow them to really ensure that they can hone their own powers and train successors. The cloaking means that any humans who try to even approach the land start to feel disoriented and sad, and then overcome with a strong urge to return home that they can't resist. Only fae or other humans with Druid blood can make it through Vala's wards."

"Oh." If Miko and my mom were right, I could only imagine how the Shades would love to use this place for their own gain. Humans would probably overdevelop it given the chance, too, destroying any magic it once held.

I was so glad it was protected. How many other places like this were cloaked from wandering humans, I wondered.

You'd be surprised. Miko piped up in my head. *Places like this are everywhere. The world is a far bigger and more magical place than most humans imagine. He's not telling you this, maybe he doesn't know, but the lake also acts as a conduit to other lakes and wells throughout both Earth and Aeden. Vala uses it to communicate with the Light Council and other Druid keepers. Shades lost the ability to use the waters that way centuries ago, when the water sprites decided to side with the Light.*

"Penny for your thoughts?" Rowan reached out and took me by the hand.

"Why?" The word slipped out before I even realized. The question was meant for Miko, but Rowan thought I was addressing him and looked at me strangely.

They both answered me at once.

Because the Shades abused the waters one too many times.

"No reason, just a question, Serious." Rowan dropped my hand and walked over to the fountain. He sat and trailed his hand in the water. I followed, my footsteps crunching over the gravel.

"I'm sorry, I didn't mean it like that..." I paused, not sure how to continue. "I, um, I meant to ask why the Druids keep watch over the land, rather than the fae. I thought it was our job to watch over the earth."

"You're right." A rich alto voice called out to me. I took a few steps to the right and peered around the fountain. The door to the house was open, and a beautiful, full-figured elderly woman with long, white hair in a messy bun atop her head waved to me.

"You must be Rowan's friend. I'm Vala, please, come in and have some tea." She angled her head towards the door indicating for us to follow, sparkling dreamcatcher earrings glinting in the light as they swayed, and she disappeared back into the house.

Rowan got to his feet and we walked to the door without looking each other in the eye. I hesitated at the door.

"Come on, don't be shy, you two. I won't bite." A hearty laugh rolled down the bright yellow hallway at me. I took a deep breath and entered. The décor was an eclectic mix of rich looking burl wood antiques, Native American artifacts, huge quartz crystals and other minerals I couldn't begin to identify, and strange paintings of swirling, spiraling shapes and animals. Carved wooden staves lined the hallway, as if waiting patiently to be claimed by the next intrepid hiker to come along. I followed the last echoes of laughter down the long hallway, stopping before an image of a massive tree, twisting and spiraling, rising from roots that formed more knot work and grew out of an upside down tree below.

Vala peeked at us around a doorway, her dark brown eyes twinkling. "Ah, you've found the Tree of Life, I see."

"I'm sorry, the what?"

"The Tree of Life. Here depicted both above and below, as it should be. Legend says that the original Tree came to this planet carrying the Fae. From its roots grew all life, and as long as it survives, so shall the Earth. Of course, the original tree is located in Valhalla, and fiercely protected. But many of its seedlings can be found here above on Earth. The Tree of Wisdom, the Tree of Peace, Tree of Enlightenment. Those are some of the more famous ones. But really you can find them all over, if you just know where to look."

"What's with all the spirals? All these paintings remind me of tattoos."

Vala laughed, her high cheekbones glowing with happiness. "Well, ain't you just something? Yes, a lot of people these days are returning to the old ways. The spirals and knot work here are all part of Celtic art. More than that, the knots and symbols can be used to create protective wards or shift energy in a room, if you know what you're doing."

"But come now," she gestured to the room behind her. "Tea's on."

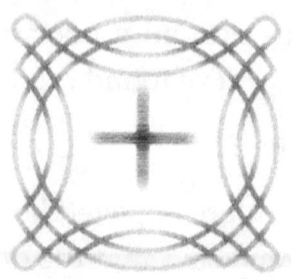

CHAPTER 22

We followed her into a sunlit room filled with more plants than I'd ever seen in one place, unless you counted botanical gardens. Or a plant nursery. Seriously. The lady had plants on every surface of the tables near the windows, and more on the white shelves lining the walls. Coming in a close second were the books that were stacked high in piles on the floor, and placed haphazardly on the shelves. Flowering begonias, succulent jades and unassuming violets sat atop many of the piles. The only clear surface in the room was a large round coffee table in the center of four comfy looking love seats -- each one upholstered in a different floral pattern and color. One blue, one red, one yellow, and one green.

I loved it.

This woman would definitely appreciate our Fiestaware collection.

Her tea pot cast a dignified air, a gleaming warm sterling silver, clearly well-worn and well loved, but her china was just as colorful and varied as the rest of the room. I sat on the green couch, rowan perching nearby on the arm of another sofa, while Vala settled down across from me.

"Go on," she urged. "Choose a cup and warm yourselves up. I picked up a handmade mug of swirling blues and greens and held it out for her to fill. "Sugar? Cream?"

I shook my head, inhaling the reassuring malty aroma of a rich Irish breakfast tea. "No, thank you. This is perfect."

"A good cup of tea can solve almost anything." She gazed at me warmly. She poured tea for Rowan and herself, and then settled back on the sofa cradling a small dainty pink cup in her hands.

"Now, why don't you start by telling me why you are here, Rowan."

"Well, Siri came to me yesterday, she ran all the way to my house, looking for help. Thorn and some thugs broke into their home and took her mother, she just barely managed to get away. We don't really know why, exactly, but my dad and Thorn are looking for Siri still, we think for someone on the Shade Council. I thought maybe you could help her. She didn't even know she was fae until recently, and has no idea what's going on."

"Do you, I wonder?" She mused, peering at him quizzically over her cup. She turned to me. "Siri, is it? Did you know your name means Victory?"

I just stared at her. Hello, random much?

"Never mind. It's odd that you were not raised knowing who you are. Who are your parents?"

"My mother is Fredrika Alvarsson. I don't know my father's name, but she told me he is fae. We moved here for my mother to do some security work with a guy named Frank, who's probably also fae."

"Alvarsson? Are you related to Jade Alvarsson?"

"Yes, that's my Aunt. I mean, no, she's my grandmother. Sorry, I only just found out who she is. I always thought she was just my mother's older sister."

"So you are light fae, I thought so." She narrowed her eyes at Rowan. "You brought her to your father? You let them meet?"

"I...well, yes, I didn't realize it would be a problem."

"Faelings." Vala sighed. "Don't they teach you anything anymore? You Shades are the worst, the way they keep you in the Dark."

See, I told you. They mindwash them. Miko practically yelled in my head.

"Ah. And you have a special friend?" Vala zeroed in on Miko. "Not a simple pet, eh?"

"What do you mean?" asked Rowan.

"Oh, right, Miko," I tried to cover, glaring at Vala. "He's pretty attached to me ever since I saved him from being roadkill."

"Indeed. A life debt?"

"I guess you could say that," I grumbled.

"Interesting. And you can hear him, too?" So much for my hints to Vala to keep the whole thing on the down low.

"I'm sorry, what?!" Rowan looked at the three of us in turn.

"Whelp, guess the cats out of the bag, Siri." Miko climbed down onto the sofa, jumped onto the table and grabbed a small teacake. "How about some service here?"

"Nice, Miko. Mind your manners." I laughed, and Vala pushed a small cup of cream towards him as if she had squirrels to tea on a daily basis.

"Wait, are you guys saying you can understand him?"

"Yeah, can't you?" I asked.

"Um, no, I just hear crazy squirrel chatter." He looked at Vala and I like we were nuts.

"Oh, well, yeah. He started talking to me yesterday. It kind of freaked me out, too. But he said it's part of my natural fae abilities."

"Yes, he's right. You have very strong channel lock," Vala explained, putting special emphasis on the last word. "I sensed it right away."

"I'm sorry, channel what?"

"Tenalach. It's a special word the Irish have for the relationship some people have with the air, water and land, a connection to the Earth so deep and close that you can literally hear the earth sing. When your tenalach is strong, you can speak with any animal. Some can even understand the trees themselves."

"Wow." Rowan and I said at the same time.

"Yes, it is an interesting and powerful ability. All light fae possess tenalach to some degree, but few these days can talk with the animals."

"My mother was explaining to me that we can feel when the earth is in pain. I actually started having visions last months of an earthquake, and then it happened. My mom was working on teaching me how to control my visions."

"Have you had more?"

I nodded.

"You have? Why didn't you tell me any of this?" Rowan looked hurt.

"I'm sorry, I wanted to. There just hasn't been time."

"Wait, is that what happened when you fainted in class?"

"Yeah."

"And at dinner when you felt sick?"

"Yep, then too."

Rowan looked at me like he didn't quite know who I was. Which I could totally get. I mean, I didn't feel like I knew who I was, either. He stood up stiffly and went to stand by the window, staring out over the lake.

"Don't worry, dear," Vala reassured me in a hushed voice. "It's an adjustment period for both of you. Now. I'd like to know more about these visions you have been having. Your grandmother is an old friend of mine and she is quite powerful, but even she does not talk with the animals. I think, also, that you have only just begun to uncover the extent of what you are capable of. Let's see how all this started."

She rose up gracefully and came over to sit by me. Each of her hands reached out to gently clasp one of mine.

Miko, I thought, is this legit?

"Go with it kid, she's good people, I told ya already."

"Relax, Siri, this won't hurt. And I won't see anything you don't want me to. We're just going to take a look at the visions you've already had."

"You can really do that? Like, mind-reading or something?"

"It's not really mind-reading, but more of an uplinking to the message the earth was sending you. I can, with my empathic connections, get a read on what is happening without forming a link, but this will give us a much clearer picture. Just don't let go of my hands, no matter what, okay?"

"Alright. Are we going to meditate or something? Mom was trying to get me to work on that before..."

"No, we're going to try something a little different. Rowan, do you see that small hand drum there on the table? Please come sit down and drum a steady heartbeat rhythm on the drum with that beater." Rowan did as she asked, reluctantly sitting nearby on the red sofa. "Don't worry, I know the drum looks old but you can't hurt it. My great-grandmother was also First Nation, she made that drum herself, blessing it with the spirits of our clan animals and her Abenaki ancestors. Go on, start drumming. Nice and steady."

Rowan began beating the drum in a steady, regular rhythm.

"Perfect, just like that. The drum will help connect us to the heartbeat of the earth. Did you know that the waves of energy that come from the earth resonate at 7MHz, the same frequency that most drums create? When we listen to the drumbeat, our brainwaves naturally shift from their predominant waking frequency to match that of the drum. When our brains are at 7MHz we are in a naturally receptive, creative trance state. Fae and young human children spend most of their time in that range, which is why this sort of thing comes so naturally to them, and to you. In fact, when you chose the green couch you were revealing a natural aptitude for connecting to the earth realm, whereas Rowan's abilities have more to do with shifting people's emotions and communication – as a water fae you'd be a great ambassador someday, Rowan."

He looked at her in surprise, mouth open. He came to himself and kept drumming, looking away again.

"So, now, we're just going to link hands, and close our eyes, listen to the drumming. Don't think about anything, just let your mind go and follow the drumming. That's it. Rowan, keep drumming until I ask you to stop."

We sat still for a minute, her hand warm and comforting in mine. She'd said this wasn't about meditation, but it sure felt like meditation. I zoned out, going deeper into the black behind my eyes, breathing in, and breathing out.

Breathing in, and out.

The room dropped out below me, and suddenly I was back in Rio in the early dawn light.

No one walked on the narrow stone streets, everyone was still sleeping. My heart filled with dread. Oh, no, did I really have to go through this again?

But I wasn't alone. I felt a hand squeeze mine and I turned to see Vala standing next to me. Overwhelmed with relief, I gave her a huge hug.

"It worked!"

"Yes, it did," she chuckled. "Where are we?"

"This was my first vision," I replied. We're in Rio, just before the huge earthquake they had."

Birds took off from the eaves disrupting the morning stillness.

I gripped Vala's hand, and the rumbling started, as I knew it would. Low and distant at first, and then suddenly all around us, shaking the ground below us. Buildings began to fall, one after the other like dominoes, the beautifully bright doorways splintering and cracking, while the muted screams of people awakening to the terror in the their beds echoes all around us.

When the dust began to settle, and the rumbling finally stopped, it was easier to hear the moans and soft cries for help under debris heaped on all sides.

"I told you. It has begun."

That man's voice again. I spun around, bringing Vala with me. But I couldn't see clearly.

Rage and frustration boiled up within me and I screamed, the sound echoing from stone to stone strangely.

"You! Who are you! What do you want?"

Suddenly there was thunder and we were standing in the rain. The wind howled and roared angrily, and the landscape had changed. Rich homes dotted the hillside above me and mud rushed down in rivers. One of the homes began to slide down the hill towards us, and maniacal laughter surrounded us.

"Join us Siri," he sneered. "If you do, you will have your mother unharmed. If you don't, we will bury you."

The house of glass and wood rushed at us like a living thing. Vala and I had only seconds before the home would squash us both.

"Help us change our fate, and live like a queen. Or suffer the consequences."

I rose my hands over my head and screamed—

"Siri. Come back now. Now, Siri!" The sound of the drumming called me back, reminded me to breath. I opened my eyes and it stopped.

Vala was glaring at Rowan. "I said not to stop until I told you to, boy!"

"I'm sorry, I just..." He rushed to my side and embraced me. "Are you alright? You got so pale, and still, and then you screamed..." He squeezed me tighter and buried his head in my hair.

I inhaled deeply, comforted as always by his scent and his warm, strong body, even as my stomach rebelled against his darker side.

Vala rose and walked over to the hearth, picking up a remote and turning on the modest flatscreen hanging above the fireplace. She scrolled through the news channels until she found what she wanted. Images of broken homes and slow moving rivers of mud scrolled behind the newscaster.

"It happened this morning. Your visions are truly seen. And more than that, another Earth fae is using them to connect with you."

"Do you know who?" Rowan asked, moving to sit beside me.

"I have my ideas. Siri, I would like to try something else with you." She hesitated, seeing me shrink into myself.

"It won't be the same this time," she reassured me. "We won't be going back into the visions. In fact, this time, you can simply relax into the drums. I will ride your energy to journey into the future and see if I can divine what is happening."

"Okay. I could use some relaxation," I gave a weak laugh. "But if that man comes back, I'm outta there. Deal?"

"It's a deal. Why don't you get more comfortable while I prepare?"

I shrugged and laid back against Rowan, propping my feet on the arm of the sofa. Miko jumped up onto my stomach and curled into a little ball, sending warm rumblings through me as he purred, overriding the slight unease I'd picked up from touching Rowan. Vala gathered her mother's drum and sat on the table next to us. She put a lighter to some herbs in a bowl, and used a white feather to waft the incense over us. The sweet, pungent smell calmed me.

Rowan coughed. "What is that stuff? It smells like pot."

"Everybody says that," Vala laughed. "This is smudge. Many cultures use a variety of herbal smokes to help clear their aura and create a blessed, protected environment. Here, I've mixed dreaming woman, or mugwort, with white sage and some tinder mushrooms from the forest trees."

"I like it. It smells sweet. Familiar somehow."

"The sweetness is from the tinder conk. The herby pot smell is from the mugwort and sage. They will help you both relax and stay centered during the session. Now close your eyes, you too, Rowan. Might as well. That's right. Just relax, and let your mind wander."

Vala began drumming, again a steady rhythm but in her hands the drum took on a more ethereal, echoing quality.

I instantly felt transported to a lush forest, and imagined myself running through the trees. I looked to my left, and saw Miko leaping from tree to tree, keeping pace with me above. I grinned and went faster, clearing small logs easily, scrambling and vaulting over the occasional boulder that stood in my way.

Laughter followed me, and I looked around to see who was there. It didn't sound like the horrible man from before. No, this was a deep, husky laugh that made my whole body tingle with anticipation.

Rowan, I wondered?

I kicked off a tree, spinning 360 degrees in the air, and glimpsed a dark-haired man ten feet behind, grinning as he followed.

Not Rowan.

I landed hard and kept running, my mind spinning. Who was this guy? He was shirtless, just wearing a set of loose brown shorts that blended in with our surroundings. God, he was gorgeous. Tall, lean and muscular, and even though I was running my fastest, he hadn't appeared to be breaking a sweat. His jet black hair was fine, worn shaggy below his ears. Even from a distance, I'd been able to see his bright green eyes gleaming at me in amusement.

"You can't lose me, Siri," he called out. "I'll follow you to the ends of the earth. But it's time we headed back for dinner, are you ready?"

I stopped and turned around, catching my breath and watching him approach. My breath caught, as I stared up at him. His eyes weren't just green. A violet ring around his pupil flared out into the green as he took a step closer and tucked a loose strand of hair behind my ears. My entire body sang at the light touch, and my heart felt like it had doubled in size, in a strange but oddly pleasant way.

"We'll have to do something about your hair," he mused.

And just like that, I wanted to smack him.

Chapter 23

And then I was back. Vala was looking down at me thoughtfully, with a slightly amused gleam in her eye.

"How interesting," she murmured. The drumming was over. I glanced at Rowan and saw he'd dozed off. Vala motioned for me to be quiet with a finger to her lips and nodded for me to follow her. I carefully extracted myself from the couch without disturbing Rowan, leaving Miko to nestle into the pillows beside him. Apparently, they both needed a rest.

Me, I needed a good run. The vision had invigorated me in ways sleep never had. I felt alive, buoyant, and for the first time in days, hopeful.

I walked behind Vala down the hall to a screened in porch. She walked out the door, not even checking to see if I was following. I managed to not get smacked in the face by the door as it swung back and rushed to catch up with her as she headed down to the lake. We stopped at the lake's edge, where she knelt down and trailed her hand in the water. She whispered something, waited, and then said some more words. When she stood up she dried her hand off on her skirt.

"The lake is still today, it is good."

Um. Sure. Okay. We were talking weather now? I decided to follow her lead and just gazed out over the water.

The water was still, she was right. It added to the overall sense of peace I was feeling at the moment. Which of course, made no sense, because how could a pretty lake help me or my mother in the long run. And yet, it did. Canadian geese swam slowly through the water, creating small ripples as they went, and the leaves of the trees on the other side reflected in a beautiful array of golden fire on the water's edge.

"I do not have any definite answers for you today, but I was able to see what you need to do next."

"Were you able to see my mom?"

"No, I wasn't. But I believe she is being held by the Council of the Shades. I was able to go deeper into your visions the second time around, and see that the man who appeared is a Dark leader known as Mikael Morrigan. By now, they will have moved your mother to a secure facility, so your only hope really is to appeal to Valhalla."

"Like, to the center of the Earth? How would I even get there?" I scoffed.

"You'd need to go there eventually anyway. I was able to look into your soul and connect with who you really are.

And who you are...well. Your father is in Valhalla. If you want to meet him, you will need to go. And if you want to save your mother, you must go."

"But how? I don't have the first idea how to get there, or even what it's like or anything? You expect Rowan and I to just haul off to the center of the earth?"

"No. I expect you to go. Not Rowan. He cannot enter there. Only Light fae or their descendants can go to the inner realms. Those fated to the Dark cannot enter. I will explain it to him when he awakens."

"You know, I don't believe in fate. Rowan isn't destined for anything. He told me himself, he hasn't chosen yet."

"Maybe not. It's true he still has a chance to exert free will. But right now he cannot enter the Fae realm unless he chooses the Light. The Dark is simply too deeply embedded in his DNA at this point."

"Great," I huffed. I know, I know. My body had been warning me against him all along. But it had also responded to him in positive ways, too. I mean, I wouldn't even have made it this far if it wasn't for Rowan. It didn't feel right to me that I would have to leave him behind. Assuming, of course, that he even wanted to go with me. "So, what then?

"I've contacted the Light Guard, and they will send a suitable escort. I have seen that the Dark are getting restless, and will be here in two days to question me again. Once they see that Rowan was unable to gather any useful information, they will send someone from the Council."

"Isn't that dangerous for you? I mean, aren't you supposed to be neutral?" In the short time I'd known her, I'd grown to like Vala. I didn't want to see her get hurt by Thorn and her crew.

Something flashed in Vala's eyes. Anger? Her face settled into a mask of determination. "No. I am neutral in that I will not willingly engage in actions that cause harm to either side. By helping you, I accomplish that. Everything I do, I do with the hope that eventually both sides will learn to work together again for the good of all. I am loyal, above all, to the land, and to the spiritual and physical wellness of all beings on this planet."

"But...what if they hurt you?" I asked. "Helping me can't be worth that to you."

Vala's gaze softened and she pulled me into a warm embrace. I felt like cookies and hot chocolate were being mainlined into my bloodstream, and a sense of well-being flooded me.

"Sweet child." She leaned back and placed her hands on my shoulders, looking straight into my eyes. "You are worth everything to me. I've seen that you alone will have the power to bring the fae together into the Light, or to give the Shades the final victory they have always desired. If I don't help you now, you will never make it to Aeden. The Earth will fall prey to the Shades on a scale we've not seen yet, and humanity will become mere slaves while the land is abused in ways that...well. What I saw was not a pretty sight, I'll tell you that much." She laughed mirthlessly.

"Me? But I'm no one. What can I do?" Somehow, I didn't think my martial arts trophies were going to be enough to help me here.

"It isn't my place to tell you. Your father, he must be the one. He has left you this long to figure things out on your own for a reason, perhaps to make you stronger, or so that he would not wrongly influence you. The Light tend to err on the side of fairness."

"Okay. Well, can you at least tell me his name? And what about my mom? Did she look...was she hurt?"

"You're mother looked a bit roughed up, which is to be expected given her skill at fighting. I'm sure she wasn't taken easily. They seem to be keeping her comfortable -- well, as comfortable as one can be in a cell."

Frustration hit me when I heard that. I wanted to go to her right now, and break her out. Except I didn't know where she was. My feelings must have shown clearly on my face, because Vala continued.

"You'll need a team of highly skilled fae to break her out. This is part of why you must go to Aeden, and appeal to your father, Bran Le Fay. You will meet him soon enough. For now, why don't you go shower and rest? Your ride won't be here until tomorrow morning, at the earliest. I'll put together a nice warm supper, and you can turn in early. I'm sure you are tired after all you've been through."

"Actually, what I'd really love to do is go on a run. Is it safe here? Are there any trails through the forest I can run on?"

My mind flashed back to my earlier vision. The trees had been covered in greens of every hues, and the foliage here was in its full fall glory. Wherever I'd been, it wasn't here, not today. Still. I needed to move, to feel the earth pounding under my feet and free my body.

"Yes, I have extensive walking trails through the woods. The land is protected for miles, this trust owns over 1000 acres privately, and no fae is allowed to roam freely without my permission, unless they want to find themselves at the mercy of the oaks."

"The oaks?" I looked around at some of the trees, wondering if she had some old Ents hidden among them or something.

"Yes, never you mind, they won't harm you while you are under my protection. You'll be quite safe anywhere on this property. Still. Can't be too careful right now; you'd best take Miko with you and Rowan if he's up for it."

Vala pointed out several trails leading into the woods, explaining which ones looped and the various distances each one covered. Then we walked back up to the house, where I collected my bag and she showed me the room where I'd be sleeping later so I could change.

I threw on my shorts from the day before and sat on the bed to tie on my running shoes. The room had a beautiful eastern view overlooking the forest and part of the lake. I'd be up early with the sun, since the room only had thin white curtains. I guessed Vala liked her guests to be up for breakfast. The walls were painted a pale peach color, and all the furniture was made of rich burl wood, just like downstairs.

They had some serious antiques in this house. Even the bedding was ancient, with a handstitched quilt decorated with a square knot filled with swirls, much like the knot work downstairs, colored in burnt orange, yellow and peach. I imagined that the early morning sun would light up the room like it was on fire.

Rowan was still sleeping when I made way downstairs. Poor guy. Miko opened his eyes and I waved for him to come along. He scampered down the hallway after me and I opened the door for us to go out on the lawn.

What's up? Miko looked at me with his head tilted to one side.

"I thought I'd go on a run. You up for it? Vala thought you should keep me company, just in case."

"Oh yeah, I'd love a good chase. Haven't been out in the trees for too long. Let's go!"

He bounded off across the lawn towards one of the forest trails.

"That trail loops around the lake in a two mile loop, is that too far for you?"

"No way, I can outrun you all day, any day, just wait and see." He ran up a tree and out across a limb, leaping to the next tree down the trail.

"Ha!" I barked at him as I followed, we'd see about that.

The thing was though, he wasn't wrong. Up in the canopy, he was able to soar over obstacles in ways my freerunning-self envied and admired. He was incredibly agile, and obviously used to running all day long. He was able to process variables in jumps that I was still learning to master. After the first mile, I gave up trying to race him and started focusing more on honing my parkour skills, running alongside the trail instead of on it, so that I would have more obstacles to conquer.

All too soon, we emerged from the trail, having run all the way around the little lake. I wasn't even close to being tired, and started to run over to another trail, one that Vala had said traveled several miles over some small hills in a closed loop.

"Siri, wait up!" I heard Rowan yell. I looked around and spotted him heading over across the soft grass. "I was hoping you'd run back through here. Want some company?"

We headed into the woods, running companionably together. Rowan was able to keep up with me with no problem, but it wasn't like running with the guy in my vision. We stayed quiet and serious. I sort of forgot Rowan was even there as I replayed the events of the weekend in my head. I tried to come up with a plan for how to find my mom, but I couldn't even begin to imagine where I would be going next or what would happen.

Frustrated, I put everything from my head and pushed myself to run faster, barely noticing that I was losing Rowan and Miko as I ran. It was just me and the forest. Nothing else existed.

Fae problems could wait. Vala and her guard rescuer could wait. The visions could wait. My mother, too. She would have to wait, there was nothing I could do. Not now.

So I just pounded the earth with my feet, running flat out, reveling in the strength of my body and the promise it held.

I would become faster. Stronger. And the next time a Shade crossed me, I wouldn't lose.

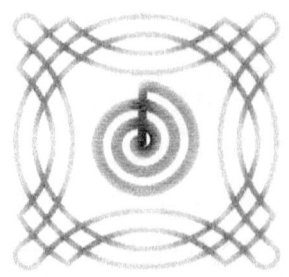

CHAPTER 24

I woke up the next morning to a sliver of orange light blazing into my eye. Argh. I rolled over and pulled a pillow over my head. I'd expected this to happen, since the curtains in the room were basically non-existent, but I had kind of hoped to sleep in a little longer.

After my run the evening before, I'd showered and joined the others for a quiet dinner. The physical exertion had cleared my head, and all the questions I'd had earlier had fled my mind. Food and shelter. Training. Finding my mom. Those were my only concerns now.

I felt a strange distance from Rowan and the others, even Miko. I heard Vala whisper words of comfort to Rowan about me being in shock, but that wasn't it. It was like I had turned off part of myself. I felt no fear anymore, but I also felt removed. Remote. Like my emotions were on ice. I ate without tasting anything, and when I finished I excused myself to go to bed early.

Not that I'd gotten much rest.

Conflicting dreams had kept me awake all night. Dreams where I fought faceless fighters made of smoke and darkness, and other dreams where I ran laughing through the steamy forests, chased by smiling green eyes.

I flopped over and stared at the ceiling, testing my mood. The morning sun hadn't changed anything. I still didn't feel anything, except a driving sense of purpose to train, run, and move. I wasn't even tired. I couldn't wait till this guardian guy showed up and things started happening. I needed to be on the move. I needed to feel like I was doing something.

I threw on some yoga pants and a tee shirt, being careful not to wake Miko, laced up my sneakers and snuck outside with an apple in hand to watch the sunrise come up.

Even while I was eating and trying to Zen out on the dawn, I couldn't stay still, going through a series of stretches and sun salutations. After a few minutes I tossed the apple core into some bushes and jogged off into the woods to check out what Vala had said was the longest trail covering steep inclines and a small boulder field.

Two hours later, I came back out of the forest covered in sweat and feeling fantastic. That had been a killer run, and the boulder field made an awesome parkour training course. My body felt like it was singing.

Rowan was sitting on the back steps, coffee in hand, watching me approach. Worry was clearly etched across his face.

I felt a twinge of guilt, realizing I hadn't left a note or anything to explain my absence.

"Vala said you went out running."

"She did?" His comment surprised me, until I remembered she was a seer. I guessed she could sense most of what happened on her land.

"Yeah, but I was still worried. You didn't even bring Miko." He nodded at Miko who was in a tree by the woods happily eating his way through a massive walnut.

"Sorry," I said without really meaning it. "I needed to get outside." And once I said it I realized that exercise had only been just a part of it.

Being outside in the forest, being in nature, had revitalized me in a way it never had before. I felt like I could go run for another two hours, no problem. The birds sang, and I could hear the song of each one separately, and understand what they were saying. They sang of the fresh sun, of the new squirrel who was just visiting, of how bright the light shone from the funny running fae when she had fewer thoughts in her head than the deer at rest, and when a gentle rain would fall the next day.

Wait. I had light shining from me? What the hell? I looked down at my arms, but they looked normal to me. Maybe it was just an avian turn of phrase.

"I still feel pretty jazzed. Since you're up...Didn't you used to do martial arts?"

"Yeah," Rowan eyed me warily.

"Wanna spar? I promise I'll go easy on you," I sassed.

"How could I refuse an offer like that? Sure, why not," he chuckled.

I kicked off my shoes, walking to the center of the lawn, and he followed suit.

"Ok, light contact only, since we don't have any gear. And no head shots."

"Deal." He bounced back into a respectable fighting stance and put his hands up. "Ready when you are."

We started with a volley of light punches. I saw he could hold his own, and started mixing in some kicks, careful not to hit any marks too hard. He knew me well, even though we'd never fought before, and was able to anticipate a lot of my simpler moves.

Our sparring slowly evolved into more of a dance, with Rowan giving me the space I needed to work out my some of my energy. Whenever I made contact he looked at me not with anger or frustration, but with admiration. He moved gracefully, and the graceful flow of our fighting inspired me to mix in new capoeira moves I'd been studying, cartwheels and rotations that looks deceivingly slow and harmless, but actually combined evasion and attack techniques in a beautiful way.

"What the hell was that?" Rowan grunted, speaking for the first time. I'd just knocked him back a few feet with a macaco roundoff ending in a kick to his shoulder.

"Capoeira," I grinned. The same relaxed, almost joyful energy I'd had after running still flowed through me. It dawned on me that I was actually having fun for the first time in days.

Rowan's eyes got a new gleam in them, and he closed the space between us, growling. "Guess I better not give you too much room."

"Oh, ok." I pretended to struggle for a moment as his arms came around me, giving him a few moments to feel some victory before I responded with a few staple Krav Maga moves. Stunned, Rowan looked up at me from the ground. "And that was?"

"Israeli army self-defense," I smiled down at him.

"How could I have forgotten, my girl knows Krav Maga?" He closed his eyes and threw his arms out wide across the grass. "I surrender."

The sound of clapping made me drop into a defensive stance. I had been reaching down to help Rowan back up, but now I was braced for whatever was coming.

At least, that's what I thought. In truth, nothing could have prepared me for what I saw.

Leaning against the back door, his inky black hair in deep contrast with the crisp white trim on the house, was one of the hottest guys I'd ever seen. Somehow, the fact that he was hot just pissed me off. I glared at him, and he broke into amused laughter.

"That was awesome!" He clapped a few more times. "I don't think I've seen anyone get owned like that in at least a year." I heard Rowan growl behind me as he struggled back to his feet.

"Can we help you?" I demanded coldly.

"On the contrary," he said, pushing away lazily from the building and walking down the steps. "I believe I am here to help you." He grinned arrogantly at me as he walked across the lawn, looking overly pleased with himself.

"Really?" Rowan drawled. "And how could you possibly help us? Vala sent for a trained Light Guard. You want us to believe they sent you instead? You don't look any older than us."

I watched the guy get closer. He moved as if he was totally relaxed, but with the same sort of awareness of his surroundings that my mother always had. I could tell he'd had training. But had he had enough?

I hadn't dropped my stance, so I decided to give him a little test.

"He has a point. Show us what you can do," I said, stretching out my hand and beckoning him with a gesture Bruce Lee would have been proud of.

If anything, his grin got even wider.

I only had a moment to reflect on the dazzling effect it had on me before he launched into a series of moves that defied categorization. I didn't recognize any of the forms, but managed to avoid his first few punches and kicks. I felt a proud thrill when I evaded his grasp as he twirled behind me and reached for my arms.

A moment later, flat on my back, I realized his grab had been a diversion. He'd used my defensive momentum to flip my legs out from under me, throwing me to the ground and pinning me down as he nimbly settled astride my hips.

It was the fastest take-down I'd ever experienced, at least from anyone other than my mom.

I probably should have been annoyed. But I wasn't. Surprised, definitely. And...oddly warm. In fact, I felt happy again, giddy almost, like my heart was ready to explode out of my chest with excitement. Breathless.

We locked eyes. Mine, curious. His, green and twinkling.

Wait.

Green?

Even with his back to the sun, I could see that his eyes were a vibrant green with the same enchanting violet ring around their center. The man from my vision.

Again, annoyance replaced joy. My body reacted instinctively to the information, and I tried to buck him off me. Too late, I realized that unbreakable tendrils of plants had come from the earth to hold me in place. They wrapped around my legs and knees, around my arms and shoulders. I lifted my head up and glared at him.

"Let. Me. Go."

"Not until you concede defeat." If he kept smiling at me, I swore I would find a way to kill him. Some day. Some time. Very soon.

"Clearly, you win," I ground out.

He stood up, and watched me, considering. I grew warmer under his inspection, my skin flushing and betraying me even as I grew more frustrated with him.

"You heard her," Rowan stepped forward, his hands fisting at his sides. "Let her up."

"Ah, are you going to make me?" The man turned on Rowan, towering over him by several inches. "Don't forget, I am already familiar with your fighting style." He put derisive emphasis on the last word.

Rowan narrowed his eyes and folded his arms over his chest, standing his ground. "Just let her up."

"I don't think so," he mused, looking thoughtful.

Miko started chattering furiously from the tree where he'd been eating, clearly not happy with how the situation was progressing.

"I think, we should see what else she can do."

He knelt down next to me and put his hand on my arm. It was the first real skin to skin contact we had made and it felt like a blast of sunshine was riding through my entire body, lighting up every cell and filling me with an intense desire to get closer to him. I struggled more against my bonds, but this time, it wasn't because I want to get up. I just wanted to get more. More of whatever it was he was serving up.

And then it was gone. He snatched his hand back, as if he'd burned, and looking at it in wonder. When he looked back at me his eyes were filled with suspicion and resentment. Relief flooded me as I realized that the vines had been the only thing saving me from a very embarrassing moment. What had come over me? I prayed it had looked like I was just struggling to get free.

"Who are you?" he asked, squinting at me as if bringing me into clearer focus might answer all his questions. He managed to sound like somehow I was the one who had suddenly appeared and now held him captive, and not the other way around.

"Who am I? Who the hell are you?" I retorted. "And when are you going to let me up?"

"Right, sorry." He shrugged. "I wanted to see if you could do it yourself. Vala said you were showing Earth powers. Is that true?"

"Um, yes, I think so. I mean, that's what everybody says."

"Okay, so let's see if you can do this. I need to you to quiet your mind."

"Easier said than done," I muttered. "Can you, maybe, back up a little bit. You're kind of freaking me out still."

"Okay, sure." He moved back to stand with Rowan, who was doing his best to ignore the guy and look supportively at me.

"Better?"

I nodded.

"Good. So, now, quiet your mind. Just relax. Take a few deep breaths in and out, and push your energy out to the vines. Thank them and ask them to release you."

Was he kidding? I was familiar with Qi Kung exercises, so I tried to push out my Qi that way, but nothing happened. I thought for a minute, not sure how to proceed. Then I remembered what the birds had sung about me shining. I tried to imagine my thoughts as rays of light, expanding out from my head.

That's the way, Miko whispered in my head.

Shhh, I thought back, distracted. I started over again, and imagined my yellow rays reaching out around me and shining into the green pools of energy of the plants surrounding me. I thanked them for their oxygen-giving ways, and asked them if they wouldn't mind terribly letting me go now?

Slowly, and ever so gently, the tendrils unwound from my body and retreated back into the ground. When the last one had disappeared, I let out a huge breath. I hadn't even realized I was holding it.

"Wow." Rowan whispered. "That was so cool."

I kipped up onto my feet and brushed off some imaginary dirt on my pants.

"Thanks." I smiled at Rowan appreciatively before I looked over at my nameless supposed escort. "I didn't know I could do stuff like that. Will I be able to call them up like you did, too?"

"Definitely. I think you'll be able to do that, and a whole lot more," he said like he wasn't entirely sure he was happy about it. We watched each other for a moment in silence. He shook himself out of it first, thrusting out a hand to me in greeting.

"The name's Alec Ward."

"Siri Alvarsson," I answered, grasping his hand. The warm sunshine on a beach feeling returned and it took all my effort not to pull him closer to me.

He dropped my hand quickly and turned to Rowan. With the loss of contact, I felt like the day had gone cloudy, but no, the sun was still out and the birds were still singing. What was wrong with me? I focused on the guys, watching Alec stare down Rowan.

"And you would be?"

"The boyfriend, Rowan Carey," he said, holding Alec's hand in a vise-like grip. Whoa, really? I mean, we hadn't actually had that conversation yet. Alec hissed and yanked his hand out of Rowan's grip. In a flash he was behind him, restraining both his arms

"You're a Shade! Why are you here?"

"Easy dude, Rowan is not a Shade." I rushed to Alec, putting my hand on his shoulder.

"He is, I sensed it the moment I touched him," Alec sneered and shrugged off my hand. "He's been lying to you. Besides, he's a Carey. They're all dark."

"Look, Alec, I promise, Rowan is not dark. He hasn't even chosen yet."

"Get off me, you jerk," Rowan tried to shake him off, and Alec's grip tightened.

`My voice rose in frustration. "You can't blame him for who his parents are!"

Alec hesitated, clearly doubting my judgment.

"Stand down, Ward!" Vala called from one of the windows on the first floor. "The girl is right. He's proven himself trustworthy, so far."

"How do you know it's not a trap?" Alec called back to her over her shoulder.

"You dare question my judgement? Have you been having your own visions now, Alec?" She chuckled. "Let the poor boy go. If he'd wanted to harm her, he could have handed her over days ago."

Vala's head ducked back out of sight and Alec groaned in frustration, clearly thinking we were all out of our minds as he shoved Rowan away from himself in disgust.

Rowan stumbled against me. I hugged him to me for a moment, my stomach rolling with tension, but he shrugged me off and stalked into the woods. I started to follow him but Vala called me back. "Let him go, child. His pride's been broken, let him have some time to put it back together."

"Fine," I muttered, kicking at a dandelion. "Miko, can you go with him? I still don't think it's safe for him to be out there alone." Miko bounded through the forest canopy, griping the whole time about demanding humans.

"You can talk to the animals?" Alec demanded from over my shoulder as I stared forlornly after Miko and Rowan. "How long have you been with the Light?"

"I'm not with the Light. I didn't even know I was fae until recently, and I don't turn eighteen until January."

Alec didn't respond, so I turned to look at him. "What?"

He was staring at me like I'd just grown another head.

"But then how did you-" he broke off, shook his head and started again. "How long have you been manifesting abilities for?"

"A few weeks. So? I mean, my mom said it was a little early, but it can't be that unusual, can it?"

"It's completely unusual. I don't know anyone who manifested before they turned eighteen, other than the Elders."

"And here I thought my mom was just putting off telling me about this fae stuff because she didn't want to face me getting older." I laughed. "But she really was telling the truth... she really thought she'd have more time..." I trailed off. It hit me that she might not have any time, period. The weight of what was happening to me crashed down on me again.

"Hey," Alec said, his arms appearing instantly around me, enveloping me with his warm, hard body. "Don't worry about your mother. We're going to figure this all out, I swear. You will have the best resources behind you, and we will find Fredrika."

He set me back from him and smiled gently at me, like I was a frail mental patient that could become unhinged at any time. Which, I suppose, wasn't too far off at the moment, considering the way my moods kept shifting.

"She trained me, you know."

I looked him up and down doubtfully. She certainly hadn't shown me any of his moves.

"Obviously she taught us different things."

"No really, she did. The Guard has their own style of martial fighting, but Fredrika leads training seminars every year or so to help catch us up on human fighting techniques. I've taken several of her workshops. It's important for us to know how to deal with any opponent."

"Well, you seem to have it down," I ceded. I wasn't sure if I should be more annoyed that my mom's "teaching trips" had involved meeting up with lots more fae, or that she hadn't taught me any of these Guard techniques. Just another thing she had hidden from me. Part of me felt kind of jealous and resentful, that people like this guy had gotten to know my mom in an entirely different way than me. But another part of me just felt ambivalent.

Either way, it didn't matter what she had hidden from me. Since being fae had led to everything that had gone down this weekend, I could totally get why she'd done it. None of it really mattered. I just had to find her and get her back safe. I wasn't ready to lose my mom yet.

Rowan returned, just as Vala's call to come in for brunch pulled me out of my musings. Alec strode quickly ahead of Rowan and I, not bothering to hold the door open for us. Clearly, he was still miffed about the whole Shade thing. Rowan linked arms with me, ambling along slowly.

When we got to the house, he placed his palm against the door and held it closed for a moment, turning to face me. "Siri, I want you to know. Whatever everyone thinks about Shades, I swear, it doesn't matter what my DNA says. I will never be like my dad. You matter to me more than anything. You will always be able to trust me, you know that right? I could never, ever, hurt you."

"Well, yeah, I mean, you couldn't hurt ever your own girlfriend, right?" I winked at him, emphasizing the word girlfriend, making light of what he'd just said. Plus, I couldn't resist teasing him. "Remind me again when I agreed to that, how long has it been now?"

He had the good grace to blush, but he gazed back at me not bothering to hide it. "Hmm, I suppose it's been, what, about ten seconds now?"

"Hmm, yes, I suppose it has." I leaned up and gave him a light kiss. "Lucky for you, I've always had a thing for bad boys. Now come on Romeo, I'm starved."

"Me, too, Serious. Me, too." From the way he looked me up and down, I could tell he didn't mean food. I gave him a look like, really? I mean, come on, now wasn't exactly the ideal time to get lost in making out. Or maybe it was. What would I know about it, anyway? But he got my meaning and opened the door, gesturing for me to enter first.

Whatever his parents were, they'd certainly raised a gentleman. That had to count for something. At least, I fervently hoped so.

We joined Vala and Alec at the table. I started to dig in, but Vala gave a slight cough and nodded at Alec, who had bowed his head.

What was it with fae and the whole grace thing? My mom had never bothered with it. I was starting to get the idea that maybe she was a lapsed fae. Was that even a thing, like a Catholic who stopped going to church?

Alec's deep voice washed over the table. I felt graced alright, just by the musical lilt of his voice and his presence.

"We accept this feast today with gratitude to all the beings who contributed to its bounty, the animals and plants, the farmers and the land itself. May it fill our hearts, bodies and minds with the blessings and the radiance of Aeden, aho-em."

I couldn't help but think back to Sullivan Carey's grace just days before, and how different it was.

"Penny for your thoughts, Siri?" Vala asked as she passed around a huge bowl of Caesar salad.

"I was just thinking back to the last time I heard a fae say grace. Do all fae say grace in Aeden?" I looked at Alec as I spooned the fruit salad onto my plate, making sure I gave myself an overabundance of strawberry and mango.

"We all bless our food in pretty much the same way. When we make our food, we also usually bless and energize it."

I looked at Rowan, wondering if I should share what I'd noticed. But surely he had noticed, too?

"But, well, you talked about thanks and gratitude. The other fae I heard thanked his Lord for dominion over the earth and for his help in seeking the light."

"Dark fae." Alec sneered, his knuckles turning white as his hand tightened around the salad tongs.

"Easy, Alec," Vala cautioned, "You don't want to bruise the fruit, now, do you?"

He let up on the tongs, but he and Rowan continued to glare at each other.

"Okay," I plowed on, "but now I am wondering who is the Lord that they were thanking – was it a deity all the fae worship, or is it someone like Mikael, the man who's currently holding my mom prisoner?" Rowan looked stunned, like he had never thought about it. And he probably hadn't.

"It's just grace, Siri. My dad says the same thing at every meal."

"Yeah, but think about it. It sounds all nice and god-like, but even before I knew Sully was Dark fae it creeped me out a little. I thought you guys were Lutheran or something with all that talk about dominion and toil."

Rowan's face tightened in anger. I gave him an apologetic look and shrugged.

"Look, I don't want to upset you, I'm just curious, okay?" I turned to Alec, "My mom never said grace, except at Thanksgiving. This is all still so new to me. But it seems obvious now that when his dad spoke about finding the light with the Lord's blessing, he was actually talking about finding Light fae, not radiance like you just talked about. So who is this Lord? Is it a god or a person?"

"As far as I know, no fae believe in any specific god. Not the Dark, and not the Light. We believe in Spirit, a unifying energy behind all existence and matter, and we are able to harness that energy, but any Lord Sullivan mentioned probably had to do with the leader of the Dark fae council. Here in the Americas, that would be Mikael."

I blanched.

"Every continent has their own council," Alec continued. "Each leader of the local council serves on a high council that rules all Shades. There is no one leader of the Shades, they all mistrust each other too much to bow to one leader. Our intel, however, indicates that Mikael would like to change all that."

"And you think my father is helping him with that? You think my family is part of this, that the Shades hunt Light fae for fun?"

"Easy Rowan, no one's talking about your family." I tried to reassure him, "Alec is just telling me what he knows about the Dark council."

"Actually," admonished Alec, "the Dark do hunt the light for fun. Every Shade warrior that I've gone up against seems to thoroughly enjoy the pain they inflict on the innocent, whether they are Light fae or just unlucky humans who've gotten in the way." Anguish flitted across his face, there and gone so quickly I could almost believe I'd imagined it. "If your father is working with Mikael, then he is directly involved in the hunting of Light fae."

"Alec." Vala shook her head in warning. "This is not the time."

"Really, Vala, then when is the time? I'm not going to lie to her, and I'm not going to let this darkling get away with believing whatever crap his parents have told him; she asked a question and she deserves an honest answer. The Light does not shield faelings from the truth, no matter how painful or ugly it might be. We give them the benefit of an upbringing steeped in truth and honesty."

He turned to me, searing me with a look that managed to both freeze me and set me on fire at the same. His natural easy manner was gone, and all that was left was a cold, hard fighter. It was a look that I was familiar with, a look I'd come across in tournament after tournament, a look that told me there would be no quarter given, no easy win, no mercy. It was a look I knew, because it was a look that I had used myself enough times.

"The fae have always been heart-centered, trusting, giving people. The Light fae still hold to those values. We are quick to forgive, and slow to hate." He paused, and his gaze intensified. I had to hold myself still, refusing to squirm under his sudden scrutiny. "When love comes, it comes instantly. We hold nothing back."

I swallowed, unable to tear my eyes away from his, yet knowing I totally should, because I could feel Rowan staring at me, too. I had to look away, it was only right that I look away. But I couldn't.

"The Dark have taken everything that comes naturally to us and distorted it. Where we trust, they take advantage. Where we love, they consume. Where we forgive, they hate and seek revenge. Where we protect, they abuse. Where we value honesty, they lie. Where we seek harmony, they sow discord and lust for power. There is nothing honorable left in the Dark. They have twisted everything that we hold dear. Every Light fae who has ever trusted a Shade has come to regret it."

He turned and speared Rowan with a pitying look, and I followed his gaze, helpless to watch. "Every. Single. One."

Rowan looked back at him with pure hate, his eyes the darkest midnight.

"That will never happen." He ground out. "I will never give Siri a reason to regret trusting me. She is everything to me, more important than my family, more important than anything on the planet."

"And that is how you will fail her." Alec whispered. "No Light fae would ever even think to make such a promise. Nothing is more important than our charge. Nothing is more important than the whole of the planet. It is the core of our soul." He looked back at me, pleading with me to understand, apology clear in his eyes for the pain he knew he'd caused. "Our love for every facet of the Earth is the same as our love for ourselves, for our mates, for our children. We cannot separate ourselves from that love because it is all of who and what we are. So you see, you can never keep the promises you are making, because the very nature of them betrays you for what you really are."

Rowan held on to the edge of the table like it was supporting him, his knuckles turning white in his grip. I could tell he was just moments away from launching himself at Alec. Vala saved the day with a gentle cough as she rose from the table, clearing her and Rowan's plates.

"Alec, can you grab Siri's plate please? The second course should be ready now." Somehow she managed to sound like nothing out of the ordinary was going on.

Rowan and I were left in at the table in a wake of awkwardness. I played with my napkin, wondering how I could improve the situation.

"It's not true, you know. That won't ever happen. I won't let it happen, what he said." Rowan's words tumbled over themselves in rush, filling the space of our silence.

"I know," I answered. "I do trust you. But I get what he's saying, too. Now that I've started to connect with my abilities, now that I can feel the energy coming from the plants and the earth...I know what he means. It's like everything is a part of me. I can't imagine wanting to strip-mine the planet or cause anything living pain. I'm not even sure how much longer I'll be able to continue eating meat, at this rate. It's like even the fruit salad has a heartbeat."

"I can't feel what you're feeling, not yet. But I know that I want to. And I know that I feel more for you than anyone I've ever met before. There is no place I'd rather be than by your side Siri, I swear it."

"I know, Rowan. I believe you," I replied. I feared it might not be enough. But what could I say? He was making promises against the future, and neither of us had any idea what that really meant.

Alec and Vala came back into the room, Vala making a big fuss over presenting the steaming strawberry-stuffed French toast and pure Vermont maple syrup, trying to smooth over the previous awkwardness. Alec attacked his plate for the rest of his meal, eating several helpings of breakfast, which was probably for the best since it left his mouth too full to talk. The rest of us tried to maintain a stilted conversation centered around the work with plants that Vala did on the estate.

Brunch ended, and it was time for us to go. I went upstairs, took a quick shower and changed, putting on my favorite skinny jeans, my silver hi-tops, a tank top and hoodie. In Arizona a lot of my friends had driven motorcycles; since the weather was always fair there it was the perfect cheap ride for a teenager. I was looking forward to being on one again. At least the weather was warm and sunny, as good as you could get for October in Vermont. Everything was happening so quickly. I wasn't even sure where we were headed.

Rowan was sitting at the bottom of the stairs when I returned. He watched me walk down the steps, drinking me in like he was trying to memorize my face, like it was the last time he would ever see me. Maybe it was.

"They're waiting outside. I think Vala is giving him some last minute tips."

Words eluded me, so I just gave him a tight smile. I was nervous and excited all at the same time. I was scared to lose him, to lose my mom, and Rose, and the new life I had just started getting used to. I wasn't ready to shift gears so suddenly, not yet. I wasn't sure what awaited me. I was excited to meet my dad, I knew that much. But everything else was just a big question mark to me right now.

He stood up when I reached the bottom step, holding me close.

"You don't have to do this, you know. You don't have to go with him. We can go somewhere, just you and me. We can leave all of this behind. The Light, the Dark, everything. Just go somewhere where no one knows us."

For a moment, my heart leapt at the idea. I could still have a normal life. Go to school. Hang out. Get a job.

Reality crashed back, accompanied by the butterflies on my stomach that I always felt when Rowan was near. The butterflies reminding me who he was, and who I was. Fluttering softly, whispering that I'd never see my mom again if I did what he was asking of me.

I hugged him as tight as I could, never wanting to let him go.

"You know I can't." I sighed, resting my cheek against his chest. I could hear his heart beating strongly. "I have to go. But I will be thinking of you every day, I promise. Do cell phones even work in Aeden?" I half-groaned, half laughed.

"I don't think so," he chuckled. "Vala should be able to get any messages to me though, through the waters."

I breathed in his scent one last time, trying to memorize it, the underlying spiciness, the warmth of him. Even if he couldn't come with me, I wanted to carry that feeling with me, wherever I was headed. I gave him another squeeze, and separated myself from his arms.

I took a deep breath, and opened the door to walk outside. This was it. I knew that the moment I stepped outside this house, things would never be the same. Everything was changing so much, there had been so many shifts to the fabric of my reality. And today, now, here was another one.

The sun had come out in full force, and for a moment I was blinded by its radiance. I held a hand up over my eyes and stepped out into the driveway, into my future.

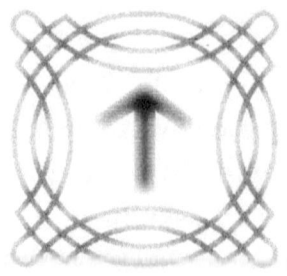

CHAPTER 25

The first thing I noticed was that Vala held Alec's hands in hers, and they were deep in conversation. He looked resigned, and she was smiling warmly at him.

The second thing I noticed was the naked bike next to them, the raw Ducati Monster painted an understated matte black and outfitted with mean-looking all-terrain tires.

Oh, this was going to be fun.

Miko ran past me and hopped up onto the bike.

Really, he looked at me, *fun? Where am I supposed to sit?*

He had a point. My backpack was totally full, there wasn't room for him in there. Then I remembered the small messenger-style bag Rowan had stowed my toiletries in.

Don't worry, I thought, *I have the perfect thing*. I opened the bags, repacked my toothbrush and things in the front pocket of the pack, and slung the bag over my head across my body, followed by the pack over both shoulders.

Hmm? What do you think? I modeled the bag for him.

It'll do, he acquiesced. I leaned down and picked him up, gently placing him inside the bag.

"Okay, we're ready." I smiled bravely at everyone, hiding my nerves.

Vala rushed over to me and gave me long, comforting hug. I wondered if she had read that Facebook post about hugs longer than twenty seconds releasing endorphins in the body to lower stress. Whether she had or not, it was definitely working. I'd almost forgotten what it was like to hug someone and just feel simple comfort. No overwhelming fae feelings. No stomach flopping. Just a good, plain old hug. Wonderful.

Then she backed up and held my hands as she had with Alec, looking into my eyes. Searching.

"I'm going to be thinking of you Siri, all the time. You stay safe now, and let me know anything I can do to help you. Speak with the trees, the winds and the waters, and they will find a way to get your message to me."

"I will, I-"

Suddenly I was back at school, the building was teeming with kids rushing the halls, slamming lockers, sneaking kisses, on their way to class.

Oh no. Not again.

I was in another vision. Vala must have sparked it somehow.

I stood by the entry doors, watching everyone. The lucky humans, and a few fae, too, walking around, just living their lives. Why couldn't I be so lucky? All I'd ever wanted was to have a real home, fit in, be normal. Would I ever have that?

The lights in the hall way flickered. Students looked up, and the lights came back on.

I heard something hit the glass doors behind me and looked over my shoulder. A few leaves and small branches floated by on the wind. Nothing there.

I turned back to look at the students. Jealousy filled me. I wanted what they had. Schoolwork. Home. Normal days. Normal families. I saw Cooper and Holly laughing by her locker, and then froze in shock as Rowan joined them, followed by Emelie. This was the future. Where was I? Still in Aeden, still traveling, or worse, caught by the Dark?

As if in answer, the lights flickered again, and then went off, plunging the hall into gloomy shadows.

"Come to the Shades, Siri. Join us, or die."

Again, with the eerie voice? Really?

"Seriously, Mikael, you need a new bag of tricks," I called out, taking a stab in the dark.

In answer, a long hiss sounded around me.

"So, you know who I am. Good. And I know who you are. We will find you, and you will join us. It is your only option. Join us, or die."

"Well, now, see that's where you are wrong. You just gave me two options. And you know what? I think I'd rather die. But not before I find you, and take you with me. I'm coming for you, you bastard, and there's nowhere you can hide."

Okay, so I don't know where exactly I pulled that from, but hey, it sounded good. I hoped it was true, too.

He didn't answer me. He didn't need to. A screaming roar ripped through the school, and everyone cowered, screaming as the glass shattered into the building, and wind tore through the rooms. A massive groan shook the building and the roof above our head was torn off. Students, one by one, followed the cement blocks into the sky, into the yawning chasm of what I could only guess what a cat 4 or 5 tornado.

Over the scream of the wind, I heard a woman's voice, riding like a banshee on the storm, "You will save your mother, but you will lose another. There must be balance."

I stumbled backwards, catching the steel door frame and wrapping my legs around it as the storm tried to suck me into its blackness. Down the hall, I saw Rowan reaching frantically for Holly, his screams muted by the dark abyss cycling above us, and then, she was gone, rising like a leaf the storm.

Tears filled my eyes,

and I blinked staring into Vala's wide eyes before me. I was back.

"Did you see?"

She nodded.

"Yes, I saw. I will make sure that doesn't happen. That was no natural disaster, and I can work with the elementals to ensure that it cannot come to pass. Don't worry. I will protect the people you can't." She reached out and put an arm around Rowan. "We both will. Don't waste a single moment worrying about us."

Rowan looked at us both uncertainly, not knowing what we'd just seen.

"He knows you are coming now. He will strengthen his defenses." Vala warned. She closed her eyes, and breathed deeply. "But he does not know everything. You have more power than he knows."

"You can see that? What else do you see?"

"The winds of time blow and change at a whim. I cannot see everything, but I have faith, and I know that you will prevail. It can't be any other way. You must trust, always. Fear is the one true enemy, it leads to all conflict in the world. It is the root of all evil, not greed. Look closely at what triggers you, personally, and what fear it stems from. True empathy, true light, comes from within by imagining yourself in another's shoes, feeling their pain as your own, their joy as your own. When we face our fears head on, then we can be truly empowered and follow our soul's purpose here on earth. Our hearts open up, our minds become unclouded and we can see our way more clearly. Trust is the key. Hold onto that, and you will be fine."

She hugged me again briefly and stepped back, bring Rowan with her.

Alec got on the bike, putting a black helmet on over his head and handed me its twin. I put it on and climbed behind him. There weren't any grip bars that I could reach easily, so I arranged Miko's pouch on my hip and leaned forward, wrapping a hand loosely around Alec's waist. I tried really hard not to notice the fact that his muscles were rock hard and trim under his light tee shirt. He gunned the engine and roared down the driveway, while I turned and held up my hand in farewell. Rowan and Vala mirrored me, saluting me with one-armed waves, Vala, smiling, Rowan's face a mask of loss and anguish.

We were off, and I didn't even know where we were headed. I faced front again, and placed my other hand on Alex's hip.

"You're going to have to hold on," he shouted over the noise of the engine. He reached down and grabbed my right hand, pulling me closer, wrapping my arm around his waist so that my chest was pressed up against his back. He grabbed my other hand and guided it to clasp my right arm, holding his hand over mine for a moment as if he doubted I would keep it there once he put his own hand back on the handlebar.

He was right. I didn't. I started to pull my hands away, to move them back down to the safety of his hips, so that I could put some more distance between our bodies, when the bike hit some ruts in the dirt road and practically bounced me off the seat.

"I told you, hold on!" He yelled again, sounding annoyed with me again.

He had a point. I reached back around him quickly and sank into him, surrendering to the comfort his body offered, allowing the strange feelings of instant peace and light wash over me. Without meaning to, I sighed in relief, and then instantly felt grateful that he couldn't hear me over the roar of the engine. But maybe somehow he had, because for the briefest moment I felt his gloved hand squeeze over mine, as if in answer. As if he, too, was feeling the relief I felt.

Moments later we were turning off the dirt driveway, out into the even pavement, heading into the unknown. The ride smoothed out, but I kept my arms around Alec, closing my eyes and leaning my head against his back. If a tiny part of me felt guilty to be relieved we were on our way, if a part of me felt bad for feeling so good as I left Rowan behind, I didn't want to know.

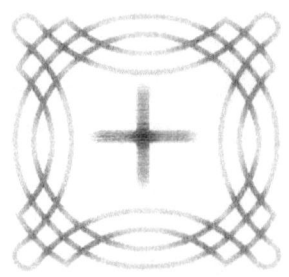

CHAPTER 26

We rode for several hours, stopping once to refuel and use the bathroom. As relaxed and close as I felt to Alec when we were riding, the moment we got off the bike it was like we were strangers again. He avoided eye contact with me and got straight to the business of getting gas. I shook out my hair, reveling in the feel of the breeze against my skin after the heat and confinement of the helmet. I headed into the truck stop to find a bathroom and some gloves. As warm as Alec and the October weather were, my fingers still felt frozen from the cool wind after an hour and half on the highway.

Finding everything I needed I grabbed a couple of small coffees and headed back outside. The heat from the coffees did wonders to thaw out my hands. Smiling, I approached Alec and held out the coffee as a peace offering.

"Coffee? I added a touch of sugar and some milk to cool it down, hope you don't mind."

"Thanks," he smiled back at me, reaching out to take the coffee. We stood in silence, taking tentative sips from the coffee. It wasn't the best, but it was good road fuel.

"So, um, how much further do we have to go?"

"We're almost at the Canadian border, and then it's another half hour to Montreal, at least. There's a safe-house there where we can stay overnight. We'll ditch the motorcycle and switch to something more suitable for the terrain we'll be covering. We'll have about half a day's drive tomorrow on some pretty rough roads. Speaking of which, we should get going," he finished the rest of his coffee and chucked it in the trash, holding out his hand impatiently to take mine as well.

I took my time drinking down the rest of it, holding his gaze the whole time. He might be my guardian and keeper for the time being, but I'd be damned if I was going to let him boss me around. I wasn't sure why, but he was able to get under my skin with the slightest of things.

He watched me, only the smallest twitch of his lips betraying the smile he was trying to hide.

"You do realize, don't you, that right now, at this very moment while we stand out here in the open, the leader of all the Shades on the American continent has every dark fae in the area searching for you?"

My eyes widened over the rim of my cup, but I kept drinking. Once every drop was gone, I handed the cup to him, and he tossed it over his shoulder neatly into the small trashcan without even looking.

"Sorry," I shrugged. "I'm trying to exercise my trust, since I've been told that fear is my only true enemy."

Alec snorted. "Trust and faith are all well and good, but believe me, we'd rather not want to get caught out here alone with the Dark. I'll feel a lot more comfortable when we get to Montreal. There are more of us at the safe-house, and very few Dark live that far north."

"Hey, I can take care of myself you know."

"Really? Like you took care of yourself back there at Vala's?" He took a step toward me, a threatening look in his eye. "Do you want to try again, maybe prove to me just how well you can take of yourself?"

I swallowed, but I stood my ground, determined to make Vala proud. "I'm not afraid of you. Even if you can take me down, you don't scare me."

He took another step closer, coming toe to toe with me. "Well, you scare the hell outta me," he muttered.

He gazed down at me, and my breath caught. In a flash, he had turned and mounted the bike. "C'mon. Time to go."

Confused by his words, I grabbed my helmet and climbed up behind him. No sooner had I placed my hands around him than we were gone, tearing down the road as if the Shades were right on our heels.

We passed through the border without incident, and arrived in Montreal in the late afternoon. I marveled at the beauty of the city. I'd never been to Canada before and I was surprised at how foreign it actually felt. I'd expected it to be like the U.S., just colder. Maybe more bearded men. More flannel. But Montreal looked more like Europe, a crazy blend of ultra-modern towers, Parisian architecture and old cobblestone streets. It was stunning. Most of the street signs were in French, although a lot of the shop signs were in English, or both.

I couldn't wait to get off the bike and explore. Surely Alec wouldn't make me sit in the safe-house all night long, not when we were in Montreal of all places. Then again, he probably would. Maybe I could sneak out after he'd fallen asleep. Given how moody he was, I figured he could use a good nap.

We entered a neighborhood lined with Victorian row houses, many of them painted in bright colors much like San Francisco. Little shops and cafes lined some of the streets, their signage clearly indicating that we had entered a pretty trendy, multicultural area. The explorative urge I was feeling tripled.

Alec guided the bike onto a side street and slowly entered an alley between two homes. The door to a small underground garage opened as we approached, and we parked inside between a flashier looking Ducati and a positively ancient yellow and white International Scout. Several bicycles hung on the walls. After the door automatically lowered noiselessly behind us, my eyes slowly adjusted to the darkness of the garage, illuminated only by a small glowing light switch by a door. I climbed off the bike gingerly, testing my legs before I stood up and readjusting my bags on my shoulders.

Alec opened the door, leading the way inside up some steps. The muted beats of house music and laughter floated down from above. Someone was obviously home.

The door at the top of the stair flung open before we reached it, and a slight Asian girl stood there with her hand on her hip.

"About time! What'd you do, stop for lunch?" She eyed me over Alec's shoulder. "This the girl?"

"Yeah, we had brunch at Vala's." The girl moaned. Apparently she liked Vala's cooking, because she muttered "Lucky" under her breath.

"Siri, this is Amber Slaight. Amber, Siri Alvarsson." We walked into a sunlit room decorated in brilliant, functional white with green accents. The kitchen, dining room and living room all shared an open layout. Everything gleamed, with Amber standing in stark contrast to the room, clad entirely in black, from her platform Docs and tight leather pants to the off the shoulder sweatshirt and heavy emo eyeliner rimming her deep brown eyes. Her long black hair was up in high pigtails streaked with deep purple. Her only jewelry was a dagger necklace that I suspected was more than ornamental. She was a manga dream.

Alec nodded at a red-headed lumberjack in torn jeans, work boots and blue flannel lying on the couch. "That big oaf over there's Ewan Patterson. Dude, get your shoes off the couch, you know Mitch'll have your head if he sees you."

"Och, serves him right, outfittin' this place all in white. What does he think this is, the damn Ritz or somethin'?" The boy left his feet up, but scooted a bit so his shoes hung off the couch.

"Not everyone has your taste for corduroy and flannel, Ewan." Amber flounced over to a chair nearby and flopped down.

Alec walked over to the huge glass refrigerator and took out two bottles of flavored seltzer, tossing one to me.

I followed him over to other couch and sat down, taking off my bags. Miko emerged and yawned.

Any water for me?

"Sure," I answered him. "Is it okay if I get some water for Miko?"

"Oh, yeah, I forgot he was even with you. What does he want, is a bowl good?"

Miko chittered excitedly and I translated for him, "No, just run the tap for him. He says he'd like to wash up a bit, too."

Alec nodded and went over to the sink, turning on a thin stream of water. Miko immediately jumped into the sink, using his hands to cup water to his mouth, and then carefully washing his arms and face in the stream. When he was finished, he hopped up on the counter and set himself to the task of grooming his fur. Alec turned off the tap, thoughtfully poured out some trail mix onto a small plate in case Miko was hungry and rejoined us.

"Okay, so just to clarify – did you just have a conversation with that squirrel?" Amber leaned forward on her knees.

"Who, Miko? Sure. Can you understand him?"

"No, of course not. Even in Aeden there are only a handful of fae who can talk with the animals. Well, other than the Ancients, of course." She looked at me thoughtfully.

"My mom told me not too many fae can talk with animals, but I wouldn't really know. Miko says that he can hear what any animal or person in thinking, though."

"Really?" Ewan sat up a bit so he could see me better. "Is he some kind of special squirrel?"

Miko snorted loudly and started chattering again.

"Oh, yeah right." I answered Miko and turned back to Ewan. "He says he's not special, that all animals can hear all other animals' thoughts. It's just the humans and the fae who have interbred with them that have lost that ability. He calls it animal-speak. Oh, and he wants you all to know that he is my personal guardian for the next eleven months, so not to get any ideas about leaving him behind when I go to Aeden."

"I'm sorry, what?" Alec interjected.

I sighed. "It's kind of a long story, but a few weeks ago, I was driving behind this huge truck near Mount Snow and saw it swerve in the road to hit Miko. I actually think it might have been Sullivan Carey driving, but I'm not sure." I paused, not sure how much I should share. These were other Light fae, like my mom, and right now the only ones who might have all the answers I needed, so I decided not to hold back. "Anyway, I felt really bad and stopped to see how badly the squirrel was hurt. He was unconscious and I held him for a while... Miko actually says he was almost dead but somehow I healed him or something and after a while he ran away fine. A couple weeks later he showed up near my house, and he's the one who distracted the Shades who busted into our house so I could get away. Now he says he owes me a year of service, some sort of squirrel code of honor or something."

"Wait, so you can talk to animals, and you have healing abilities?" Amber clapped her hands and bounced up and down in her seat. "So it's true then. You really are Bran's daughter."

"Um, I guess? Vala said that was my dad's name. My mom never knew who my dad was, they met on a military mission and they all had code names, so...What?"

All three of the Light fae in the room were staring at me slack jawed.

Alec recovered first. "Sorry, it's just-"

"Every fae in Aeden knows who Bran Le Fay is," Amber interrupted. "You're telling me your mom didn't recognize him?"

Alec glared at Amber. "Jade raised Fredrika here, above below, remember? Without knowing his name, how would she have known? Fred never comes to Aeden, I don't know if she ever has."

"Why would my aunt, I mean, sorry, my grandmother, have kept her out of Aeden?"

"Most fae stay above below, or in Aeden. The only ones who regularly travel back and forth are fae like us," Alec gestured to Ewan and Amber.

"Fae like you?"

"Light Guards," Ewan yawned.

"But, my mom said that she was a guardian, too. That our whole family stayed here to guard the earth from the dark."

"She's a guardian. We are Light Guard. Big difference." Amber sank back into her chair again. "The Light Guard is the elite of all the guardians. We keep Aeden safe against unwelcome intruders, and we protect the Light council. We are Aeden's first line defense. I guess you could call us the fae Marines, you know, the best of the best. Hooo yah!" She pumped her fist and laughed at her own antics. "Guardians are skilled, too, don't get me wrong, but they focus more on the day-to-day livelihood of the humans and animals above below than we do."

"Okay, so then you're saying Bran is what, a Light Guard?"

"As if! Bran Le Fay isn't a Light Guard, he's one of the most powerful a-"

"Amber," Alec interrupted her, spearing her with a glance. "Now is not the time."

He turned to me with an apologetic smile. "Look, I'm sorry, I know you have questions, but your dad, he asked us to just focus on getting you back safely, and leave any debriefing to him. He wants a chance to explain everything to you himself."

I folded my arms over my chest and narrowed my eyes. "Oh really, you guys talked about this? You think it's your right to keep me in the dark more than I have been already? Fine. Keep your little fae secrets. Whatever." I jumped up and started pacing.

"You know, you think this is easy for me? You think I give a crap about who my dad might be?" I ranted. "My mom is missing. Missing! Probably being tortured and abused by some Dark psychopath as we speak, and where has he been all these years? I never asked for any of this, I never even had any inkling about this whole, above below bull you guys are talking about. Light fae, dark fae, shades, druid seers. Ugh! I suppose next maybe we can go fight some witches and vampires or something?"

"Actually," Ewan drawled, "most witches are just watered-down fae human hybrids. Of course, there are the Druids, but they are pretty much just humans with heightened senses of telepathy and divination."

I glared at him. "Gee, thanks, I feel so much better now."

"No sweat. Vampires, now that's a different story, those stories all stem from the way the Dark can use their energetic connections to drain life force from humans. And werewolves are just a branch of fae who can shift, too."

"Right, like Fenrir. Miko told me about him." I sighed and sat down on the arm of his couch. "So, you really think this Bran guy is my dad? I know, I know, you can't tell me about him. Can you at least tell me if he's going to be able to help us, I mean, help me and my mom?" I could hear the desperation in my own voice, and hated it.

Ewan reach up and placed a hand on my arm, smiling kindly at me. "Don't worry, little girl. We will all be helpin' you. Bran will make sure of it. You'll see, he is the best help you could have hoped for."

"Little girl, are you kidding me? What are you, twenty two?"

Ewan laughed, rubbing his hand up and down my arm. It felt comforting. My stomach didn't react at all, although I felt a warm glow spread through my body. That was it, though. No fireworks, no sunlight, no joy like when Alec had touched me. Apparently, I wouldn't have to suffer huge bodily mood swings every time a fae touched me. I exhaled, thankful, and couldn't help letting my eyes slide over to look at Alec. He was staring at me grimly, his mouth set in a line while a small muscle twitched along his jaw. I couldn't imagine what the problem was now.

Ewan's deep voice pulled my attention back to him. "Sorry, force of habit. You remind me of my youngest sister back home, she's sixteen. But to answer your question, I'm thirty four, and six foot five, both of which pretty much qualify you as little in my eyes, sorry. You want to talk to a twenty two year old, go bug the young twig over there." He pointed at Alec, who didn't look any more amused than he had a minute ago.

I smiled back down at Ewan. "Ok, Redwood. You got it."

"Ha, nice one. Redwood, old and tall. I like it." Amber laughed and wiggled her eyebrows, making Ewan and I join in. Alec made a face and got up.

"Come on, I'll show you where you'll be staying tonight."

I shrugged and followed him down the hall, grabbing my bags on the way. We passed a couple of closed doors and Alec pointed out the bathroom. He opened the door at the end of the hall, revealing a deep green room with a plush navy blue rug. The dark wooden bed had a canopy over it draped with a simple dark fabric that evoked the night sky. A couple guitars leaned in the corner and a pile of books sat on the floor by the bed. Otherwise, the room was relatively uncluttered.

"Wow, this is great. Thanks."

I sat down on the edge of the bed and bounced a little, testing it out. "Oh, yeah. This is perfect."

Alec watched me, his gaze unreadable.

"Right. Well. I'll just leave you to freshen up then. Feel free to take a nap if you want, you must be tired after the long ride. Dinner isn't for a couple hours."

He closed the door behind him and I flopped back on the bed. Oh, this was a dream. The bed was heavenly soft. I hadn't thought I was tired, but now I realized a nap would suit me just fine. I kicked off my shoes and crawled up towards the pillows, burrowing my way under the covers. Mmm. My last thought as I tumbled into a dreamless sleep was that I needed to get the brand of their laundry detergent. The pillow and comforter smelled like rich forest air, bringing to mind freshly crushed pine needles with a hint of coriander.

CHAPTER 27

I was running through the woods again, but I wasn't scared. I was happy.

Alec was following me, and again, we were racing through a forest, laughing and vaulting over and around obstacles.

After a mile of cross-country parkour, I stopped and waited for him to catch up. I was out of breath, but I could tell he wasn't even winded. As he approached, his bright emerald eyes held mine entranced. He tucked an errant strand of my hair behind my ear, returning his gaze to mine. The violet rings around his pupils expanded with desire as he lowered his eyes to my mouth and caught my chin in my hand, gently running his thumb over my lower lip. As always, my body hummed merrily in response to his touch.

"It's time for dinner," he whispered.

A knocking sound in the trees startled me.

"Siri! It's time for dinner, can I come in?" Amber knocked on the door again.

"Yeah, sure, come on in." I called out, sitting up and stretching as she flicked on the lights. I felt totally refreshed. Better than refreshed actually. My body was still humming, all my nerve endings singing happily still from my dream. I blushed, remembering the heat in Alec's eyes. I mentally instructed my body to simmer down. I had zero interest in Alec, guardian extraordinaire. Rowan was my dream guy. I didn't know why Alec kept popping up in my visions, but it was going to stop.

A pile of clothes showering over the bottom of the bed brought me out of my head.

"What's all this?"

"I saw that little backpack you had with you, and figured you must have had to leave behind most of your clothes. And hey, a girl's gotta dress the part, right? We keep a ton of clothes here for missions, gear in every style for every occasion. These are the ones that looked like your size."

"Oh wow, thanks. I have a few outfits with me, though, I don't really need all this."

"Nonsense." She sniffed, and started digging through the pile. "My job, so far as I see it, is to make sure you are properly taken care of. I figured you could probably stand to let off a little steam, so we're going dancing after we eat."

I glanced at the dark windows. "What time is it, anyway?"

"It's after ten." So much for exploring the city, I thought as she went on, "I guess you really did need the rest. I sent the guys out to grab some Poutine, you can't come to Montreal without having it, it's, like, a law or something." She held up a shirt against my skin and shook her head, tossing it over her shoulder.

"If you say so. Sounds like something you'd find in a portolet."

"Ew, no! Poutine, it's fries and fresh cheese and gravy. Trust me, it's the perfect pre-dancing food."

She held out a silky forest green camisole with delicate silver edging and a sequined leaf on the front. "Hmm, this will look great with your shoes and these pants." She threw some gunmetal vinyl pants at me.

"Um, I don't know if vinyl is really my style, no offense, and don't you think the shirt is a little too, I don't know, girly?"

"Just try them on." She bossed, bouncing up and down on the bed. I could see that Amber was a non-stop whirlwind of energy. I doubted I'd even be able to get the pants on, but I could tell she wasn't the sort to take no for an answer so I stripped down and tried everything on.

"Oh, it's perfect. Now the shoes!"

I sighed and laced up my vans, surprised at how comfortable the pants actually were. I doubted the cami would be warm enough for a night on the town in Canada, though. "Is there a jacket somewhere in this pile? Or should I just wear my hoodie? What do you think?"

"Ew, a hoodie? No, no way. No hoodies allowed where we are going, not with me around. Here, try this on." She tossed a cropped black jacket at me. "That should do it."

It fit perfectly. I shook out my hair and walked over to the mirror hanging on the closet door. My nap had infused my face with a natural blush, replacing the tired look I'd been wearing for days with a fresh glow. The pants looked great, I had to admit. And the top, paired the way it was, looked more edgy than girly.

"Okay, you can dress me every day from now on," I said, laughing as I turned around to check out the view from behind. Not bad at all.

"Great! I haven't had a girl to hang out with in ages, and Ewan gets so stuffy sometimes. Here, hold still, you just need some mascara." She dabbed some of the pearlized black makeup on my lashes. "Perfect."

"We're back!" Ewan called from the hall, a door slamming behind him. "Come and get it!"

Amber squealed and rushed from the room, yelling for me to follow. I laughed, shaking my head. Who would have thought such a tiny girl would have such an appetite for cheesy fries?

Ten minutes later, licking my lips appreciatively, I had to concede. These had been no regular cheesy fries. Poutine was divine, artery-killing goodness, fresh fries and cheddar cheese curds drenched in homemade gravy. God bless the Canadians. Even Miko looked totally blissed out, eating his share while he sat by the window.

I caught Alec watching me. I couldn't tell what he was thinking, and it made me nervous. He hadn't said a word since he'd returned, just looked me over and dumped the bag of food on the coffee table and gotten straight down to the business of eating. Actually, the whole group had fallen to eating their containers of poutine with near-religious fervor.

I wasn't sure what I had expected. It's not like I had dressed up to impress him or anything. But when he returned I had felt a flood of relief, like I had missed him in his absence and not even known it. The feeling was irksome.

While we wrapped up eating, Amber started hounding the guys about going out.

"Come on, I know you guys said you were just going to hang out and play Skyrim," she rolled her eyes at the mere thought of playing a video game instead of dancing, "but you really owe Siri a good night on the town."

Ewan huffed and went over to the Xbox, clearly determined to ignore her.

"Yeah, you're right," Alec spoke up. "After all, the Shades are after Siri, it's not safe, even here in Canada. We're in." Alec stood up and dusted some imaginary crumbs off his pants. "I'll just go change. Come on, Ewan."

"What? Aw, come on, you promised." It was funny to see such a large burly man reduced to whining. He followed Alec reluctantly down the hall, grumbling all the way.

After a while they returned and stood by the couches, allowing Amber to circle them. Apparently everyone had to have their outfits approved by Amber, not just me.

"Not bad," she told Ewan, eyeing his light gray slacks, some classic black and white Adidas sneakers and the white v-neck tee that hugged his shoulders. It was simple, but it was a definite step up from the lumberjack vibe he'd had going before. Amber masked it quickly, but I could see a gleam come and go in her eyes as she circled behind him.

Moving on to Alec, she made a small noise of approval. Clad entirely in black, from his jeans and military style black boots to his tight black tee, Alec looked lethally hot. Amber quirked her lips in thought, and reached up to run her fingers through his hair, effortlessly mussing his fine dark locks so that it looked like he'd just gotten out of bed. Annoyance stabbed through me, but I wasn't sure if it was because she'd touched him or because he had the gall to look like something that stepped out of a Calvin Klein ad.

He caught my look, and grinned back at me like he knew what I was thinking, a dimple glorifying his left cheek. Jerk. My fingers twitched, itching to slap the arrogant smile of his face. Suddenly I couldn't wait to get out of there and get dancing.

Amber followed his gaze and looked back over her shoulder at me. "What do you think, Siri, do they make the grade?"

I swallowed and struggled for nonchalance. "Yeah, they'll do."

"Okay," she flashed a brilliant smile at everyone. "We approve. My favorite DJ is spinning tonight at Zora, so let's get a move on. I wanna get there before the first set ends."

She pushed the guys out the front door, holding the door open for me and waiting so she could lock up. As I brushed by her she whispered in my ear, "Oh, by the way, Alec's favorite color is green."

She locked up and tucked her arm in mine.

"What was that supposed to mean?" I hissed at her.

"Oh, nothing," she sang quietly. The guys were ten feet ahead of us, but I was glad she was keeping her voice down. Subtlety didn't seem to be Amber's strong suit. "Just, you know, in case you wanted to know. I thought maybe I sensed something between the two of you. I'm a Water Fae, I can sense changes in people's emotions. Affect them, too." She winked at me.

"Well, there's nothing going on with us. I have a boyfriend."

"Another fae?"

"Yeah, although I didn't know that until recently. I met him last month. He's really sweet. He's the one who helped me get to Vala's."

"And he didn't mind you taking off with Al?" she whispered dubiously.

"Actually, he did mind. But he couldn't come, so, there wasn't much he could do about it. He's really worried about my mom and me, though."

"If he wanted to come, why didn't he?"

"His family works with the Shade Council," I whispered. Amber gasped. I rushed explain, "But he's good, like I said. Sweet. He wants to choose the Light when he turns eighteen."

"Well, that's good, I guess." She didn't sound convinced.

"Anyway, how about you?" I asked, changing the subject. "I saw the way you looked at Ewan earlier. Are you guys together?"

"Pfft, no. He thinks I'm too young and pure to sully with his elderly self. He says I need to live a little, make sure I'm not going to change my mind. Rumor has it he was burned pretty badly when he was young. But I've never felt the surge with anyone like I do with him. Plus, I just really like him, you know?"

"He seems like a big sweetheart. I still can't believe he's thirty four. How old are you?"

"Nineteen," she sighed. We walked in silence for a minute, each of us thinking about our relationship difficulties, no doubt.

"What's a surge?"

"Oh, you know, that warm fuzzy feeling you get when you touch another fae, times like a hundred. Sometimes, with the right guy, or I guess girl if that was your thing, it's like both your bodies light up. Like the sun is shining through you, you know?" She sighed again, this time more dreamily. "But you must know. Didn't you feel that way with your guy?"

"Sort of. I always feel really comforted by his touch. But my stomach goes kind of wild, too, and not in the best way."

"Oh," Amber's face clouded, "right. That's because he's a darkling you know that, right? I mean, if he chooses Light that effect will go away, but until he does, his Dark DNA casts that feeling. It's your body's way of warning you. It's even worse when they are full-fledged Shades."

"Yeah, I know. That's what Miko said." This time, we sighed together. The guys had stopped and we practically ran into their backs, which made Amber and I crack up.

"Whoops, sorry!" Amber apologized when she could catch a breath. Then she looked up. "Oh, we're here!" She tugged Ewan's bare arm and dragged him inside an unmarked door to a large commercial building with blacked out windows. I watched, bemused. Right now, her bare hand was transmitting the surge through her body, and most likely Ewan's, too.

Alec looked at me, his hands in his pockets. "After you."

The others were already at the door, and when they opened it I could hear the unmistakable sound of thumping tribal bass trickling out the door.

Excited, I hurried up the stairs after them. They must have soundproofed the building, it was so quiet out on the street. Once inside, I could hear the music, but it was still muted. We'd entered a long hallway that ran parallel with the outer wall. I checked my jacket and walked down the hall to the small line by another inner door. No wonder it was so quiet outside. The club was virtually invisible, I wondered how people even knew it was here. Even the typically long bouncer lines would be indoors here, rather than on the street.

"Is this place a private club or something?" I asked Alec.

"Zora? Nah. Anyone can come here, although it is a something of a favorite for all the local Light fae, more than any other club. The owners are fae, and most of the employees, too. There are quite a few of us in Montreal, since it's so close to an Aeden portal."

Amber's long pigtails bounced as she bumped and wiggled to the music.

"Hey Amber, what's up?" The huge bouncer's face lit up when he saw her. "Tribe is spinning something fierce tonight. Ewan, Alec. Go on in." The bouncer barely looked at us, waving our group in through the door. Apparently drinking ages were for mortals, not fae.

Once inside, the loud, thumping music washed over me in waves. Native American pow-wow singing blended with a strong bass and fast beats. I itched to dance.

"I'll get the first round," Ewan yelled over the music. Amber grabbed my hand and dragged me along, pushing her way through the crowd of dancers.

Somehow, she managed to find a relatively clear spot, and turned to face me, grinning widely. She let out a wild scream and started to move. I hadn't been to a good club in months, and it didn't take me more than moment to follow her lead, losing myself in the deep tribal beats. She hadn't been kidding, this DJ was amazing.

I lost track of the time as we danced. All my cares and worries dissolved, shaken out of my system as I moved. It felt so good to be free like this, and the energy of the crowd was contagious. Amber was the most amazing dancer I'd ever seen, like a prima ballerina hip hop artist rave girl, all rolled into one. I tried my best to keep up, knowing that my moves were rougher, more primal, but not really caring.

I'd forgotten how good of a release dancing was. I should tell my mom, maybe we could work it into our training program somehow-

I'd forgotten. Just like that, the world came crashing back down. I couldn't tell my mom, because my mom was a prisoner of the Dark. The music receded and the room turned dark.

Join us, or die.

I froze. I couldn't tell if the voice was real, or just a memory.

Someone put their hands on my arms and I whirled, ready to fight. But it wasn't an enemy. It was Alec. He pulled me to him, holding me protectively with one arm, scanning the room for danger. Amber was still dancing, oblivious.

The cold seeped from my body, replaced by a thrumming stream of energy that set my body on fire. It started in my arm, where Alec's hand was resting, and flowed through my entire being like a ray of sunshine. I felt like a sunflower – I would follow that ray anywhere, it was like chocolate for my soul.

The surge.

I leaned my head against his chest, taking advantage of his preoccupation with my safety while I tried to steady my senses. But it was a mistake. All at once I felt enveloped by the forest, by the scent of freshly crushed pine needles and a hint of coriander. He smelled the same as the sheets in my room, and I leaned back, peering up at him in a daze.

"What detergent do you guys use?" I asked. Hello, random. Had I really just said that?

"Huh?" He looked down at me, confused. "Some generic brand, I think. I don't know, Amber does all the laundry. Are you okay? You looked..."

"Yeah, I'm fine." The first set had just ended and some psytrance was just starting to ramp up, slow, yearning beats straining under a haunted melody. I started to sway, the surge taking hold of me again, driving me to move and release and invest all that gorgeous pure energy flowing through my body.

The violet rings within Alec's eyes fluoresced brightly under the blacklights. He was still holding me, and had no choice but to sway with me. He moved his hands down to my hips, pulling me against him roughly as we moved in concert. The sudden lack of skin-to-skin contact was like the sun going behind a dark cloud. Alec growled in frustration and brushed his thumbs up under my camisole, gently rubbing the smooth skin above my belt. Overwhelmed, I leaned into him, resting my head against his chest.

"What is this?" I moaned. The music continued on, slow and hypnotizing, while my body soared.

Alec's breath hitched. A tremor went through him and suddenly he set me away from him. The loss of contact was stunning.

"I need a drink," Alec ground out, that muscle in his jaw jumping again. "Come on."

He spun on his heel and stalked off the dance floor. Well. Alrighty then. Maybe it wasn't the surge after all. And even if it was, I had Rowan, and Alec had...well, Alec had an attitude problem.

I thought about staying on the dance floor with Amber, because who did he think he was, but when I looked around I saw she was already cavorting at the bar with Ewan. The same bar that Alec was fast approaching. I licked my lips. Well, I was thirsty. I supposed I could use a drink.

I walked up behind Amber, who had her arm around Ewan and was giggling. Alec was already nursing a beer on Ewan's other side, glaring morosely down into its depths. Yeah, I didn't need to go there. Whatever was going on between us, I really wasn't up for the drama. I squeezed up next to Amber, pushing aside the guy on her other side who had clearly been trying to get her attention. Good luck with that one, buddy, I thought.

"Hey, girl," she exclaimed. "Here, we've been saving these for you." She pushed two amber shots towards me, and a tall glass of water. I eyed the shots warily. I wasn't much of a drinker, and I usually stayed away from hard alcohol.

"I don't know if our caretakin' duties extend to gettin' the faeling drunk, luv," Ewan admonished.

Amber protested, and irritation swept through me.

"Well, I think I deserve a little fun."

I downed both shots, one after the other. The liquid burned, making me cough. Over Ewan's shoulder, I could see Alec's mouth twitching as he restrained a smile. Was the conceited ass laughing at me? Annoyed, I waved the bartender over.

"Another round for all of us." I held up the shot glass, and gestured to the four of us. The guy nodded and grabbed a bottle of high-end Tequila, pouring out four more shots.

"Siri, I don't think—" Alec started. I threatened him with a look and grabbed one of the tiny glasses.

"Cheers!" I said, smiling sweetly at him with a wink, and downed the shot. This time, I didn't cough. Alec watched me, amusement dancing in his eyes even as he tried to school his face into a look of disapproval.

The DJ announced the start of his second set and Amber grabbed my arm. "Hold on!" I yelled over the loud house music that was gearing up, gulping down my water in several long swallows. "Alright, let's go."

I allowed her to drag me back onto the dance floor and let the music pound into me. I let everything go, all my frustration, my anger, my confusion. Soon, Amber and I had attracted several guys over to us. Whenever one got to handsy I would dance out of reach. Eventually they all got the message and kept their paws to themselves, although Amber didn't seem to want to discourage her admirer. She leaned back against him, allowing his hands to roam over her waist, dancing suggestively behind her while she kept her eyes on the bar. I glanced behind me, and saw Ewan watching her from his stool, stoic.

Finally, his eyes narrowed and he marched over to her, pulling her away from the guy she'd been dancing with.

"Hey!" The guy protested. Ewan ignored him, focusing only on Amber.

"You're playing a dangerous game here, luv."

"Yeah?" She tilted her head and batted her eyelashes up at him. "Think I'll win?"

I held my breath while he just stared at her, his face unreadable. Suddenly he reached down, threw her over his shoulder, and stalked off toward the exit. Amber didn't

274

seem to mind. "See you later, Siri!" Her laughter echoed through the club while people watched, bemused. In my heart, I wished them both luck. I wasn't sure who would need it more.

The guy she'd been dancing with shrugged and got back down to business, eyeing me and closing in. Apparently, I was a good runner up for his attentions. I let him approach, but danced away when he tried to get too close. I made my way up near the DJ stand where a group of girls my age were dancing and edged into the group. They didn't seem to mind, all their focus on grabbing the DJs attention. I set my mind and body to dancing, and forgot everything else.

My muscles were rubbery and I'd worked up a serious sweat by the time the music wound down. Last call had flown by unnoticed, the girls around me had all left. There were a few stragglers at the bar arguing with the bartender for just one more drink. The clock over the bar showed three o'clock. I didn't see Alec anywhere, and wondered if he'd left me.

Thirsty, I sat down and got one last glass of water from the bartender. What now? I hadn't paid any attention on the walk to the Zora and I doubted I'd be able to find my way back to the safe house.

Still brooding, I felt someone drape a jacket over my shoulders, and the slight brush of a hand against my arm left a warm tingle that confirmed it was Alec.

"Ready?" he asked.

I nodded, finishing my water.

We walked in silence back to the house. Several times he looked like he would say something, but never did. That was fine by me. I wasn't sure that any conversation between us at the moment could have a good ending.

We separated at the door and I peeled off the vinyl pants, collapsing straight into bed in an exhausted heap. Yet when I closed my eyes, I couldn't sleep. All around me, the scent of pine and coriander teased. It's just detergent, I scolded myself. Nothing to get worked up about. I forced myself to think about Rowan, about citrus and spice.

But when I finally drifted off to sleep, it was visions of the forest that chased me through my dreams, laughing green eyes running on my heels.

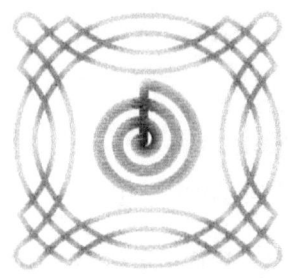

Chapter 28

The next morning, I woke to the sound of people arguing. I pulled on some sweats and trudged into the living room, running a hand through my hair.

"Hey, what's all the racket?"

I surveyed the room. Alec was lounging on one of the couches with a blanket and pillow, as if he'd slept there all night. Ewan was sitting on one of the chairs, his head in his hands. Amber was practically toe to toe with an older man who looked around fifty.

"You don't get to tell me what to do, not on this," Amber yelled at the man.

"Look, Amber, your mom trusts me to keep you safe. When you signed up to be a Guardian, I promised her I would do my best to keep you out of trouble."

Alec laughed heartily, "Well, there was your first mistake."

Amber and the man didn't even bother to look at him as they replied in unison, "Shut up."

"Look Mitch, who I have a relationship with is none of your damned business. My parents want me alive, not celibate."

Ewan groaned, sinking his head even further into his hands.

"Oh, it's a relationship now, is it?" Mitch snorted.

I crept over to Alec and sat on the floor next to him. "What happened?" I whispered.

"Word seems to have traveled about Ewan carrying Amber out of Zora last night, Mitch heard all about it at the coffee shop on his way here. He's pretty pissed at both of them. Guardians aren't really supposed to date, at least not openly. Plus, Mitch is Amber's uncle, not just the leader of the Guardians. That's part of why Ewan's been trying to keep his distance until Amber's older. But the surge is pretty hard to ignore when it's strong."

I kept my eyes on the argument, not daring to see if Alec was looking at me or not.

"Ewan, what do you have to say about this?" If looks could kill, Ewan would have been dead by now. He managed to look pretty brave in spite of his impending mortality, however. He leaned back, giving the question some thought.

"Well, you know how Amber is, sir. Once she has her mind set on somethin', it's useless to stand her way." She harrumphed, crossing her arms. Now poor Ewan had two angry fae staring him down. It didn't seem to faze him.

"I've been tryin' to resist her for well over a year now. I'm through with that. Amber is the woman for me," he said simply. "There is no other."

She yipped, and jumped straight into his lap, throwing her arms around him as he fell back against the sofa.

Mitch sighed. "It's your funeral. I'll put in a good word for you with her father, see if we can't keep you alive for the rest of the relationship," he smirked. His eyes drifted over to Alec on the sofa, and he seemed to notice me for the first time.

"Well, hello there. Sorry if we woke you. As you can see, we had a little bit of family drama to sort out this morning." He walked over holding out his hand and I jumped up, placing my hand in his.

"It's nice to meet you, Sir. I'm Siri Alvarsson."

"Yes, I know. You look very much like your mother. She was a student of mine years ago. Wonderful girl."

He smiled warmly at me as I wondered just how old he could be, that he considered my mother, at fifty eight, a girl.

"What about you Alec, why are you on the couch, couldn't you make it to your room last night? Just how drunk were you all?"

"No, sir," Alec answered him calmly while he stood to fold his blankets. "Siri slept in my room. I only had a couple drinks last night, in case any situations arose."

Mitch looked behind him, watching Amber nuzzling Ewan's neck, and shut his eyes tightly as if in pain. "Well, it seems a situation did arise, unfortunately."

I coughed into my hand to cover the laugh that escaped.

"Yes, sir, sorry about that, sir. I felt it prudent to focus my attention on Siri." Alec seemed to be fighting a smile as well, but managed to keep a straight face.

"Yes. Well. About that. We think we have found where they are hiding Fredrika, we have some operatives getting in position now. Ewan, you're going to stay here with me and wait so we can escort the team back to Aeden, assuming all goes well. Amber, you are going to ride back with Alec and Siri."

"Yeah, like I didn't see that coming from a mile away," she muttered. "Just can't wait to split us up, can you, Uncle?"

Mitch shook his head. "Look, you are still a Guardian. Your new relationship is going to have to take a backseat to getting Siri safely back to Bran in Valhalla. The Shades have got to know we are closing in, and they're going to be getting desperate. We can't risk losing her when she's so close to safety."

"Fine," she looked at me guiltily. "You're right, sorry Siri. I wasn't thinking. Can't have my new best bud getting snatched by the Dark, now can I? Besides, I think we have some catching up to do." She winked at me.

Alec groaned and shuffled off down the hall, muttering about being stuck with gossiping girls, and what did he do to deserve being stuck with two faelings.

"Hey now, I heard that," Amber yelled after him. "I'm not a faeling, you gloob!"

"Gloob?"

"It's a pasty, stinky, foul little creature that hangs out under rocks in the swamplands of Aeden."

I shook my head, giggling, and went to my room to grab some clothes for the shower. Still smiling, I opened the door to the room. Alec turned away from the closet, holding a pair of jeans in one hand. Other than some boxer briefs, he wasn't wearing any clothes. All too late, I remembered what he'd had said about this being his room.

I couldn't get out any words. Sure, I'd seen naked guys before. I'd done my fair share of skinny dipping in out west. But this felt different. The room felt...charged. I wanted to look. I wanted to spend the next hour, just staring.

"Sorry," Alec spoke, bringing me out of my reverie. "I'll get out of your way." He grabbed a shirt and some socks, brushing by me on his way down out.

I shut the door the minute he left, slamming it without meaning to. Collapsing back against the door, I struggled to breath. When he'd brushed by me, arm to arm, I'd felt the surge again, more powerfully than ever before, even if it was just for an instant. I took a deep breath in, and caught a whiff of forest in the air, that intoxicating smell, again.

And I realized. It wasn't detergent. It wasn't some fancy soap the fae brigade was using to wash their clothes and sheets. It was just Alec. Pure him.

I took a few more deep breaths, talking myself down from my pheromone high.

I was with Rowan. I was on a mission. The only thing that mattered were getting to Aeden and getting my mom back. Once he and Amber delivered me to Aeden, Alec would probably be sent on another assignment and I'd never even see him again. Whatever this surge thing was, it was just hormones. It had nothing to do with compatibility, or feelings, or real life. It could be overcome, just like any other obstacle. I repeated these things to myself over and over again, until I heard someone walk by the door, bringing me to my senses.

I needed a shower. I needed a change of clothes. And we needed to get on the road. I pushed away from the door and set about getting ready.

The shower confirmed what I'd already figured out – there wasn't any pine-scented soap in the bathroom, no coriander cologne. Some Irish Springs soap and shea butter salon hair products were about all I could even find.

I went through the clothes Amber had brought in, keeping some items and folding the rest on a chair. I rolled everything up tightly, an old military trick my mom had taught me, and was able to squeeze it all into the pack.

Everyone stood up when I rejoined the group. Mitch walked over and shook my hand.

"Siri, it's been a pleasure to meet you. I want you to know that I am doing my best to retrieve your mother quickly and safely. We'll see you soon, I have no doubt. Please, try not to worry too much, and listen to your Guards. Even though they may not look it," he paused here to squint at Amber, clearly at a loss to even begin to understand her outfit of striped leggings, doc boots, and a Hello Kitty sweater topped with two tight buns on top of her head. "Amber and Alec are two of the best fighters we have. Trust them to see you safely home."

Home, I thought. If only it were so. Out loud, I thanked him and assured him I had great faith in his team. Amber winked at me behind his back and I had to smother a laugh.

I turned and hugged Ewan goodbye, whispering so only he could hear, "You've got a good one there, don't judge Amber by her age. I think you are perfect for each other."

"Ain't that the truth," he chuckled in my ear, picking me up and practically squeezing the life out of me. "Take care of yourself, little girl."

"Same goes for you, Redwood."

Alec grabbed my bag, and I scooped up Miko, who'd been unusually quiet since we got to Montreal. I supposed that this was all a fair amount of excitement for a squirrel. He scampered up on to my shoulder, his claws anchoring him gently to my t-shirt.

Don't think I haven't heard everything that you're thinking about this new guy.

Shh, I hushed him, just in case anyone else in the room was an animal communicator.

They can't hear me, only you. And let me tell you…if you could hear all their thoughts. Wowza. This is one X-rated group, I gotta tell ya!

My thoughts immediately went to Alec.

Yep, him, too. Trust me, he's as into you as you are into him. And as confused about it.

"I don't even want to know," I answered.

"What's that?" Alec paused on the stairs to the garage, looking back up at me.

"Oh, nothing. Nothing, I'm good, just telling Miko here I don't want to know where he's been going to bathroom since we got here."

Nice. Real nice, kid. Just throw me under the bus, why don't ya.

Sorry, I shrugged.

We piled into the '66 Scout – apparently it was Ewan's baby, which we'd promised to be very, very gentle with. Alec and Amber sat up front and Miko and I sprawled across the backseat. We'd hardly been on the road for two minutes before my stomach growled loudly.

"Dude, was that you?" Amber turned around and looked at me in awe.

"I guess so," I grimaced, placing a hand over my abdomen. "I haven't eaten anything since last night's poutine, what about you guys?"

"Nah, me neither," Amber replied. "My uncle kind of found us before Ewan and I had a chance to put anything together."

"Oh, I don't know, I think you guys had plenty of luck putting things together, if you know what I mean." Alec waggled his eyebrows at her with a leer.

"Ew! You are such a skag." She swatted him. "Alright, change of plans, let's take Siri over to Chez Boris for some breakfast beignets and cocoa. You are going to love this place, they have the best doughnuts in all of Montreal; they even make doughnut sandwiches."

"I like the way you think, Amber." Alec said, turning the car around to head south. He parked the Scout after we'd traveled several blocks.

"It's just around the corner here," Amber rubbed her hands together. "Come on, donuts wait for no man!"

The café looked adorable, with functional red benches outside. Even before we entered, I could smell caramelized sugar and baked goodness wafting out the door. A couple of guys sat on one of the benches, looking at pictures on a phone together while they sipped their coffee. Inside, the tables were all lined with old maps and newspapers. I would have loved to stay and absorb some of the local ambiance, but Alec thought it best we eat on the road. We got a box of twelve assorted donuts, all carefully chosen by Amber, several breakfast 'beignewiches' and three extra-large hot chocolates which Amber assured me were better than anything I'd ever find south of the Canadian border.

I grabbed a donut for the walk to the car, moaning at the spiced cinnamon perfection as we walked outside. The guys at the table looked up at the noise, amused at my pleasure. The blonde one nudged his friend to look at the phone again. People and their phones, I thought. I hoped it was interesting.

I followed Alec and Amber around the corner towards our car, when all of a sudden hands grabbed my arms from behind, pulling my donut away from my mouth. Oh, hell no. Someone did not just make me drop my donut.

I yelled, more in frustration than fear or anger, and pulled forward into a crouch, flipping whoever it was over my shoulder on their back. I stared into the face of my attacker, shocked to see that it was one of the guys from outside Chez Boris. For a brief moment, I wondered insanely if we'd somehow bought the last donuts of the day, and this guy was looking for payback.

Then he reached to grab me by the neck and a wave of icy cold gripped my insides as my stomach lurched.

Dark fae.

I allowed him to pull my head down, as I snapped my shoulder forward, jabbing my elbow into his face. His head fell back on the concrete with a satisfying thump. I looked up, just in time to see Amber leap over my head aiming a flying kick at someone behind me. I heard a sickening crunch, followed by another thud on the pavement. I turned as Amber aimed another quick kick to the guy's head, knocking him out, too.

Alec reached down to help me stand. "We've got to get out of here, others might be on the way already. Not to mention, we have a bit of an audience."

Indeed, a couple of young girls were filming us with their cameras from across the street.

"Oh, fans!" Amber gave them a wide smile and a dainty bow. She laughed and waved goodbye to the girls as she threaded her arm through mine, whispering in my ear. "Don't worry, our IT guys will have scrubbed the video from the internet by lunchtime."

We hustled back to the car and took off. Luckily, the rest of breakfast had survived the commotion and we all dug in. This time, I'd wound up in the front with Alec, Amber claiming she needed to get some shut-eye on the road.

Alec drove as fast as traffic would allow. Soon enough, we were out on the open road, heading north into the wilderness.

CHAPTER 29

"I'm sorry for what happened back there," Alec said.

We'd been driving for hours, and Amber had succumbed to a food coma in the back with Miko draped around her neck.

"It's not like it was your fault."

"No, but I should have been paying more attention. Mitch warned us there might be danger. And I should never have let you walk by yourself behind us like that." His face grim, he gripped the steering wheel tightly, turning his hands white at the knuckles.

"Hey now, I think I took care of myself pretty well back there. I might not know all your fancy moves, but I was trained by the best, you know." I teased him, and was rewarded by a small, tight smile.

"Yeah, but not the best of the best," he teased back, and turned serious again. "We will remedy that in Valhalla. I have a feeling you are going to need that training before too long. Besides," his smile came back, "how else will you be able to hold your own in a spar with me?"

"Oh, I can think of some ways, don't worry." I would have been annoyed by his sass, but right now all that mattered was seeing that smile on his face. I liked happy Alec way more than brooding Alec. Today just didn't seem to be my day, though, I thought as his face shuttered in once more.

"Those guys, we were lucky, they don't seem to have been well-trained," he mused.

"I saw them looking at their phones when we came out from the doughnut shop, I think maybe they were looking at a picture of me. Is that possible?"

"Yeah, the Dark is probably broadcasting your face to every Shade that has a phone, probably with some kind of reward. We were lucky."

"Well, I'd like to think skill had at least a little bit to do with it."

"No," Alec shook his head, "you don't understand. As good as the Light Guardians are, the Shades have trained fighters who are just as good. Some of them are so twisted and evil, it is almost impossible to fight them. Some of them feel no pain, and are fueled by pure bloodlust. They revel in it." Sadness and loss suffused his voice, making my heart feel like it would break with empathy.

I reached out and placed my hand on his arm, not thinking about the result. Warmth and comfort flowed through me, and I hoped Alec was feeling some of the same. I concentrated on sending the compassion I felt back to him as I talked. "You sound like you're talking from personal experience. I'm sorry if taking care of me is bringing up some bad memories."

"Thanks," he smiled crookedly at me, his eyes flitting toward my hand on his arm, being careful not to take his eyes off the road for more than a moment. I waited, wondering if he would feel comfortable enough to share his pain with me. When it seemed like he wouldn't say anymore, I removed my hand, feeling a little awkward. I stared out the window, watching the fields and trees whir by. It was a beautiful, clear day, and I could see hills rising in the distance.

"It happened when I was just a boy." His quiet voice pulled my gaze back towards him. "My father fell in love with a human, my mother. He left Aeden and fae politics behind him to make her happy. Before, he'd been with the Guardians, but we lived in Boston for most of my childhood. He trained me from an early age, a lot like how your mom trained you. My sister hated fighting, all she ever wanted to do was dance, and he let her. She was three years younger than me."

He stopped, and I watched him, waiting for him to go on.

"One day, the Dark sent men to our house to capture my dad. He may have put fae matters aside, but his name was still in their records as an operative, and they'd found him. We were out fishing. It was a gorgeous day, a lot like this one. I'd caught five trout all by myself, and I felt so proud coming home to show my mom. But when we got there, my mother and sister were dead. They'd been tortured, beaten and killed without remorse. The house was covered in blood. We didn't even get to bury them, my father packed

290

me back in the car immediately and took me to Aeden to live. I was only ten, but I dedicated my life to becoming a Guardian that day."

"Oh Alec, I'm so sorry. All this time, I never thought anyone could understand how I am feeling about my mom, but this has got to be so difficult for you, bringing it all back."

He shrugged. "The Dark stopped scaring me a long time ago. I didn't think they could ever hurt me again. But the thought of them getting to you...I won't let that happen."

"Is that the surge talking, or some Guardian kind of honor code?" My mouth let out the words before I could even think them through. I winced, clapping a hand over my mouth. God, had I really just said that? I'd pretty much just admitted what I felt every time we touched. How mortifying.

"I don't know," he answered carefully, keeping his eyes on the road. "I want to protect you. Discovering you with a darkling made me want to rip your friend's head off, and not just because I hate the Dark. But your father is Bran, so I think...I think you must be meant for something bigger, given who your family is, and the way Mikael is hunting for you. I'm not sure we could ever-"

A loud yawn from the backseat interrupted him. "Whatcha guys talking about. Is he schooling you on the ways of the Dark?" Amber rubbed her eyes and leaned over the seat. I'd totally forgotten she was even in the car, I'd been so focused on the words coming out of Alec's mouth. "What'd I miss?"

Hmm, let's see, I thought. Alec has some sort of feelings for me, but he may or may not feel the surge the way I do, I don't know, because you and your annoying mouth just interrupted him.

"Nothing," Alec and I answered at the same time. Miko snorted, obviously catching my thoughts in his head. I reached out to him to see if he knew what Alec had been about to say.

Sorry doll, not a clue. All I'm getting from him now is intense relief at having been interrupted.

Well, that was reassuring. Not.

"Okay," Amber looked at each of us, clearly sensing that something was up. "How long was I out?"

"A few hours," Alec answered. "We're almost at camp."

"Camp?" I started. "Please tell me we aren't going to be sleeping outside."

I could only begin to imagine the size of the bears in these Northern woods.

"No way, too cold!" Amber shuddered. "We own a private camp near here, the land contains some caves that lead into Aeden."

"Tell me again how the Dark can't follow us here?"

"Oh, they can come here, the land isn't protected from them or anything, although it is private property. But no one except the Light can actually enter Aeden. This entrance wasn't discovered until after the divide, and we've kept it a secret from the Dark. That's the main reason we lived in Boston when I was a kid, so we would never be more than a day's travel from the portal."

He went quiet again, and I resisted the urge to put my hand on his knee.

"Okay, but can't they just make a blockade or something, to keep us from getting there?"

He laughed mirthlessly. "They could try."

"Gee, that makes me feel much, much better."

"Don't worry so much, Siri." Amber clapped me on the shoulder. "We'll be fine. We're using a secret entrance that practically no one even knows about, certainly no one Dark."

"If you say so." I knew she was trying to comfort me, but I couldn't shake the feeling of dread that was crowding me in. I watched a few more miles of fir and pine pass us by.

"Almost there," Alec said, turning onto an almost invisible rough track through the trees. I was glad we'd switched to the Scout; I couldn't imagine how the Ducati would have fared traveling this terrain. Every once in a while we'd slow down to gingerly traverse ruts in the road, or climb over small tree limbs that had fallen across our path.

"Doesn't anyone maintain this place?" I asked.

"Not much. We like to keep it off the map, if we take too much care of it we start to get poachers and squatters, and that could attract attention from the Dark. The locals think this land is owned by a small, crazy family of Americans, and we try to keep it that way."

"Ah," I said, like I followed their logic.

We pulled up in front of a tiny, ancient wood cabin. "Don't worry," Amber whispered in my ear, "the cabin's just for show. We almost never stay in it."

"Speak for yourself, girly girl," Alec mocked. "I love staying out here. It's really quiet, if you know what I mean."

"Oh I totally get you," she rolled her eyes, "I love the quiet when you stay out here, too."

I couldn't help it, I had to laugh. I wondered if Alec realized that while he'd lost one sister in Boston, he'd gained another with Amber.

Alec pulled the car behind the cabin, camouflaging it slightly by parking between several large hemlock bushes. I slung my bag over my shoulder, eyeing the woods with a mixture of excitement and trepidation.

This was it. No turning back now.

Alec grabbed my pack and Amber stuffed the remaining bag of donuts into her own messenger bag. Miko raced into the trees, clearly reveling in his return to nature.

Amber strode confidently into the woods, following a trail that apparently only she could see. I followed her a few feet behind while Alec brought up the rear and Miko trailed us in the canopy above. If my mood had been different, if I hadn't been nervous about wasting time, I would have challenged Amber to a footrace. I was itching to run, the woods calling to me with their siren whisper.

I zoned out for a while, just allowing my feet to fall where Amber's had been.

You can't hide from us, Siri. We will have you. Join us, or die.

I stumbled. No way was Mikael here. Amber had said we were safe. A few crows cawed in the distance. Maybe I was just imagining things, my nerves getting the better of me.

Just as I had that thought, Miko started chattering frantically.

"Siri, there's danger up ahead," Miko warned. "The woods are alive with the news. The birds say there are five Shades in the clearing by the caves."

I stopped abruptly and Alec crashed into me, grabbing my waist to keep me from falling.

"Amber!" I hissed, but she didn't hear me.

"What is it?" Alec whispered in my ear, sending a shiver of tingles down my spine. Oh, but this was so not the time for that.

"Shades, five of them, up ahead."

"How do you-"

"Miko," I nodded up at the trees.

"Okay. Stay out of the clearing. I'm going to go around and close the circle from behind. Whatever you do, don't follow Amber. She can take care of herself."

"Whatever you say, oh Captain my Captain." Either he missed my Dead Poet's reference, or he didn't hear me, because the only response was the rustling of a leaf as he disappeared out of sight.

"Miko, come down here," I whispered, feeling a bit out of my element. He dropped down gently onto my shoulder from a branch above. "Can you tell what the Shades are doing?"

"They're just hanging out in front of the cave. As far as I can tell, no one else is in the forest. Typical Shade behavior, relying on brute aggression rather than employing any finesse or strategy," he sniffed disdainfully.

I resisted the urge to chuckle as I crept up behind a large boulder on the edge of the clearing. Amber had just walked into the clearing and was doing her best lost hiker impression. She was so small and young looking, I could see how easy it would be to fall for her act. Four men and a woman stood in a semi-circle before her. The men watched her with varying degrees of boredom and appreciation, while the woman looked intelligent enough to suspect that Amber's act wasn't on the up and up.

"Hey guys, I'm supposed to be meeting my boyfriend at a campsite here, at least, I thought it was here." Amber giggled. "We're playing hide and seek with our GPS, see?" She rolled her eyes and held up her phone, quickly putting it back in her pocket.

"I think you must be lost, girl." A particularly rough looking Shade with a half shaved head stepped forward, cracking his knuckles.

"Oh, um, okay. I'll just be on my way then," she took a step backward, staying on her toes as if she meant to run.

"I don't think so." A second Shade stepped forward, a massive First Nations youth with long black hair and tribal tattoos.

"Now, now, boys, is that any way to invite a lady to dance? This is dangerous country for a girl to be out all alone." The red-headed woman pushed Long Hair out of the way and approached Amber, putting out her hand. "I'm Giselle."

Amber eyed the hand distastefully.

"Come now, don't be rude. Where are your manners?" Red sneered.

"Oh, right!" Amber said in her best Valley Girl voice. "Like, I totally forgot. Here they are!"

She placed her hand in Red's, watching her eyes widen fractionally as they recognized Amber's Light, and pulled her forward suddenly, breaking the woman's nose with a vicious head butt.

The woman howled with rage and charged Amber head on. Amber, however, had clearly been schooled by the same trainer as Alec. If anything, her moves were more fluid, more graceful. In a flurry of kicks and twirls, hair flying loose from her buns, she decimated her opponent. Long Hair snarled and Rough Guy cracked his knuckles and his neck at the same time, the two of them converging on Amber.

"Oh, yay. Is it time to dance now?" Amber wriggled her hips. "Bring it, boys."

Again, her feet flew, faster almost than my eyes could track her. But the guys weren't planning a fair fight. Even as they received blow after blow, they remained standing. It was clear that they both had vast reserves of strength and endurance. And now, I could see that the other two men from the group were circling around, trying to get the jump on her.

"Miko, I'm going in." I whispered. "Stay here."

Oh really, you want me to obey you, when you are planning to go against orders yourself. Well, ain't that just peachy.

"Just stay, alright?" I hissed, crawling forward. The youngest of the group, a surprisingly clean cut blonde kid, was crouching behind Amber now, obviously hoping to trip her the next time she came too close. Hah. Not on my watch. I reached down and grabbed a long stick from the ground. Weapons were always useful.

The boy beckoned his friend to him, gesturing at Amber. All they needed was one good push and she'd stumble backward right over him. It was now or never. I slipped up quickly behind him, rapping him on the head and knocking him onto his stomach. I gave him a second whack on the base of his skull, just to make sure he stayed down.

Suddenly, I was at the center of the attack. Now that the Shades had seen me, their fighting became more focused, more virulent. The staff helped keep them at arms' length as Amber and I took position together, readying ourselves to fight back to back. Amber knocked out Rough Guy as he lunged for me from the side.

Which was great, really, it was, except that Red was starting to wake up, and where the hell was Alec?

Red, Long Hair and a small weasel of a man formed a triangle around us, slowly circling. Weasel kicked Rough Guy when he stepped over him.

"Stupid git," he muttered. "Get the hell up."

"Wow, some friend you are." I couldn't help it. Sometimes things just popped out of my mouth. My hippie friends in Arizona blamed my zodiac sign. Really, though, I just had no filter sometimes.

"He's not my friend. And neither are you." Weasel came at me. He was surprisingly fast and efficient in his moves. I guess they'd been saving the best for last.

He grabbed me, and the force of his energy punched me like a sword in the gut. Coldness seeped through all my pores. The forest went still and dark around me. My stomach heaved and I fought to stay focused, to not vomit at his feet. A breeze ruffled my hair, and suddenly the light and sounds of the forest returned. My vision cleared, and Weasel started to fall backwards away from me, a small dagger protruding from his eye. I looked over my shoulder and saw Alec perched on a rock. He locked eyes with me for a moment, relief naked in his gaze. Then he was running into the clearing, daggers flying from his hands. In moments, every shade was down. They would not be getting back up.

"Nice work, Bruce Lee. I was wondering when you'd show up," Amber quipped.

Alec ignored her and strode directly to me. He cradled my face roughly in one hand.

"What the hell happened back there? You stopped fighting. Why? And why were you fighting in the first place? What about 'stay here' did you not understand?"

It was like being lectured by my mom when I fell out of a tree in Ireland and she couldn't decide whether to be worried or mad. I couldn't muster an ounce of irritation in response, not when Alec was touching me and all my endorphins were flowing after the fight.

I reached up and placed two fingers over his lips, a tiny shock going through me at the contact. "Shh. It's okay." I removed my fingers. "I'm okay."

"But you-"

You know what they say about not starting relationships in life or death situations? Yeah. Screw it. My blood was coursing through my body furiously, pulling me to one source, and suddenly I understood what they meant when they called it the surge. Because that's what it felt like, all the energy in my being, all my light, surging forward to crash into his like two ocean waves colliding. I reached around his head and pulled him down as I rose up to meet him, kissing him square on the lips.

For a moment, there was just the surge, the two forces of light connecting. The quiet before the storm. I had a split second to question the wisdom of what I'd just started. This was how tsunamis were made. And then he was pulling me to him, literally crashing into me. It was a kiss that poured every bit of his soul into mine, every moment of yearning I'd had for the last two days. It stole away every ounce of my resistance, every thought I had of why this couldn't work, and set every fiber of my being on fire. Time stopped, and we restarted it. Better. Stronger. Brighter.

Amber started clapping.

We pulled apart, and the entire forest looked greener. More in focus. Yet I only had eyes for Alec. He stared at me in wonder.

"That was. Amazing," I murmured as I tried to catch my breath.

"Woo hoo, Alec and the commander's daughter, this is going to be awesome!" Amber laughed.

Alec's face clouded and he backed away from me, dropping his hands from my arms. Just like that, the world was a colder, darker place to be in.

"I'm sorry, I shouldn't have...I mean, we can't-" he began.

"Hey, whatever, you didn't do anything. Forget it." I leaned down and grabbed the knife from Weasel's eye, wiping it on the ground and sticking it in my boot. "If you don't mind, I'll keep this until you can deliver me to my father."

"Siri, look, let's talk." He frowned at me like I was a stubborn toddler.

"Hey, there's nothing to talk about. You're just doing your job, and I have a darkling boyfriend, remember? Come on, Amber, let's walk." I turned to her and grabbed an arm, dragging her toward the cave. I whistled for Miko and he climbed up my jeans and into my bag. I refused to give Alec the satisfaction of turning around to see if he was coming.

After all, he had to follow.

It was his job.

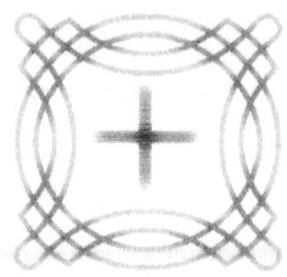

CHAPTER 30

The cave should have seemed dark, even with the bright LED flashlight Amber switched on to light the way. But it wasn't, really. I could see every crack in the rocks, every bit of moss, every pebble in the dirt floors.

I wondered briefly if Alec had somehow awakened more of my fae-ness with his kiss. Had I connected with his energy enough to truly acquire some of it as my own? That sounded dangerous, and unlikely. I mean, then, fae people would hardly be able to go around kissing just anyone. No, more likely it was just a coincidence. Maybe a reaction to the adrenaline from our little battle. I supposed that as an Earth fae that I should have the ability to see it clearly, even when I was under it.

I felt like we'd walked over a mile when Amber finally broke the silence.

"So, dish. What was that back there?" she whispered. I looked over my shoulder, and Alec trailed us by thirty feet, which seemed out of earshot, even for a master fae such as himself.

"I don't know, just the thrill of the battle, I think."

Amber snorted. "Looked like a lot more than that. Looked like the surge to me."

"Yeah, well, I don't think Alec thought so."

"Aw, just give him some time. Alec takes his duties very seriously, and your father was his mentor when he first started training. Your dads are practically brothers, they are such close friends. Plus, I think he's worried about how things might change when we get down below."

"What do you mean?" I asked, worried. I wasn't sure how much more change I could handle.

"Look, there's no sense worrying about anything now," she waved my question away. "What will be, will be, I always say. Or, it is what it is. Something like that. Anyway, you get the point. Just focus on one step at a time."

"Like you and Ewan?" I jibed.

"Exactly," she purred. "Things have a way of working out, even when they don't seem like they are. Just give time a chance to work its magic."

"Wow, I had no idea you were such a guru," I teased.

"I know, right," she hip-checked me as we turned a corner. A wall of heat hit me and I tugged on her arm.

"I don't think we should go any further," I warned.

"Oh, that's just the barrier. Sorry, I should have warned you. The enchanted barrier keeps everyone out of Aeden, unless they are pledged to the Light. If you weren't a faeling, you wouldn't even be able to see that the tunnel continues on, it would just look and feel like a wall of rock to you. Even Miko, if he wasn't honor bound to you, wouldn't usually be able to enter. Come on, we're halfway there."

She pulled me forward, picking up the pace. I heard Alec approaching, and hoped he hadn't heard any of our earlier conversation.

After another ten minutes of walking we came to a large open cavern. A massive tunnel opened on the other side like a huge, yawning mouth of darkness.

"Please tell me we aren't going in there?"

"Yep, we are. Trust me, it's totally safe." She walked over to some ultra-modern golden snowmobiles sitting along the cave walls. "Here, you can ride with me."

"Um...don't we need snow to ride these?"

Amber laughed like that was the funniest thing she's heard all day. "Girl, you crack me up. Hop on, wear these and use the safety harness."

I climbed on behind her, putting on the goggles she handed me and clicking a belt around my waist as she gunned the engine. Alec walked into the cavern and climbed onto one of the machines, too.

"Alright, here we go! You might want to hang on, too."

The machine rose suddenly into the air, swaying gently as Amber adjusted herself in the seat. Miko broke into my own shocked thoughts, asking what was going on. I filled him in on our new gravitational situation, and told him to stay safe in the bag. I wrapped my arms around Amber, holding on tightly.

"You sure this is safe?" I questioned. Her slight build didn't quite feel as reassuring as Alec's, and I couldn't help wishing that I was riding with him.

"Safe as pie. I'm the best gravicycle flyer in the Guardians."

We set off, slowly picking up speed as we entered the dark tunnel that supposedly led to Aeden. The dim headlights of the gravicycle seemed to run on a UV frequency, lighting up the rocks around us in vivid greens, whites and purples. Our speed continued to increase. The corridor started to take on the appearance of space mountain, the lights streaming by in a blur. I leaned over Amber's shoulder to view the terrain ahead of us, but she was moving so fast I didn't see how she could even navigate the twists and turns of the tunnel, wide or not. The only thing I knew for certain was that we were heading ever steadily downward.

I looked over my shoulder into the light of Alec's cycle, but was unable to see his shape in the dimness that ranged behind the light.

We continued on this way for a long time, so long in fact that I lost track of time as I tranced out on the beautiful crystalline light show. At some point, we seemed to change direction, climbing upward instead of down. I had no way to gauge the speed we traveled at for sure, but I guessed we were going well over legal highway limits.

Finally, a light loomed ahead. I expected Amber to slow down as we approached its source, but as usual she reacted contrary to all rational expectation. She leaned down lower over the handlebars and gunned the motor, increasing our speed. We burst out of the tunnel into the sky as she let go of the handlebars and threw her hands up in the air, whooping loudly.

God love her, but she was crazy.

She returned her attention to steering as we zoomed through space, breaking through misty pink clouds high above a lush forest canopy below. A warm, red sun lit the land, presumably the source of the strawberry and salmon colored cumulus. The air was hot and humid, with an incredibly clean ozone tang to it. It was the Amazon rainforest mixed with the clarity and freshness of Alaska and the colors of a Hawaiian sunset.

I heard a rumble beside us and looked over to Alec pulling even with us. He grinned at Amber, saluting her, and sped ahead.

"Oh no you don't!" she yelled, racing to catch up with him.

I probably should have been terrified, hundreds of feet about the trees, riding a flying snowmobile without a helmet going one hundred and thirty miles per hour. But I wasn't.

I was captivated. I'd never smelled air without pollution, not even in the most remote wilderness. I'd never realized what real, clean air really smelled or felt like. I felt alive in ways I never had before. The trees below, while they seemed to form recognizable shapes, sported foliage ranging from bright cerulean blue to deep indigo and violet. Every once in a while I would see small flashes of glittering silvery white liquid waterways and pools, reflecting the red shimmer of the sun above. Gentle hills and valleys shaped the landscape.

A raucous yell brought my mind back to the present moment and I looked ahead at Alec, standing on his cycle, arms spread wide, head thrown back. I really hoped these things had auto-steering.

"Don't even think about it!" I warned Amber.

"Hey, even I'm not that crazy," she laughed.

Alec climbed down from his perch, bringing my heartrate back down with him, and I went back to watching the land below.

I started noticing that some of the darker streams were actually roads. Occasionally the roof of a house would peek out from the trees. Eventually, the forest gave way to plowed fields and larger villages. Most of the buildings I saw were round and looked like they were made of stone. The larger ones had stacked, peaked conical roofs reminiscent of Japanese pagodas, made from dark, almost black material.

"Almost home," Amber yelled to me, pointing ahead.

Seven huge glittering, twisting golden spires rose in the distance, the warm sunlight glinting off of them. They almost seemed to dance as the reflections moved along them. At their center, an impossibly tall Sequoia tree towered above them. Smaller domes of white and gold covered the wide valley around the spires, ranging ever outward. The smaller rivers and streams all fed into a large river delta to one side of the city on the edge of a smooth silver sea.

As fast as we were going, the city rapidly grew in size. Within minutes we were rushing over the buildings, not so small or insignificant anymore, and approaching the golden spires. Instead of decreasing altitude, Alec's cycle rose higher, Amber following in its wake. Our speed dropped as we closed in on one of the spires. As we got closer, I was able to discern many small balconies jutting from the building, all made from the same shining gold material. Strangely, I didn't see any windows or doors in the walls.

We slowed and circled around the spire, gently easing down onto a particularly large balcony. It was empty except for several more gravicycles parked near one railing. Amber helped me unclip myself from the cycle while Miko peeked out of the bag at our surroundings. I petted him, needing some reassurance myself.

"Welcome to Valhalla!" a smooth voice called. I looked up and saw a gorgeous, tall thin brunette walking across the balcony towards us. Behind her, a panel in the golden wall was sliding shut, revealing only the barest of visible seams. She placed her hands together and bowed, much like some of the yoga teachers I'd had in the past.

"You must be Siri. I am Mireia. Your father was hoping to be here to welcome you, but he has been called into council to deal with another matter. Please, why don't you come with me and I can show you to your room so you can freshen up. I am sure by the time you are finished he will be available to see you all." She smiled at us all, and turned to the wall again, not pausing to wait for the wall to open as she approached. Apparently that just happened automatically here, although I didn't see any sort of sensor mat on the floor or motion detector on the wall.

Inside, the halls were carpeted with a strange, thick blue plush that reminded me of the forest colors we'd seen from the air. I noticed that the others removed their shoes, carrying them as they walked, so I paused to do the same. When I put my feet down on the carpet, the strangest feeling washed through me, cool and invigorating. It was rather like taking a sip of cold lemonade on a hot day, but through my feet.

"What kind of carpet is this?" I asked.

"Carpet? I'm sorry, I'm not familiar with that word," Mireia replied.

"We don't use carpets in Aeden, we use cala" Alec supplied. "What you are walking on right now is actually a hybrid cross between the plant you call grass and a thick ground clover. It's pretty hardy, but walking shoeless helps it stay healthy. We all have a deep connection to the plant life in Aeden. Can you feel how it nourishes you? Right now, your immune system is actually regenerating your cells at a faster speed because of the biosynthesis going on between you and the cala."

"Wow, cool." I stopped to wiggle my toes in the cala, reveling in the strange sensations it created, almost as it was caressing my feet. Forget pedicures, cala was so the next big spa thing.

Mireia smiled at me indulgently and waited until I was ready to move on. As we walked down a few more corridors,

I noticed that many doors were marked with strange symbols that reminded me of cuneiform. I couldn't imagine what they said, or how I'd ever find my way in this strange maze of a building. Finally, we came to a room with no markings on it all, save for a small triskele. I was familiar with triskeles, ancient Celtic symbols consisting of a triple spiral, from my time in Ireland. They were supposed to represent the divine trinity, or past, present and future.

I hoped this was my room – I might actually be able to find it again. Mireia asked me to put my hand on the triskele, and placed hers over mine. A moment later the door slid open. "There, now the door is keyed to your hand, it will open only for you and your companion from now on."

"My companion?" I looked at Alec and Amber, wondering which of them would be staying with me.

"Yes, Auroreis will keep your things in order, as well as help you adjust during your stay here." She gestured into the room where a young girl was waiting. She couldn't have been more than fourteen.

"Um, okay," I replied. "I don't really need a servant, you know. We don't really do that where I come from."

"Yes, well here I assure you it is completely normal." Amber rolled her eyes at me as Mireia walked over to the far wall and placed her hand against it, causing a shield to rise and allow the warm sunlight to penetrate the room. I stifled a laugh and took in my surroundings.

The walls were just as golden as the spires themselves. The floor was covered in light blue cala, and the spare furnishings consisted of simple violet lounges and ebony tables. A bowl of foreign looking pink and white fruits sat on the table.

Auroreis curtsied and asked if I would like a bath. I nodded, and she retreated to another room, which I could only assume held the bed and bath.

"We will leave you now. I will return in one hour to collect you." Mireia nodded at Alec and Amber for them to leave with her. Amber gave me a hug, and whispered, "I'm just a couple of hallways away. I'll come find you later, okay?"

"Okay." I gave her a tight squeeze and she left the room with Mireia, leaving Alec and I in awkward silence.

"So, a red sun and purple trees, huh?" I waved at the scene outside the window. "You know, you guys could have warned me about some of this."

"Would you have believed me?"

"Hmm, let's see. We just came fifty miles through the earth's mantle, and we're in a giant gold castle watching the sun set from inside the earth? Um, no, I guess not."

"Actually, the sun never sets here in Aeden, and it was more like two hundred miles." He quirked a smile at me. "It's part of why the fae here live longer. The lack of ways to mark the passage of our days affects how our minds, and thus our bodies, view time. It is a perfect power source, too, and it's also why you won't see many windows on the buildings that can't be completely sealed from the light."

"So, now what? Are you going to stick around, like Amber? Or are you going right back to the surface?" I tried to sound casual, like it didn't really matter to me.

311

"I'm not sure," he answered, running a hand through his already wildly tousled hair. "I have to debrief first with my commander."

"You mean my father?"

"Yeah, that, too." He sighed.

"Amber mentioned our families were really close. I guess that means we're practically cousins, right?" I laughed, trying to keep breathing, trying not to care. I flopped down on one of the chairs and gazed up at him from under my curtain of wind-abused hair. "Look, just so we're clear, I didn't mean to cause you any trouble back there, you know, above below or whatever. I know you were just doing your job. Okay?"

"Don't worry about it," he said stiffly, shoving his hands in his pockets. "I handled that badly. I don't want you to think I took advantage of you. I really...well, look, like you said, you have a guy already. You've been attacked three times in as many days. I was supposed to be taking care of you, not-"

"Yeah, yeah, I get it." I stood up again and marched up to his face. "I'm just a faeling you'd rather not be babysitting." My voice rose, dripping with sarcasm. "I'm oh so sorry to have caused you all this trouble. At least you can go debrief now and get rid of all this drama, go back above below and save someone else now." I pushed him away from me.

A muscle twitched in Alec's jaw and I almost apologized. Since I was a child I had been schooled about keeping my hands to myself. What was it about Alec that made me want to deck him or jump him?

"Look here, Siri," he warned, taking a step towards me. The violet ring of light in his eyes shimmered with frustration and expanded, the emerald green gone as they turned a dark blue from the Aeden sunlight. Suddenly, I missed the green in his eyes. I missed the easy banter we'd had between us so often.

I missed him. And I barely even knew him.

Sorrow lined my soul, and I wasn't sure anymore how to handle this, how to do anything in this strange new world.

An answering expression of pain flickered across his face, and he took another step towards me. "Please, can't we just talk?"

"I-"

Saved from whatever I was about to say, because no matter what, it was sure to have been the wrong thing, I was interrupted by Auroreis.

"Your bath, miss, it's ready for you." She glanced uncertainly between Alec and I. "You should probably go now, sir."

Alec sighed, and closed the distance between us. He didn't touch me, just leaned forward and whispered in my ear. I took advantage of the moment to inhale deeply, trying to memorize his sweet, wild scent.

"This isn't over. Think about what you want to say to me while I am gone. Because, as much as I would like otherwise, I will be thinking about you."

My mind whirled. He was thinking of me? Wait, what, he didn't want to be? What the hell? What was that supposed to mean?

I started to think of plenty of things I wanted to say to him at the moment, but by the time I opened my mouth to speak he was gone, the door sliding soundlessly shut behind him.

CHAPTER 31

"Your bath, miss," Auroreis gently reminded me as I stood staring at the door.

"What? Oh, right." I padded over the soft cala to follow her through the bedroom into the bathroom. The bedroom was a repeat of the living room, with dark, almost black wood furniture crafted with neat, spare lines and violet linens.

The bathroom itself was a study in opposites. The walls were the same golden material as the rest of the suite, but the fixtures were all made of gleaming silver. In the floor, a massive round tub large enough for four people shone like liquid mercury. Fluffy grey towels sat folded by the edge.

Auroreis started to tug my shirt over my head. "Hey! What are you doing?" I exclaimed.

"I'm helping you disrobe, miss." She looked at me like this was obvious.

"No offense or anything, but where I come from people undress themselves. Do you mind?" I looked pointedly at the exit and she giggled.

"Of course, miss. I'll be in the receiving room should you need any assistance."

"Thanks," I spoke in relief.

As soon as she left I tore off my clothes and sank into the pool of warm inviting water. Something in my body responded immediately to the water, almost like when I touched other Light fae. I felt relaxed and happy. Did everything here have healing properties?

I sank under the surface, allowing the water to soak my hair. The tub was large enough to float freely in. When the water began to cool I looked around and found a bar of soap. I didn't see any shampoo or conditioner bottles, so I figured it must be multi-purpose and lathered up. It had a mellow scent that reminded me of flowers and sandalwood.

After I rinsed off I wrapped in the warm towels and walked out to the bedroom. Auroreis had left my backpack on the bed next to a silky silver outfit. I tugged on clean underwear from my pack, and examined the fae clothing.

There were two pieces, consisting of wrap pants and a short stretchy top. The pants were wide, tying at the waist and ankles and overlapping at the sides, leaving vents at the side that allowed in cooling air as I walked. The tight sleeveless top came down to my waistband and had a small circular neckline. It seemed to feature some type of built in support so I didn't even need to wear a bra. I tucked Alec's knife into a hidden pocket along one seam, just in case.

Enjoying the new comfy clothes, even if they weren't quite my style, I went through my pack to grab my toothbrush and comb. I didn't have anything to dry my hair with so I just threw it up in a ponytail and checked out my reflection in the mirror. After the bath, I looked remarkably refreshed. I certainly didn't look like I had traveled through two hundred miles of the earth's crust. I even had some color in my cheeks.

I heard a loud rapping at the outer door and returned to the living room, or as Auroreis had called it, the receiving room. Mireia stood at attention, waiting.

"Are you ready? I hope you enjoyed your bath, and that our clothes are to your liking." I noticed for the first time that she was wearing a similar outfit, except hers had sleeves and was made of a soft taupe material.

"Yes, thanks, it was great," I smiled back at her.

"Wonderful. Then, if you are ready, we will go meet Commander Le Fay."

"Ready as ever," I replied. Nerves filled me, but almost as fast as they came the cala helped soothe them away. Still, I scooped up Miko from the couch where he was napping, feeling like I might need some moral support.

We walked down the hallway, coming out to a wide circular staircase. As we approached I saw that the stairs moved slowly like an escalator, one stair twining downwards while the other spiraled up. At the landing the stairs flattened out, three lining up with each other to create a wide, safe platform for entering and exiting. We stepped on, one after the other, and rode the escalator up another two floors.

This floor didn't have multiple hallways leading away from the stairs, the way my floor did. Instead, just two doors led from the landing on opposite sides. One had a spiral symbol on it with a line struck through it, while the other was marked with a plus sign.

Both had a pair of guards stationed outside. We walked to the door with the plus sign and my eyes widened as I recognized Alec standing at attention. He stared straight ahead, not making eye contact. I was reminded of the sentries at Buckingham Palace. When we had visited the London landmark I had tried my best to get them to laugh or smile, but, nothing. They were like statues. At least here Alec didn't have to wear a stuffy black hat. He was dressed in a tight green sleeveless shirt, much like my own, and some loose brown shorts that fell below his knees. The other guard was similarly dressed, white linen gorgeously setting off his mocha skin and curly blonde hair.

Mireia barely spared the guards a glance as she placed her hand on the door's surface. It slid open, revealing a gigantic wooden round table dominating the room. Emblazoned across it was the same plus sign, one line painted in gold, the other silver. A man sat to one side at the table staring into a crystalline bowl of water.

Was this my father? I watched him, taking in his blonde-white hair, brushed back from his face in a low ponytail, small strands escaping and leaning forward as he gazed into the bowl, talking to himself quietly. He wore a loose gray shirt.

Mireia coughed and the man looked up, recognition flitting across his features when he saw me. He waved a hand over the water and stood, his eyes flashing liquid silver.

"Siri?" He came to stand in front of me, nodding at Mireia in dismissal. I heard her footsteps recede as she left the room. His arms came up, as if to touch me, and then changed direction as he clasped his hands behind his back. He smiled warmly down at me. "You look so much like your mother when she was young."

"Thanks, I guess. All except her hair and eyes, I guess." I fidgeted under his gaze.

"No, you have my mother's hair." His eyes twinkled, and I realized with a flash that they mirrored my own. "She will be here next week, and will be excited to see that she's finally passed something on to one of her descendants. My father's genes have always seemed to hold dominant," he chuckled.

"But where are my manners?" he continued. "I am Bran Le Fay, Commander of the Light Guards, Son of Yvain Le Fay and Kalila Norna. And, apparently, your father. I'm sorry that I've missed your childhood, but I do hope that I will be able to be a part of your life moving forward."

"That would be nice," I couldn't help smiling back at him. The man looked like a god, like some huge, brawny middle-aged version of Thor. No wonder my mom had fallen for him so hard. If I'd been her, I probably wouldn't have dated anyone after him, either. It was hard to process the fact that this guy was my dad, he barely looked past thirty five. "How old are you, anyway?"

I blurted the question out before I could stop myself, and he laughed, grabbing me in a huge bear hug. "I see you really are just like your mom, honest and forthright. That is good. I am a hundred and fifty four."

"But you don't look old at all, not like Mitch. Are you an Ancient?"

"No, but we have very pure fae blood in my family, both my grandmothers were Ancients, so we tend to age more slowly than most. But that isn't important now. What matters is what has brought you here, and why the Shades are after you."

"Oh." I could feel my face fall at the introduction of this new topic. "Right. Do you have news about my mom? Is she here yet?"

He sighed and led me over to the chair where he'd been sitting.

"Why don't you sit down?" he asked. Oh no, I thought, that never boded well.

I collapsed into the chair, stroking Miko's fur.

"Ah, who is this little guy?" Bran asked.

"This is Mikowa, or Miko for short. I healed him and saved his life, it's kind of a long story, but he says he's honor bound to serve me for a year now."

"You healed him? And you can talk to animals?"

"Yeah, mostly just him so far, it all started a few weeks ago. Can't you? I sort of assumed I got the ability from you."

"No, not me. I am an Earth fae, but my power works better with rocks. Very few fae can talk to animals these days, but your great-grandmother, Morgaine, she had the gift." He paused, looking at the bowl of water as if it held some sort of wisdom.

"Your mother is on her way here right now, she should arrive within the next few hours."

"But, that's great!" I caught the sadness in his eyes. "Isn't it?"

"Yes, this is the safest place for her now. I wish I had known about you, if I had I would have sent for you both sooner, and we could have avoided all this." He leaned back in his chair and stared at the ceiling for a minute. "The thing is, Mikael did something to your mother. No one has been able to wake her up. We've known for some time that the Shades have been developing a Light anti-serum that forces our body into a hibernation state, and we've been trying to formulate an antidote but with no luck. We assume, however that the Shades must have one, or else they wouldn't have used it on your mother, not when they were trying to gain your cooperation. We are trying to figure out now where it might be hidden."

"But what about my mother? What's going to happen to her?" I asked frantically.

"She will sleep. She isn't suffering at all, but she will continue to age at a slow rate while she sleeps. We've seen this before, in fact, we have a few other fae in the sanatorium who've been affected by the anti-serum in the last year. They all continue to sleep deeply, but are thriving on daily doses of IV fluids."

"Whatever you are doing, I want to help. I want to be part of it. This guy Mikael has come after me, and he's threatened my friends. I want in."

Bran reached out, holding my hand in his. It was the first time we had touched, and it felt like hot cocoa on a warm day. It was comforting, but it made me miss my mom all the more.

"I had a feeling you would say that, given what Guard Ward reported earlier. I understand you've already had quite a bit of training with your mother?" I nodded. "She is a formidable fighter. We've arranged for you to start your training right away with Amber. You'll go see her when we finish."

"Okay, but there's one thing I still don't understand. Why does Mikael want me so badly?"

"There is an old Druid prophecy about a descendent who will bring together the bloodlines of three families. This descendent will decide the war between the Dark and the Light, either returning peace above and below, or bringing about an era of world slavery and domination by the Dark."

"Okay, so? What's the point?"

"The point, my young daughter, is that you bring together all three of the bloodlines. On your mother's side, you are descended from Tyr, who was honorable and brave, and had the uncanny ability to decide battles. Through my mother, you gain the sight of the Skuld Norna, one of the three most powerful Ancient fates. You've seen events before they occur, right? Vala already filled us in on that. Blended with your Earth powers, it is a powerful gift. Finally, through my father's line from Morgaine Le Fay, you obtain the abilities to heal and to end cycles through the manipulation of fate. You are the one prophesied.

Somehow, the Dark came to know about your existence before we did, I'm still trying to work that part out."

"My visions...since the beginning, Mikael has been tapping into them somehow."

"Ah, yes, he comes from another Norn bloodline, that of Verdandi. His visions are rooted in the present, he must be using them somehow to be seeing what you are seeing, when you see it."

"At first, I thought maybe he was sending the visions to me somehow." I was both relieved to know he wasn't, and grossed out to think that he could get in my head like that.

"No...Vala and I don't believe so."

"Still, I don't get it. I'm not that powerful. How can I possibly decide the fate of the fae?"

"Your powers are only beginning to develop. Most faelings your age don't even start tapping into their abilities until after their Choosing. The fact that you are manifesting early is a good indicator that the prophecy holds some truth. Regardless, Mikael believes it is true. Word on the street has it that as soon as he entered the visions of an unallied Norn, he began tracking them all down. It was simply bad luck that he found you and your mother so easily."

I thought back to that weekend, and realized that it hadn't been just bad luck. Sullivan Carey had led the Shades to my mom.

"You said you talked to Vala, how? Can I talk to her? I promised I would send a friend a message when I was safe."

"Your darkling friend?" he asked doubtfully.

"Don't call him that," I chided him. "Rowan is good. He got me out of there, if it wasn't for him I wouldn't be here." My words held more truth than he knew. If it hadn't been for Rowan, I would never have met his dad, and I would never have led the Shades to my mother.

Tears pricked my eyes and I held up my chin defiantly, determined not to cry. "I know he's going to be worried about me. I at least owe him the courtesy of letting him know I am okay."

"Alright. Here."

He pushed the bowl of water towards me.

"What am I supposed to do with this?" I asked, completely boggled.

"You've heard stories about gazing balls and the wells of old? This is what they are based on. The waters of Valhalla hold special qualities, both for healing and for communicating. There are certain spots throughout your world that also hold these qualities, and we can connect to those channels using the water of Valhalla. Simply look in the water and call out with your mind to the person you are wanting to speak with. The keepers of the water, Druids like Vala, can sense and answer our call. Sometimes it can take a while for them to make their way to the water source, but Vala said she is staying nearby while she gardens today. It should only take a moment."

"Wow, seriously?" The whole thing sounded crazy to me, but he looked so earnest I didn't have the heart to laugh at him. I placed my hands around the bowl and concentrated on Vala. A minute later, her face appeared in the water, and I could hear her voice in my mind.

Siri, dear, how are you? Her face shimmered through the liquid.

"I'm good. I'm here, safe."

Bran told me as much. What can I do for you?

"I need to talk to Rowan. Is he there?"

No, he's not. But he should be back tomorrow afternoon, his father has him checking in with me regularly for news, not that I would give him any. Do you have a message you'd like me to pass on to him?

"No, just tell him I am safe. I'll try to contact you again tomorrow."

Vala's face faded from view, leaving me alone for a moment with my father and Miko at my side.

Still holding the bowl, I felt a sudden compulsion to speak with Rowan. I wished he was here. I had so many confusing feelings in me, I didn't know what to do, or what I would say when I saw him. If he was here, it would be so much easier. Suddenly, his face swam into view.

"Rowan! Where are you?"

Siri? No way! I'm at the falls, I missed you, and I came out here by myself to think. I was just looking at the water, remembering our first date, thinking about...

"I was thinking about you, too! I can't believe we got this water thing to work! Well, Vala did say you were a water fae," I beamed at him and then glanced at my dad, feeling pretty proud of myself. The look on his face didn't seem to echo my feelings, though.

"Is he alone?" he asked urgently. "Are you sure this is a safe line of communication?"

I waved his concerns away. "Bran, you can trust Rowan, I told you. Do you think I could talk to him alone? Please?" I gave him my best puppy dog eyes and he sighed, getting up and leaving the room.

As soon as he left, I turned back to the bowl.

So, was that your dad?

"Oh my god, yes, I'm sorry, I totally should have introduced you!"

That's okay. He didn't sound too excited to see me.

"Yeah, well, we weren't expecting you. I was just finishing talking to Vala when you appeared in the bowl...So, how is everything? Are you okay with your dad?"

I'm okay. My dad is really pissed, but he's almost never home. He thinks I am helping him look for you, he has no idea I helped you get to Vala's, or that Vala helped you, either. What about you? I heard my dad talking about some botched attempts to capture you up in Canada. And are you really in Aeden? It's really real?

"Alec and his friend Amber took care of it, everything worked out fine. And yeah, Aeden is totally real, and it is so strange! Rowan, there's a mini sun in the middle of the earth, who knew??" I laughed crazily. "It's pretty amazing here. I'm in this city called Valhalla, and they rescued my mom, she's on her way here. We just have to figure out a way to wake her up. Have you ever heard of an anti-serum that puts Light fae into suspended animation? They used it on my mom and we're going to need to find the antidote."

No, I've never heard of anything like that. But I'll see what I can find out.

Okay, just be careful. I don't want you to get hurt, too.

I'll be careful. I'm more worried about you. I miss you.

"I miss you, too. But I don't have any idea when I'll be back up there. My dad's talking about getting me trained in combat like Alec, and-"

Alec again, huh? You spending a lot of time with him?

"What? No! I mean...well, sort of. I mean, he was the Guard responsible for getting me here, so yeah, I guess. I doubt I'll be seeing him much anymore, though." As much as I tried, I couldn't keep the tone of sadness from creeping into my voice.

I see. And I was afraid that maybe he did, because even through the water I could see the same sadness reflected in his eyes. Then his mouth tightened a bit, and he sat up.

Look, I should get going. His voice sounded rougher, angry. *I'm glad we got to talk. I'm fine here without you, everything is pretty much back to normal already at school, you really don't need to worry about me, okay? You don't owe me anything.*

"Rowan, I-"

I get it, okay? Even though I am fae, I'm not welcome in Aeden, and it sounds you have a lot to keep you busy with your new friends. His face twisted with pain, and then smoothed out into a cold mask. *I think with everything going on, it's best if we just take a break. I'll see what I can find out about the antidote, and in the meantime, you should probably focus on your training. I'm sure Alec will be able to help you out with that,* he ended with touch of sarcasm.

"But-"

I have to go, Siri. If you need to reach me, just send me a message through Vala, okay? I don't know when I'll be able to get back here.

"Okay," I answered in a small voice, stunned. The bowl went blank and I struggled to blink away tears. Had he just dumped me?

Looks that way, kiddo. Miko piped up, wiping my cheeks gently with his tail as he nestled under my chin.

"Ugh, you could hear all that?"

Yep. But don't worry, your secrets are safe with me.

"Yeah, but how safe are you with me, I wonder? You might have been better off staying in the forest at home. I'm sorry you've been dragged all this way."

Are you kidding me? This is the most exciting thing that could have ever happened to me. Plus, I hear they have some awesome cocoa-like nuts here. I'm not leaving until I've sampled everything.

I laughed, grateful for my small, furry friend. "You're a good friend, Miko."

Right back atcha, kiddo.

I stood up and walked out of the room, surprised to see that the guards had changed while I was inside. Alec was nowhere to be seen, and Bran had gone, too.

"Um, I'm supposed to train with Amber now, I think?" I asked the guards, hoping one would relent and point me the right way at least. They surprised me by stepping away from the walls toward me.

"Actually, we were instructed to wait for you and escort you to the sanatorium. It's in the next tower, if you will just come with us. Your mother has arrived."

One of the guards gestured toward the escalator, following behind me while the other walked ahead. We rode the stairs down, Miko and I sandwiched between them in silence. Apparently these two took their duties very seriously.

By the time we had ridden the spiral all the way to the bottom of the tower, I expected to feel majorly dizzy, but I wasn't. I asked the blonde guard, who said his name was Dorian, about it, and he shrugged, saying no one ever got dizzy. When pressed further on the matter, he reminded me that fae had exceptional balance and dizziness was a human weakness.

Nice, right? I forgot to feel outraged when we stepped outside the building into the plaza centered among the spires. I'd noticed the huge tree at the middle on our earlier flight in, but now I stood in awe, taking in the sheer enormity of the trunk in front of me. Gazing up, I couldn't even begin to see where it ended. I'd seen sequoias before in California, but never anything like this.

"Wow. This tree is amazing. It's a sequoia, right?" Miko chittered excitedly, scampering over to the tree and climbing up and disappearing into the canopy above. Apparently, he thought his time would be better spent communing with the local wildlife. His parting words reassured me that he'd catch up with me later.

Dorian stood behind me while his friend Barit tapped a foot impatiently several yards away.

"It's an ancestor of the sequoias, yes, although they are rather poor copies. This is the Tree of Life, the origin of our species and everything else on Earth. Indeed, it was the very seed for Earth itself. The planet grew out of the tree."

"Grew out of the tree? But how is that even possible?" It just didn't make any sense to me.

"These gold towers you see here are not actually separate buildings. They are but pieces of a whole, the outer hulls of a primeval starship that housed this tree and the seeds of life. Legend says that when our first world was destroyed, the Ancients created this ship much like Noah created the arc. Set on autopilot, it wandered the heavens for eons. When it finally found a hospitable solar system, it placed itself at an optimal orbit and began the process of creating Aeden and the world above. The Tree of Life anchors the cold fusion star above us, which in turn fuels the particles that are needed to sustain life on this planet. Without it, life on earth would cease to exist."

"That's...that's just...wow. Okay. That's incredible. How tall is it?"

"Bigger than any regular Sequoia, that's for sure. The trunk is exactly forty four meters in diameter, and the tree itself measures three hundred meters tall."

"But that's more than nine hundred feet! It's almost the same height as the Eiffel Tower in Paris!"

Dorian just smirked at me and asked if I was ready to move on.

Feeling a bit like a bumpkin country cousin, I started walking, staring around me all the while. There was so much to look at.

The plaza was filled with magnificent flower gardens, cascading with gorgeous roses and gleaming fountains. Birds of every color frolicked among the plants, filling the yard with unfamiliar songs. I watched a pair of indigo jays bathing in the water, and was reminded of my conversation with Rowan. Suddenly I felt small and alone in this strange place, and just a little bit sorry for myself. I hurried on, not wanting to see anymore new things, yet knowing it was inevitable as I trailed Barit's impatient form.

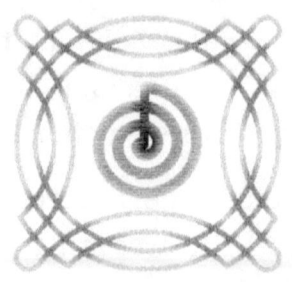

Chapter 32

We entered the tower to our left, which I noted had four dots above its door, apparently denoting its number. Dorian pointed to the tower we had come from, Tower Three, explaining that it had three dots, and housed all the defense, intelligence and military training facilities of Valhalla. Tower Four contained not only the sanatorium, but also the medical research and clinical facilities of Valhalla. Tower One housed the ruling families and remaining Ancients, Tower Two contained the Council Chambers, Tower Five held the schools, Tower Six was a giant indoor marketplace and Tower Seven was set aside for all other research and development. I wondered what else they could possibly dream up in Tower Seven – it seemed like they already had the tech to do whatever they wanted.

Inside, Tower Four looked more or less like Tower Three, but with a lot more people walking around. Most people seemed to be in a hurry with some place to go, although some looked sad or lost while they milled aimlessly about. In that respect, it was pretty much like every other hospital I'd ever seen on television. Of course, the gleaming gold walls, strange hieroglyphs carved into doors and the spiraling escalators pretty much ensured I'd never forget I wasn't on Earth anymore. No. I was in it.

We rode the stairs to the top floor. The further up we'd gone, the fewer people we passed coming back down. Dorian whispered that the Sanatorium cared for long-term patients, unlike the emergency services and basic health care wards below. The top floor, where we were going, was reserved for the most serious cases, the ones who needed the most isolation and rest. With a pang, I realized what that said about my mother's condition.

A small waiting area with soft pleather chairs surrounded the staircases. I saw Bran in one of them flipping through some papers and rushed over to pepper him with questions.

"Have you seen her? Where is she? How does she look?"

He looked up, a world weary smile on his face. "I have. She looks...a little older than I remember, but good. Peaceful. As far as she's concerned, she's just sleeping. Honestly, she's probably doing better than the rest of us. I was just going through her file now to make sure the doctors are following protocol for the anti-serum."

"Bran? Can I ask you something personal?"

"Of course. I want to get to know you, and I hope you feel like you can do the same with me. Ask away."

"Well, it seems like you might have had feelings for my mom when you...when you guys were on mission together. She tried to find you afterwards, did you know that?"

From the way his face paled, I knew he hadn't. I pushed on before he could answer. "How come you never tried to find her?"

"When we met, I was in the middle of a long black op. I was sent from place to place for three years, never anywhere for more than a few days, never any contact with Aeden other than my coded instructions. By the time I finished, the time I'd spent with Fredrika seemed like a dream. When I returned I was thrown right onto the fast track to command. I convinced myself that whatever I thought I'd felt, she hadn't felt the same, or that she'd moved on. I figured if she was looking for me, I would hear about it. I'm sorry if I was wrong."

"She didn't talk about you much, but I know she tried. She told me she didn't want to come to Aeden because she wanted me to have a taste of human freedom before my Choosing. But there was a moment, you know, before she was taken, that she talked about how you guys connected. How she just knew it was right, in her heart. She was talking about the surge, wasn't she?"

"What do you know about the surge?" he eyed me suspiciously, the way I expected most fathers would if they knew their daughters had been kissing boys. I didn't think he'd earned the right to look at me that way yet, and I gave him a look that let him know it.

"Well, was she?"

"Yes, I think so. At least, I thought so. But the surge is no guarantee. It's just an indicator of mental, physical, and spiritual compatibility."

"Gee, is that all? What if you don't like the person? Can you experience the surge with someone else?"

"It's rare enough to find the first one, but yes, you could find another surge connection. And plenty of fae fall in love and have families without ever experiencing the surge. In some circles, it's even believed to be a bit of a fairy tale, like love at first sight."

I snorted.

"Well, we know that's not true," I muttered.

"Do we now?" He eyed me speculatively.

"Can you use the energy rush of the surge to wake her?"

"No, we've tried that before with another patient, and I felt nothing just now when I was in her room, not even the normal indication that you get when you have contact with another fae. The anti-serum suppresses the energy flow of our light when it's used, so the surge is disabled. But how do you—"

Before he could finished his question I deflected his attention by asking if I could see my mother now. Forgetting his budding paternal inclinations, he apologized and showed me to my mother's room. He excused himself at the door, promising to send Amber to collect me in a half hour.

I placed my palm against the door, took a deep breath and stepped into my mom's room just before it closed shut again. Her room was bathed in beautiful pink light reflected by the clouds. Bran was right, she did look peaceful, I thought as I approached her bedside. Her face, even without the sun's glow, held a slight blush and her breathing was steady.

Her auburn hair fanned out prettily on her pillow, and I wondered who had arranged it that way. Had it been my father? Somehow, I thought maybe it had. I'd seen the tenderness in his eyes when he spoke of her, the regret when he realized the time he'd lost with her.

A lone IV line lay next to her on the far side of the bed, linking her to fluid sustenance. Apparently, she could exist comfortably like this for the rest of her natural life. I swore to myself she wouldn't have to.

God, I missed my mom. I missed our daily spars, our chocolate fests and movie nights. I missed her laugh and her easy ways. Rowan was right, I tended to be too serious, but my mom... She had always been my true north to happiness. She could bring me out of any funk, and make any town a home. I wanted her back more than I'd ever wanted anything before. I had a dad now, but I would have traded him in a second to get my mother back, to go back to the way things had been before.

But I knew that could never be. I could never go back. Even if I returned to Falls Depot, even if I found a cure for my mom and brought peace to the fae, I knew life would never be the same.

Yearning for simpler times, I climbed carefully up onto my mother's bed and curled myself around her. I rested my head on her chest and listened to her heartbeat, letting the sound of her blood, my blood, the earth's blood, drum my worries away.

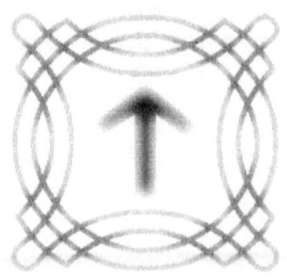

CHAPTER 33

I lay like that for a while, not quite sleeping, and not quite awake, listening to the sound of my mother's heartbeat as she breathed, in and out, in and out. That was how Amber found me, lying in bed. She placed her hand on my shoulder and gently roused me.

"Visiting hours are almost over, and it's way past dinner time. Come on, let's go get some food in you. Have you even eaten anything since the beignets?"

I shook my head, and she clucked her tongue at me like a mother hen. I kissed my mom on her forehead, smoothing her hair again, and followed Amber outside. For the first time since we had arrived, I really absorbed what Alec had meant about the sun never setting in Aeden. It hadn't budged from its spot in the sky high above the Tree of Life. Barring some unseen disaster, it never would. How did people ever sleep here? Did they get high on the sunshine the way people did in Norway and Alaska? I guessed I would find out soon enough. I'd definitely have to look into getting some kind of a watch, otherwise I'd never be able to tell what time it was.

Amber brought me to a small outdoor buffet by the school spire. I let her order for both of us, since I didn't recognize most of the fare. They served us the food and I looked at it warily as I sat down.

"So, um, the food here, is it like in all those fairytales? If I eat it, will I never be able to leave?"

Amber let out a peal of laughter. "If that was true, Alec and I would hardly be able to come and go the way we do, would we? No, the truth of it is that those warnings are made up by the Dark to keep the humans from meddling in fae affairs. Besides, you can't believe everything you hear – I mean, do you see anyone here with wings?"

"No, but I have yet to meet an ugly fae, either."

"That is true, our genetics tend to keep us looking well. Though some are better looking than others, and we definitely come in all types."

While we ate, Amber filled me in on her day, which had consisted mainly of debriefing with Bran, weapons training, more debriefing with the Council, a conversation with her father about Ewan, and tea with her mother.

I envied her the time she'd spent with her mother, but apparently the time with her dad had gone less smoothly than mine.

"So then he says he can't believe that I would do this to him. And I say, do what? I mean, it's not like I slept with my uncle, for Frigg's sake."

I spit out my fruity beverage, laughing. "Tell me you did not say that."

"I did. His reaction was not as funny as yours. He sort of turned beet red and couldn't really speak for a while, so I just left. Whatever. He'll come around. You can't fight the surge." She winked at me, and I remembered my conversation with Bran.

"My parents felt it, and my dad let her go anyway," I sighed. "But don't go by me. What do I know? I'm pretty sure Rowan just broke up with me today."

"No. Way." She leaned forward on the table. "When did you talk to him?"

"In the Light Guard meeting room. I was talking to Vala through the water, and after we finished Rowan just sort of came through. I guess we were both thinking of each other at the same time. But it didn't go too well. When I mentioned you and Alec he got really mad and basically said I should work on my training here and forget about him."

"Sounds like he's jealous," she said sagely, popping a pink fry in her mouth.

"I guess. It doesn't matter now. Who knows how long I'll be here, anyway. I may never go back to Falls Depot, and even when he chooses the Light, he might not come down to Aeden. It's over, at least for the time being."

"So, about him being jealous, do you think that maybe he's right?"

"Argh! Shut up about that, okay?" I leaned forward so we were almost nose to nose, whispering, "Alec and I, we're not anything. There's something, okay, fine, maybe it's the surge, I don't know, but he is acting really weird about it so can we just talk about something else now?"

"Sure, no problem," Amber grinned, popping another fry in her mouth. "Did you know Bran's sending him away tomorrow?"

"Who, Alec? Why would Bran do that?" I thought back to our conversation about the surge and wondered whether he'd ordered Alec away before or after our little chat.

"He's leading a team on some reconnaissance to a couple medical research labs we believe operate on Shade funding. They're hoping to find the cure for Fredrika. It was all decided during our first debriefing."

"Oh, good." I was glad he wasn't just being sent away by an overprotective father. "Is it dangerous?"

"Nah. This kind of thing is what we live for," she winked. "And, it's what you're going to start training for starting first thing tomorrow morning."

"First thing? How can you even tell what time it is here?"

"Watches, just like anyone else. Greenwich Mean Time is actually based on Aeden time. But really, for the most part, a lot of fae here just do what they want, when they want, especially the people that live outside the cities. If you want to have breakfast at night, you can, and if you need to sleep at noon, that's alright, too. Generally, no one will give you any grief over it."

"Well, that said, I'm exhausted. Think you can help me make sure I find my way home now?"

"Sure, come on. You're going to need all the rest you can get tonight." She hip checked me and laughed, grabbing our trays and walking over to place them in some bins along the wall for recycling. I silently called out to Miko by the tree and he said he'd catch up with me the next day.

Amber escorted me to my room and gave me a hug. Auroreis had already come and gone, having turned down the bed, shuttered the windows and laid out a long silky gold sheath for me to sleep in. I brushed my teeth and combed out my hair, slipping on the nightgown and crawling into bed. My eyes were closed before they hit the pillow.

Sometime later in the near darkness I awoke with a lazy, euphoric sensation cascading through my body. I smelled pine trees and sweet coriander and even before I opened my eyes I knew what I would see. In the shadowy gloom, I could just make out Alec hovering over me. His hands were by my shoulders, propping him up away from me, and his legs straddled mine, his bare calves resting hotly against my thighs where my nightgown had ridden up. Ah. So at least now I knew where the surge was coming from.

"How did you get in? Isn't the door keyed only to me and Auroreis?"

"I have my ways," he assured me. Even in the dark, I could tell he was smiling that cocky grin of his.

"I just bet you do. But, what are you doing here?"

"I wanted to talk to you before I left. I was on my way up here before, but Amber told me you'd already gone to bed. She told me what happened with you and the darkling."

"And?" I gritted out. Did he have to always call Rowan that awful name? Was it really so impossible to believe that there could be some Light left in the Dark?

"And, I went back to my room to take a nap before I leave. I decided I would talk to you when I came back. Give you some time, and hopefully bring back some good news to cheer you up."

"But you changed your mind," I whispered.

"I changed my mind," he whispered back, a smile in his voice again. "I promised you we would talk, so I'm here. To talk."

"To talk?" I asked, smiling up at him.

"Mmm, yes, to talk." He leaned down then, slowly, and kissed my neck. His lips moved down along my jaw, brushing lightly across my lips and then made their way back up to my ear, his hot breath making me feel wild. The surge was building back up inside me, and I moaned, pulling his face back to my so our lips could meet. As he kissed me, I felt our energy twine together and merge, flooding me with feelings that were not mine alone.

I couldn't read his thoughts, not like Miko's but I could feel everything that he was experiencing, like a sort of telempathy. It didn't matter now if things went unsaid, because the surge was carrying our emotions forward, stirring them together and revealing them truly for what they were. For a moment I thought of my mother and father, and I wanted to laugh at the thought that anyone could believe this was a fairytale, that the surge was made up. It was the most real thing I had ever experienced.

After I had felt all his longing, all his adoration, every ounce of his protectiveness and his wonder, we broke apart. He stared down at me, the dim light revealing only a strange purple glow around his pupils. I knew he had felt my own yearnings echoing his.

"That's it?" I teased. "Is that all you have to say?"

He laughed. "You know very well it's not. I don't want to hide how I feel about you. But I also don't know where this can go. I am half human. I'm lucky to even be here in Aeden, even luckier to have become a Light Guard. You are a full fae; your father is practically an Ancient. You should be with someone of similar bloodlines. The Council will try to arrange a better pairing for you; it's inevitable."

"Let them try," I scoffed. I relayed everything my father had said about my bloodlines ending with, "they'll never find anyone with ancestry like mine. I'm a prophecy, I'm special, unique. Which means I need a special sort of guy. A guy like you."

I pulled him down to me again, trying to show him all the ways with my lips that I could be his. A kiss here on his neck. A nibble under his ear. A flutter of kisses across his eyelids, his cheeks.

"They'll still try," he muttered.

"It won't matter," I reassured him. "I'm already yours." We kissed deeply, the surge riding the waves of our newborn love, quelling each other's innermost fears and desires.

Finally, we broke apart. Alec fell back on the bed next to me, pulling me to him and I wrapped myself along his side, sighing, reveling in the rise and fall of his chest below my head. He kissed my hair and held me as we both dropped off to sleep.

I have no idea how long I slept. Time really was meaningless here until I got my hands on a watch. The bed beside me was still warm, but it was empty. He was gone.

I didn't worry. I knew he'd be back, just like I knew he wouldn't rest until he had done everything in his power to restore my mother.

I wasn't sure what the future held. My father had plans for me, I was sure. He wanted me to train, and fulfill a prophecy. I wasn't remotely sure what that would entail.

But I knew that I would have Alec by my side when I needed him, and the rest of my new friends. I smiled, and started to drift back to sleep.

I would have faith. I would trust. I would not allow fear to determine my path. I would open my heart and the way would be clear.

I just had to trust myself, trust my friends, trust my family, and trust fate.

How hard could that be?

ACKNOWLEDGEMENTS

There were so many amazing, helpful people involved with the creation of this book, that I am not sure I will be able to thank you all. But I will try!

First off, I would like to thank Maya Cointreau and the brilliant team at Earth Lodge for giving me a chance and taking on the Inner Origins series. I could never have accomplished the editing, layout and cover design all on my own, never mind brought *Shades* to press so seamlessly. And, of course, without Earth Lodge, I would not have had access to such a phenomenal team of beta readers.

Lisa Shab, Pita Lemstra, Ellen Woolf Feichtner, Lisa Kessler, Kathy Lalonde – thank you for all your insightful comments and helping us catch the inevitable errors and typos! You helped us refine *Shades* into the story it is today, something I certainly couldn't have done without you.

I am extremely grateful to my husband and children. Your infinite patience for my love affair with my keyboard was a true blessing. Thank you for sleeping peacefully beside me while I wrote into the wee hours of the night, for all the little words of encouragement, and for the mugs of hot tea and chocolate when I needed them most. I love you all more than words can say.

Finally, I would like to thank the fae communities, both ethereal and tangible. I heard your whispers in the morning light, and found the many messages you left for me. You showed me the Light, and introduced me to my own shadow side. You inspired me time and time again, helping me to connect with the elements and showing me the inner origins of space and time.

Thank you!

ABOUT THE AUTHOR

Ellis Logan has been talking to fairies and writing stories since she was a little girl, and is ecstatic to be publishing her new fantasy series through Earth Lodge. She lives a quiet life with her family in New England, where she enjoys skiing, boxing, hiking and eating chocolate...always chocolate!

Follow Ellis on Facebook at EllisLoganBooks

and

Join Ellis's mailing list at EllisLogan.com
to stay tuned for new releases and giveaways.